Beached

by

J L Wilson

A Remembered Classics Romance, Book 8

Beached

Cover Art by *Kim Mendoza*

The Wild Rose Press, Inc.
PO Box 708
Adams Basin, NY 14410-0708
Visit us at www.thewildrosepress.com

Publishing History
First Edition, 2021
Trade Paperback ISBN 978-1-5092-3602-2
Digital ISBN 978-1-5092-3603-9

A Remembered Classics Romance, Book 8
Published in the United States of America

"To be fair, I think any partnership you come up with that involves any woman would have problems." He nodded glumly. I felt sorry for him. That's what prompted me to say, "I don't think you have much to worry about, though."

"Really?"

"Yeah. I'm not jealous material. I think you'll be okay. If you want my desserts, I'm willing to try it for a few weeks and see how it works."

He appeared relieved, and I knew I'd said the right thing. "Maybe you're right. I'm sorry I didn't finish the frosting."

"No worries. Thanks for what you did. It helps." I returned to the peony petals, working quickly so the gum paste didn't soften too much. I needed to start forming them around the center I'd already crafted, and too much handling made them malleable.

Dallas headed for the stairs, then stopped. "You're wrong."

"About what?" I asked, not looking up.

"You are."

"Are what?"

"Romantic material."

My head jerked up, and the gum paste petal split in half. "What?"

"See you tomorrow."

"Tomorrow?"

"Support group, remember? Five-thirty."

"You can't—I can't—"

"I want your desserts in my restaurant, and I won't take no for an answer." He winked. "Plus, I want your buttercream recipe." He dashed down the steps.

Dedication

To women everywhere who have struggled with self-image, only to realize they are just right just as they are.

Chapter One

"How about death by buttercream frosting?" I stepped back to view the small cake I was decorating. Sunlight angled into the room, which was the entire second floor of my lighthouse overlooking Hardscrabble Point.

"Too gooey. We'd leave fingerprints everywhere. Let's do death by offset spatula." Jamie Priest, my friend and owner of Jamie's Java Jolt, the next-door coffee shop, leaned against my stainless-steel counter and watched while I piped the last flower onto the cake. "Or death by cake leveler. We'd have to make sure he was properly sedated, otherwise it would get truly messy." He lifted the aforesaid instrument, a wicked looking contraption that combined a hacksaw blade with a C bracket to help me slice off uneven cake tops.

"I doubt we'll get close enough to him to do him in." I spun the cake on its stand, eyeing it critically. "He probably has security guards protecting him from the hoi polloi."

Jamie and I were facetiously plotting to get rid of the newest competition in the restaurant trade in our part of the world. Dallas Prinze, a hometown boy, was returning to our little metropolis of Denmark, Minnesota, population 10,000. *Prinze's Prize Catch* was set to open in a month across the bay from my

1

bakery shop, which occupied the ground floor of my lighthouse.

It was great marketing on his part. Denmark was five miles west of busy Interstate 35 and only twenty miles south of the main Twin Cities metro. An outlet mall was a few miles north of us, and several lakes were clustered around us with Spirit Lake, where my lighthouse sat, the biggest. He'd be able to draw on tourists and Twinies alike for trade.

"I still say you should call him and suggest he feature your baked goods on his menu. After all, you and he went to culinary school together. You're alums of Spirit Lake Technical College. He claims he'll only use local foods and do the whole farm-to-table thing. He could send a boat here and pick up dessert every day."

"Dallas Prinze and I attended the same school. We weren't exactly friends," I lied with casual ease as I nudged the cake to one side.

"Seriously? Come on, there must be something." Jamie bent to examine the small six-inch cake. His gray-streaked hair stood up in small tufts, typical for him by the end of the workday after running his hand through it. He was handsome in an understated way, rugged without being overbearingly masculine. "Weren't there some wild nights? Crazy parties and orgies? Tales of longing and excess?"

Thirty years of practice kept my hand steady, but it was a near thing. I almost blasted pale golden buttercream frosting all over the counter. "Come on, Jamie. You know I was as big as a whale then. Nobody would party with me." I moved the tray of rainbow Pride cupcakes into position where I could frost them, using that action to keep my face averted from his. "I didn't get the name Tugboat Giganta without reason."

"And I still say they were a bunch of stupid, ignorant assholes," he declared. "I can't believe you kept that nickname."

"I not only kept it, I embraced it." I touched the box sitting next to the cake, my signature label glued to the top. *Tug's Treats* was written in a flowing script and underneath was *Drop Anchor in our Harbor.* "It's been so long since anyone called me Theresa Gallant, I wouldn't answer to it." I quickly dolloped frosting on a dozen of the cupcakes.

"Well, as long as you're not pissed off, I won't be, either." Jamie peeked into the mixing bowl. "It was a genius idea to sell the leftover frosting spread on graham crackers. I can't believe how fast those sell out."

"I don't think it matters to Dallas Prinze if I was pissed off or not." I nudged the mixing bowl to one side, knowing how Jamie adored 'just a smidge' of frosting. "Besides, we'll never see him. He's opening a restaurant across the bay, amongst the Richers." That was our term for the folks in the Yacht Club crowd, who frequented the peninsula across Church Bay.

"It might be fun to go to his place once it opens. We can give him helpful hints about running a food business in this part of the world."

There was no way in hell I would visit Dallas Prinze at his restaurant. Despite what I said to Jamie, my memories of culinary school were problematic at best. Dallas was the Big Man on Campus, mainly because he had a modeling contract and was making enough money that he easily afforded the tuition. Most of the rest of us were scraping by, working in kitchens at menial jobs. Dallas parlayed his modeling career into a modestly successful Hollywood career and returned to the culinary world a decade ago.

I shifted the cupcakes to the staging counter and brought out the graham crackers. "Make yourself useful." I pointed Jamie to the Sanitation Station on the far wall, used for handwashing. Employees washed their hands according to my criteria before putting on gloves. Jamie wasn't an employee, but he knew the rules.

"What's the song of the day?" he asked.

"You'll see." I set a new tray of cupcakes into position. My interns baked my cupcakes and cakes in Jamie's coffeehouse, and I used my kitchen for finishing. It was an arrangement we worked out over the twenty-some years we'd been in business since I first bought the dilapidated structures and painstakingly remodeled them. Now Tug's Treats and Jamie's Java Jolt were flourishing businesses—small but debt-free. My lighthouse, painted a pale gold color with dark blue trim, was known around the lake and had become a destination stop for boaters both winter and summer.

Jamie approached the Station. The smart mirror above the sink said, "Prepare to sanitize, minion." He positioned his hands under the automatic faucet as *Ain't Too Proud to Beg* began playing. "Good one," he called over his shoulder.

"I aim to please," I called back. I watched him scrub his hands for the requisite thirty seconds, singing along to the music until it and the water stopped. It cost me a bundle to get that installed, but it was worth it. I was a stickler for sanitation.

Jamie dried his hands with paper towels before rejoining me. "Save some frosting for the crackers," he protested, eyeing the rows of Pride cupcakes lined up. "That one looks odd." He pointed to one whose colors were distinctly not-level.

"We do an assembly line, piping the layers of batters. It's pretty freakin' tedious, and I usually liven it up with television shows. A few of them are a bit lopsided, depending on what Judge Judy is adjudicating that day."

"Like some queer folk I know," Jamie said wryly. "A bit lopsided."

I grinned. "I'm proud, no pun intended, about my Pride cupcakes. Six layers of color is tough to do." I shook rainbow sprinkles on top of the frosting to add to the effect.

"It's worth the effort. Of course, it doesn't hurt that you volunteered to make the wedding cake when the asshole baker refused to make a cake for that lesbian couple." He dipped an offset spatula into the frosting bowl and spread a layer on a graham cracker.

"It was the right thing to do," I pointed out.

"And a profitable thing to do. You're now the go-to baker for funky wedding cakes for most of the gay folks in the south metro." Jamie hummed while he worked, deftly spreading frosting on a half-dozen squares and lining them up on a serving tray. "I wonder if he's gay."

"Who?"

He shot me a long-suffering look. "Dallas Prinze. Our competition." He put squares on top of the frosted ones and set out more for dolloping. "He's never married anybody."

"I've seen his name linked with a couple of high-powered actresses. Besides, he and Lily are together."

"Lily? His business manager? You're on a first name basis with her?"

I sighed. "Okay, I knew him and her. He and I were in classes together for two years or more. She was in Hospitality Management and in a few of my classes. But she was a Richer, and we didn't exactly travel in the same social circle."

"Wow. A brush with celebrity."

"A very thin brush," I assured him. "I doubt if he's gay."

"He never got married," Jamie insisted.

"I never got married and I'm not gay. Not everybody can bask in wedded bliss like you."

Jamie beamed at me. He married relatively late in life, at age forty, to Susie Deacon, a corporate exec who worked in the Cities. They had an adorable five-year-old daughter who was the center of Jamie's universe. Little Theresa was my godchild, and I thought she was pretty special, too. "I am blissful, aren't I? I sometimes think I'm the luckiest guy in the world."

"Keep telling Susie that and you'll stay the luckiest guy." I pulled up a stool and sat, my aching back telling me I'd been standing long enough. We worked in companionable silence for a time. "That should do it for tomorrow," I said, finishing the cupcakes. "Thanks for the help."

"I had time before I need to pick up Little T. Her summer camp lets out at four. Perfect timing. Susie drops her off while I'm at work in the morning, and I pick her up when I close in the afternoon." He licked the frosting off his spatula before putting it in my dishwasher. "I'm glad you decided not to stay open for the evenings."

"Desserts are what I do best. The more I considered having soup and sandwiches, the more complicated it looked." I put a layer of plastic wrap on the graham crackers which I'd sell tomorrow for fifty cents, endearing me to the children in town. The cupcakes went into a storage box with others for the early morning crowd. My assistants would come in to bake the majority of tomorrow's offerings at midnight, leaving cupcakes and cakes here to cool and be ready for me to frost most of them when I woke at five a.m. My shop staff would arrive at six to open and sell the bread and pies just out of the oven. I continued to frost and replenish supplies throughout the day, depending on how sales were going.

"I still say we need to contact your old classmate and see if we can set up an arrangement. Even if it's only the occasional pie or cake, it doesn't hurt to have your name on the display case where the Richers spend their money. And if we could put in a plug for the Jolt at the same time, I wouldn't object."

He was right, of course, but I wasn't anxious to pursue it. "I'll think about it."

"I know what that means. It means forget about it." He went to the sink and washed his hands again while I tidied up the counters. I took the storage cupcakes and went with him downstairs to the shop, which still had a couple of customers scrutinizing the displays. "I'll talk to you tomorrow," Jamie said. "And think about contacting him. It might be good for business."

"Yeah, yeah." I closed the shop door behind him. The store was starting to get that end-of-the-day feeling. We sometimes closed early when we sold out of goods, but there were still several loaves of bread and a half-dozen cupcakes. If they didn't sell by the time we closed at five, I'd donate them tomorrow to the food pantry.

Marty Temple, a student in Hospitality Management, was behind the counter. He was a big, burly guy who was as meticulous as me about keeping the area clean and spotless. Marty was my closer because he wasn't a morning person, which was tricky for someone who wanted to be a baker. This job was giving him a chance to see what the business was all about.

He gestured me nearer to the glass display case. "There's a lady on the porch who's got a beef about the bathroom," he said in a low voice.

"What about it?" I knew the tiny bathroom tucked under the stairs was clean. Either I or the staff checked it several times a day.

"She wanted to use the lady's bathroom. I told her we only had the one, and she got huffy and demanded to talk to you." Marty shrugged one massive shoulder, his sea blue baker's jacket straining across the chest. I made a mental note to get him a larger size. He pointed to the south-facing patio door. "She's the old lady in the old lady clothes."

I sighed. "Seriously? It's the only bathroom we have. I needed to make it gender neutral."

"You're preaching to the choir. This is why you're the boss and I'm a minion."

"Remember this when you set up your own bakery," I muttered.

"I'm taking notes," he assured me.

I opened the patio door and stepped into the June humidity. The veranda began at the steps leading to the dock and wrapped around half of the lighthouse. It was mostly empty at this late time of day. Two men sat at the far end where the deck turned to the east with a view of the lake. They were gazing at the water, Jolt coffee mugs in hand. A teenager was with them, hunched and focused on the phone in his hands.

I followed the curve of the deck, which had the same kind of railing used on cruise ships. I was paranoid about a kid climbing up and falling onto the rocks below, so I spent Big Money to get a system that was four feet tall, clear Plexiglas below, and seamless with no spots where a child might get a foothold. That combined with the caution signs at the entrance was the best I could do, but I still worried about a foolhardy child and a non-observant parent.

I spied the woman immediately, a table away from the two men. She wore a pale-green flowered blouse and dark-green slacks. Her white hair was scraped up into a bun, accenting the lines on her face and adding to her age, which was maybe somewhere in her seventies. She was eating a cupcake with a fork. A vanilla cupcake, I noted. No Pride cupcakes for her.

I approached her. "I'm the owner of the shop. My assistant mentioned you had a concern about the restroom accommodations. Can I help you?"

The woman twisted in the chair to view me. "You're the owner?"

"Yes, I am. Was there a problem? Was the restroom not cleaned properly?" I looked from her to the other table. The kid raised his head to regard me with incurious green eyes.

"It was acceptable," she said haughtily. "However, I think you should know that I object to using a restroom that may have also been used by a transgender or other unnatural person."

I considered and rejected a couple of simple answers. *It's the only bathroom here. Live with it.* Or perhaps, *then go next door to the Jolt, you fucking idiot.* Instead, I said, "I believe state law dictates that gender-neutral restrooms facilities must be provided if possible."

"I saw that at our local Target store," she spat. "It's disgusting. What if one of those cross-dressing people came into the bathroom?"

"Presumably, you'd be busy doing what you went there to do and wouldn't notice," I said mildly.

The kid grinned and ducked his head.

"I'm a decent Christian woman. These lax laws are tainting our society. Leviticus 18:20 states that a man shall not lie with another man because that is an abomination. Our minister says that…" Her complexion, a somewhat uniform pale color, was starting to get a bit pink.

I waited patiently for her to wrap up her diatribe. I'd heard it before, most notably from the minister who currently led my father's former church, who admonished me for catering to sinners and whores. I had my ex-communication letter from the church framed and it now hung below my business license on the bakery wall.

"Leviticus is often quoted," I said when she drew breath and I could slip a word in edgewise. "Isaiah 43:1 is often quoted by the LGBT+ community. It emphasizes God's love and protection for all his people."

"I'm sure God did not intend to include perverts in that love," she sputtered.

"Did you know that the Bible is actually two groups of documents, put together at different times? The Apocrypha includes the books that didn't make the final edit of the Bible you know today. Have you studied those books?"

"No, of course not. Those aren't accepted as gospel," she stammered.

"But which gospels? There are Synoptic Gospels, but the Gnostic Gospels should also be studied, shouldn't they? They also reflect the life and times of the apostles, don't they?"

"I haven't studied that. I don't believe those are covered in my Bible class." Her cheeks were definitely getting pinker, and I don't think it was the setting sun causing this reaction.

"We also need to consider that Jesus spoke Aramaic, and there aren't any original text of the New Testament in that language. Everything that we have now was written in Greek or an Egyptian language." I frowned, dredging up facts I'd stored away years earlier. "Coptic, I think. As you probably know, there is no word in Hebrew, Aramaic, or Greek for 'homosexual'." I smiled knowingly at her.

"I—I wasn't aware—" She sucked in a deep breath. "The disciples were charged with writing the Words of our Savior, and I think we can trust that what they wrote reflect his teachings."

I nodded. "Biblical scholars agree that Paul and many other writers of the scriptures reflect the assumptions that most Jews of the time had—because God created men and women, obviously everyone was born heterosexual."

"Absolutely," she said fervently. "Exactly what I'm talking about."

"But that's a mistake. You see, Paul based his knowledge on his world view, not on what was true. In his world, men owned woman or treated women as property. Love was not the basis of marriage and consequently, we can't use those norms as models for what we'd have today."

"There are still more precepts that we can apply," she sputtered.

"True. But it's important to understand that people are not born heterosexual. That's a construct created by society. If you were to construct a model of how the world is today, your scripture might be different." I saw a flicker of interest in the kid's eyes. "And as you know, the New Testament is not considered the Word of God. It is merely man's interpretation of the Word. In fact, the New Testament is an affirmation of love and inclusion."

The woman's mouth sagged open. "I—what—which—"

"In Galatians 3:28 it's said that 'There is neither Jew nor Greek, there is no longer slave or free, there is no longer male and female; for all of you are one in Christ Jesus.' This implies that if a person has accepted Christ as their savior, then sexuality is irrelevant."

"But that's not what that means," she said faintly.

"How do we know? We only have the words of the people who followed Christ, and we don't have all of those writings. The Bible is a carefully edited and curated set of documents, filtered by churches throughout the ages. If you want to understand the life and times of the disciples and Christ, you need to read everything." I shook my head sadly. "It's a daunting task, but we should never blindly accept what our leaders tell us, both political and religious. We need to think and form our own opinions." I was talking to the kid now, but I don't think the old lady realized it.

She folded her paper napkin very precisely, her hands trembling. "It appears you have marshalled several arguments against Christians and their teachings."

"I have a bit of an advantage." I leaned toward her and said in a conspiratorial voice, "My father was an evangelical Pentecostal minister. I was required to study the Bible day in and day out. I can quote scripture every day. And I made it a point to study *all* the scriptures, not only those approved by the church hierarchy. For every scripture you toss at me, I can toss one back. Of course, as you know, the devil can cite Scripture for his purpose. That's Shakespeare."

Her lips thinned even more. It was amazing how like a snake she appeared, with that smirky smile and beady stare. "I'm sure your father was disappointed."

I straightened. "Luckily for him, he died before he saw how I turned out. He and my mother were killed in a boating accident when I was a teenager."

This seemed to startle her. "Oh, well. That's too bad."

"It was a long time ago. Thanks for coming in today. I certainly understand if you'd prefer to avoid my shop in the future. But you're quite welcome as long as you don't try to preach to anyone here."

"I doubt if I'll return." She pushed her chair back with a screech of metal on wood. Snatching up her white handbag, she stalked off.

The teenager watched her go then grinned at me. "Good work," he muttered.

"I hope you enjoyed the show."

The two men glanced at us. "Is everything okay?" one of them asked.

The kid said, "No problem, Dad. We're good."

I went back into the shop. "Problem handled?" Marty asked.

"Yeah, we probably lost a customer, but I had fun quoting Bible crap at her."

He laughed. "That's a talent I'll never be able to master."

I waved a hand. "Don't even try." I picked up the mail from the counter and headed for the stairs. "Give me a buzz when you lock up."

"Will do." He went back to wiping the display case.

I went upstairs to my kitchen, which was spacious enough to double as my living room. This was nearly as big as the ground floor, which was thirty-by-thirty feet. I sank onto the couch to sort through the mail. One letter, the bakery name scrawled on front, caught my attention. I opened it and shook my head when I saw the contents.

Your kind of people shouldn't be allowed to have a business in Denmark. Someday something might happen to your business and to you and your queer friends.

I received similar missives almost daily for the past nine months since I catered the first gay wedding. They no longer worried me. I filed it in the folder in my desk drawer along with the others, which were equally ignored by the local police department. I suspected they were uncomfortable with the influx of gay folks to their little resort community, drawn here by my notoriety.

However, several business owners had confided to me that their trade was flourishing. Apparently, Denmark was getting a reputation as a hip, out-of-the-way spot that welcomed people regardless of race, orientation, or ethnicity. If I had helped foster such a reputation, I was thrilled. I'd been marginalized for years because of my weight, and I knew what exclusion felt like. If I could turn the tide even a tiny bit, I counted my life as worthwhile.

I cleaned the countertops in the prep area before starting the dishwasher. Then I used gum paste to press out the various flower petal sizes I'd need for upcoming cakes, putting them on a tray and popping it into the fridge for use on Tuesday.

Time for Me Time. I made a sandwich and carried it up to my third-floor bedroom, a twenty-by-twenty space with windows on each side and a narrow deck. I chose a spot on the northeast side overlooking the lake, away from the hot afternoon sun, and plopped in my zero-gravity chair to eat my turkey-and-swiss. A few minutes later, Marty texted me that he'd locked up and was heading out, stopping at the bank on the way to deposit the till.

A few minutes after that, the shop phone rang below me in my kitchen on the extension. In the distance I heard my voice say, "Sorry, we're closed now. Come back tomorrow at six o'clock and see what treats we have available." The beep sounded on the answering machine, and a voice said something I didn't catch.

Whatever it was, it would wait. I finished my sandwich then went to the second floor and spent an hour at my desk opposite the kitchen, studying menu choices and checking our supplies. A couple of wedding cakes were coming up, and I needed to plan my week to make sure I had that covered. My workers were students at the tech school. I trusted them with making the cakes and the cupcakes, but I needed to handle most of the decorating. I had a challenging week ahead, but it was only Monday. I'd get it done.

I sketched a bit on the design for one of the cakes. It had a mermaid theme because the two women getting married were avid swimmers. I experimented with my watercolors to get the correct effect, and when I was satisfied, I tacked the sketch to the large corkboard near the prep area where I could review it while I worked.

By now it was six o'clock. Cocktail hour. I poured myself two fingers of Maker's Mark and went back up to the deck, resuming my seat and stretching my legs. This was my time to relax. I stared across the bay at Anderson's Point, where Dallas' new restaurant was being constructed. It was connected by a thin thread of land to Turfmoor Peninsula, where the Yacht Club was located, south and east of where I sat and out of sight. His location was perfect and, frankly, one I envied. My lighthouse was on the poorer side of the lake, and to reach my shop folks had to drive along not-so-well-maintained roads.

Of course, a lot of my trade came from the lakeside. People drove up in their boats and anchored at the bright red dock below the lighthouse, coming up the red and white steps to the shop and sitting on the veranda below me. As though called up by my brain, a boat launched from Anderson's Point, angling across Church Bay to me. There was another public dock down the coast from me. The boat might be heading there.

I sipped my drink, eyeing the buildings a quarter mile away. Why did Dallas come back here to open a restaurant? He had one in Vegas, one in Kansas City, and one somewhere in the morass that was southern California. Why come to Minnesota? I didn't know him well. He and Lily Malone were part of the Cool Crowd at tech school. My parents died in a boating accident when I was still in high school, and my tuition was paid by a small fund established for me by my father's ministerial flock. I was seventeen and on my own, struggling to make ends meet.

Dallas' father owned one of the biggest boat emporiums on the lake, and Lily's father had a thriving business creating outdoor spas and swimming pools. Her grandmother owned a dress store in town and catered to the wealthy tourists. Dallas aspired to be a high-end chef, and Lily was into Hospitality Management, plus she was a talented singer and dancer. I envisioned them opening a high-class restaurant in the Twin Cities or maybe Chicago.

Instead, Dallas almost drowned, I saved his life, and he thought Lily was his savior because I was afraid of being seen in my plus-plus-sized swimsuit. I dragged his butt to the shallows and left before anyone spied me. Lily was the one he saw bending over him when he opened his eyes. He went to New York City and a modeling career, and Lily followed him there. I wasn't sure on the chronology of events, but I think they broke up and he eventually landed in Hollywood and an acting career. From what I read in the gossip rags, they were reunited a decade or two later, when they were partnered on one of those celebrity dancing shows. Now he was a restaurateur and she was his business, and maybe his romantic, partner.

Yeah, they left for the bright lights of New York City and Hollywood and I remained behind, nineteen years old and badly overweight. I packed on more weight, eating myself in and out of depression until I took a grip on my life.

All the girls were infatuated with Dallas back then, but he was so far out of my league I wasn't. I may as well have wished for Hugh Jackman to swoop in and whisk me away. No, I never saw Dallas as Crush Material. He was a nice guy, not The Guy. And now they were back. Thirty years had passed, and he was still amazingly handsome, if the photographs I saw in *People* magazine were to be believed. Tall and slender with broad shoulders, a long, narrow face, and thick gray hair and goatee. Voted *Sexiest Man Alive* three times, one of which was when he turned fifty.

I pushed my gray-streaked black hair behind my ears and sipped more whiskey. I wouldn't be voted Sexiest Anything, and that didn't bother me. The girl who cried because of her nickname had learned to love who she was without worrying about appearances. It took me more than ten years, but I shed about two hundred pounds, and now I was a successful businesswoman, happily single, and looking forward to my fiftieth birthday in a month.

I went to the railing, eyeing the boat coming through the chop toward me. It was a cuddy cruiser, a small, closed boat which meant I couldn't see who was inside. It was definitely heading for our dock. I glimpsed a ghostly shape moving into the shadows around the bottom of the lighthouse, one paw raised to step onto the boulders at the base.

"That damn cat," I muttered. A big tabby cat had taken to hanging around, often seen in company with a smaller version of him or herself. Jamie fed the critters occasional scraps and nicknamed the bigger one King Fisher and the little one Shrimp. They never let me get close to them, probably suspecting I'd grab them and call Animal Control.

As I watched, the bigger cat leapt from the rocks around the base of the lighthouse and meandered onto the planking. The smaller cat, intimidated by the distance, watched until finally curiosity got the better of it and it picked its way on the boulders to join its bigger self in meeting the boat which was now docked.

I finished my drink and set the glass on the plastic end table behind me. When I turned, I saw that a man and woman were exiting the boat, moving onto the dock and walking toward the steps. They were dressed in the epitome of Lake Shore Living, the man with khaki pants and a Hawaiian shirt, the woman in khaki Bermuda shorts and a similar shirt. They appeared tanned, lean, and wealthy. Just the kind of person I liked to see dock at my shop to spend a boatload of money.

The cat, playing a role of greeter, approached them. The man leaned down, and the cat rubbed against the man's hand, acting like they were best friends. When the man straightened, Shrimp bounded up to him and stropped against his legs, leaving a dusting of fur on the man's crisp khaki trousers.

The big cat approached the woman, but she shooed it away with an almost-kick. The man said something to the woman, who gestured dismissively, then he stared up, one hand shading his eyes. He spied me and waved then hurried forward. The woman made a comment and let him go ahead of her. She paused to peer up, her shoulder-length, shaggy blonde hair blowing in the breeze.

Holy crap on a cupcake. Dallas Prinze and Lily Malone. What the hell were they doing here?

Chapter Two

I raced into my bedroom and viewed myself in the pedestal mirror. What I saw wasn't a disaster, but it wasn't an example of Lake Shore Living, either. I brushed my hair and slipped on a red headband to keep it tidy, then I grabbed a clean white chef's coat to pull on over my blue tank top. I considered changing my pants but decided my denim capris were clean enough. I did get a clean pair of Crocs, though, the white ones with rainbow design on the sole. It matched the rainbow band on the exercise tracker on my wrist.

I stumbled down the stairs and got to the shop door as the first knock sounded. I opened the door, prepared to finesse through my embarrassment at greeting these ghosts from my past.

Lily thrust out her hand. "Are you Theresa Gallant? I'm Lily Monroe. I'm Dallas Prinze's business representative. I suppose you know we're opening a new restaurant near Mermaid Shores Resort. We've heard your cakes and pies are the best around."

I clasped her hand, and she gave mine a brisk shake. "I heard you were opening a shop," I said inanely. "Who told you mine were the best around?" I peeked past her to Dallas, who stood there with a bemused look on his amazingly handsome face.

Lily waved a perfectly manicured hand. She was like I remembered—chic, tall, long-legged. Lily was beautiful with a capital B. I always wondered why she never went into modeling, the way Dallas did. Her shoulder-length ash-blonde hair appeared artfully tousled, and her wide blue eyes weren't creased at the corners the way my blue eyes were. I always envied her long, lean physique. I was a Shetland pony compared to Lily's thoroughbred.

"We've done our research," she said dismissively. "We talked to people in town. We think it might be beneficial—"

I spoke past her to Dallas. "What do you think?"

He regarded me above Lily's head. "Can we come in and talk?"

"Sure." I went into the shop, my mind churning. One thing was becoming perfectly clear.

They didn't recognize me.

Lily and Dallas acted like I was a total stranger. Granted, we weren't close, but wouldn't Lily know me? After all, she and I rescued Dallas. And Dallas—my face flared with color when I remembered our naked swim. The thing was, he wouldn't remember that at all. As far as he was concerned, it was Lily who mattered that night.

Thirty years, I thought, leading the way past the empty display cases to the tables near the patio doors. Thirty years and two hundred pounds. "Have a seat." I went to the storage cabinet. "Would you like a cupcake? I have some ready for tomorrow."

Dallas pulled out a chair for Lily, who sank down with a graceful swish of fabric. "Thank you. That would be nice," she said.

"And you?" I asked Dallas.

He smiled faintly. "Thanks. Yes."

I put two Pride cupcakes on saucers and brought them to the table with forks and napkins. "What brings you to my side of the harbor?" I set the plates in front of my guests.

"As you know, our restaurant serves local ingredients, and we prefer to use local vendors if possible. We've been told you have rather good desserts, and we'd like to feature them one or two nights a week." Lily unfolded the paper napkin and settled it primly on her khaki-clad lap.

I watched Dallas' long fingers gently pull away the cupcake wrapper to reveal the multi-colored layers of the cupcake. "Interesting," he commented.

"Oh, dear," Lily said. "We couldn't serve anything like this."

"Like what?" I sank into a chair opposite Dallas, Lily on my left.

"We want to maintain a friendly presence in our restaurants. We don't take political stands." She used the fork to take a bite of the cupcake. "It's delicious. Your buttercream frosting is unique." She pushed the plate away after that one bite.

"Yeah. I'm sort of known for my buttercream." I crossed my legs, one rainbow Croc dangling on my foot. "It's not about taking a political stand. It's the law. Everybody treated equally and all that."

Lily's lips twitched and, for one second, I flashed back, remembering that condescending, *you silly, stupid child* look. "I'm sure you're right, but it's not the sort of thing that attracts customers. Regardless of one's sexual orientation, we strive to be as neutral as possible."

"I'm not gay, if that's what you're saying. And I am being neutral. I support the law, which says that

LGBT+ folks are supposed to be treated like everybody else."

"Yes, but that kind of thinking can alienate a certain clientele."

"Oh, you'd be surprised. I get lots of different clientele in my shop." I kept my voice level, but it was an effort. It was her kind of attitude that made my anger start to churn. I understood the avowedly Christian woman earlier in the day. My father had been a minister, and I knew about Church doctrine and indoctrination. Lily's prejudice wasn't like that. Hers was the kind that kowtowed to the supposedly elite, taking their opinions for her own. That more than anything pissed me off.

Dallas took a bite of his cupcake, foregoing the fork for the messy pleasure of using his fingers. "Great buttercream," he stated. "Very rich, and there's a hint of mint? Or maybe it's almond. It's hard to pin down. But the cupcake is almost too moist." I started to defend my baking skills, but he overrode me. "Of course, you're at lakeside and need to take that into account. I suppose by the end of the day, absorption occurs." He smiled a slow, engaging grin. "That's what Monsieur DePuis used to say, at least. You look great."

I leaned back, tension oozing out of me. "What gave it away?"

Dallas held up the cupcake. "Your buttercream. You excelled at buttercream. I remember that instructor—what was her name? She taught Intro to Decorating—she said your buttercream was the best she'd ever tasted. She wanted to know your secret."

"Mrs. Christian. She used to watch me make my frosting and she couldn't tell what my secret ingredient was."

Lily looked from me to Dallas. "Do you know her?"

"Yes. You know her, too, Lily. It's Tug."

"Tug?" Lily stared at me, and the shocked expression in her perfectly outlined blue eyes was sweet reward. "No, it can't be."

I raised an eyebrow. "It is."

"But you—" Her gaze swept over me. "You're thin."

"How about that? I'm thin and I'm a baker. That's an oxymoron if ever there was one."

Dallas laughed, a big guffaw that reminded me of our classroom days. He was always a clown, and his laughter was always infectious.

I was hard pressed not to join him. It was delicious to see Lily's stunned face. She squelched my humor quickly. "How interesting you're here," she said, talking through Dallas' laugh. "I'm sure we can use our former association to a marketing advantage."

"What do you mean?"

She waved an artful hand. "Local kids make good, working together at the new restaurant in town. Maybe we can employ a few of the students from the school and show how we're anxious to help our Alma Mater."

I had a vision of my employees vanishing, lured away by her promise of wealthy customers and more money. Then I gave myself a mental shake. I might lose a few, but I wouldn't worry about something that might not happen. "I'm sure it might be a good ploy, but I've been using it for years. That's how I got started."

"How did you do it?" Dallas leaned forward, pushing aside the crumbs of his cupcake. "Lose weight, open the shop, settle here?"

Lily put her hand on his wrist. "We don't have time to get caught up tonight," she said. "We have to meet Senator King for dinner."

"I'm sure the senator can wait."

She withdrew her hand. "He's rather important to our plans for a pier."

"King?" I asked. "That asshole? If he had his way, I'd be out of business, and anybody who isn't his idea of normal would be forced to work beyond the town limits, including minorities, immigrants, and LGBT+ folks."

"He's an important political figure, however," Lily said coolly. "Regardless of his beliefs, we need to work with him."

"Why don't you go without me?" Dallas suggested. "You're in charge of those kinds of things. Lily handles licensing and permits." He glanced at her hand on his wrist. She removed it. "She's great at handling infrastructure details."

Because his gaze was fixed on me, he didn't see the flash of resentment that I saw in her cool, sea-blue eyes. Then her façade slid back into place. "Maybe Tug is busy tonight and doesn't have time to reminisce. After all, she has a business to run, too." Lily smiled perfunctorily at me while pushing her chair back from the table.

"No, nothing planned." I relaxed, trying to look the picture of a woman with all the time in the world. "I do keep baker's hours, though," I warned. "Early to bed, early to rise."

Dallas laughed. "I hated that. I never got used to going to bed before the sun set."

"I don't go to bed that early. I have students from the school who are on internships. They come in and do the baking. I do the finishing." I regarded Lily, who stood and tucked her handbag under her arm. "I'd be interested in seeing a business proposal about a possible opportunity at your new place."

"We'll get something to you in the next day or two." She put her hand on Dallas' shoulder. "We need to get going."

"I told you, Lily. I think I'll stay and chat."

She lifted her hand as though scalded. "I can't drive the boat. You'll need to take me. Perhaps you can come back and get caught up with Tug another day." She went to the door.

Dallas watched her, his face cold. Then he relaxed. "That's not a problem. I'll call Nate at Pride of the Sea. He'll pick you up and leave a boat for me." Dallas pulled a cell phone from his shirt pocket. "You remember Nate, don't you? He used to work for Dad." He tapped something on his phone while he talked. "He loaned me a boat for tonight. He bought Dad's business when Dad died." Dallas leaned back in his chair, phone to his ear.

I looked at Lily, who stood at the shop door. It was like she'd been turned to stone, her face a mask of fury. I tidied up the remains of their cupcakes and took the plates to the counter. I was sure that if I said anything, she might erupt into Lord knows what kind of temper tantrum. I vaguely remembered her pulling that kind of shit when we were younger. *Lily has anger issues,* a teacher told me once. Looking at her now, I guessed she hadn't solved that problem through the years.

Dallas finished his call and stood. "All set. Nate will be here in a few minutes."

"Are you sure?" Lily asked, her voice as sweet as honey. "We have a lot of details to discuss and—"

"I thought the licensing was taken care of. You're in charge of that. I want to take a break. I've gone back and forth between here and Vegas for the past month. I'm focusing on one location for a change." Dallas joined me at the counter, touching my shop logo on one of the napkins. "I can't believe you kept that name."

"Why not? A tugboat is small, powerful, and pushes around the bigger boats." I tucked the used dishes off to one side. "That's not a bad image."

"Perhaps you can escort me to the dock," Lily said frostily. "We can discuss how I should handle Senator King."

Dallas' lips thinned. "Sure," he snapped. "Let's do that. I'll be right back, Tug."

"No hurry." I let them out the shop door, then I raced upstairs, going to the window to watch them. This was interesting. Apparently, Dallas didn't like Lily bossing him around, and he was using me as an excuse to draw a line in the sand. That hinted at a relationship dynamic that was at odds with my idea of the perfect Hollywood couple.

They were on the steps to the dock. Lily stalked ahead of Dallas, saying something over her shoulder. As she did, the tabby cat—King Fisher—darted out from the rocks that held back the bluff where the lighthouse sat. He trotted onto the step ahead of her. She nudged the cat and caught him on the butt, making him scramble. It wasn't a full-blow kick, but it was enough to make me long to slap her. Nobody did that kind of shit to smaller creatures when I was around, even if it was to a mangy interloper.

Dallas said something to her and she whirled to confront him. If I opened the window wider, I might be able to hear what they were saying. The wind was in my favor. I decided I didn't want to know, and besides, it wasn't anything to do with me.

I saw my sandwich plate. If Dallas was missing dinner, maybe I should make him a sandwich. I put together another turkey-and-swiss on our special rye bread and added a few potato chips on the side. About the time I finished I heard a boat nearing the shore. I went to the window and watched a man approach the dock on the opposite side from the small cruiser. Dallas took the bowline from him and secured the runabout, typically used for puttering around on the lake. The man leapt from the boat and they shook hands, Dallas gesturing to the cruiser. I glimpsed Lily sitting with her back to the two men.

I took the sandwich and went downstairs, going on the porch to put the plate on one of our tables. Dallas came up the lakeside steps a few minutes later. "Out here," I called.

He came through the screen door, the tabby cat close on his heels. "You're welcome, not the cat," I said when the creature attempted to ooze in behind him.

"Sorry, buddy." Dallas shooed the cat back outside and joined me. "I figured it was your cat."

"Nope. He's only a beach bum. I made you a sandwich. I figured it was the least I could do since you're missing dinner." I nudged the plate toward his side of the table, and he sat. "Do you want something to drink? I have water, bourbon, or lemonade."

"That's an interesting selection." He took a bite of the sandwich. "Lemonade would be nice."

I went into the shop and poured him a glass of lemonade from the big urn we kept in the cooler. I set the aluminum glass in front of him and resumed my seat. "I won't stock anything in plastic bottles, and that limits my choices. Most folks get their coffee at the Jolt then come here for their treat, or vice versa. The bourbon isn't normally offered to customers." I winked at him.

"I figured that." He took a sip of the lemonade. "I'm sorry about Lily. She gets wrapped up in work and forgets how to be social sometimes."

"She's your business manager?" I asked.

"She manages a portion of my business operations." He gazed around the porch. "You've got a good spot here, Tug. Nice breezes off the lake."

"It was awfully run down when I first saw it. It took me two years to get it back into shape. I didn't do it alone. Jamie Priest owns the Jolt, next door. I worked out of his shop until the lighthouse was habitable." I grimaced, remembering those days of back-breaking repairs and baking, trying to create a home while starting a business.

"Does it still have the lamp? Can you lure ships to their doom?"

"No, it was decommissioned a long time ago. There is a high intensity lamp I use now and then, when I know someone's coming to visit when it's getting dark. Mostly I just try to make sure no birds are getting too comfortable."

"Where have you been since graduation?" He took another bite of his sandwich, his eyes fixed on me.

I leaned back, not sure where to begin. "I guess it started with a mentor I had. She was so—" I stared at the lake, the setting sun making it glint and sparkle. "Madame Marcelle was the *pâtissier* at my first professional bakery job in Paris."

"You were in Paris?" Dallas asked, his head jerking up in shock.

"First Paris, then D.C., then Seattle, until I finally came back here. Anyway, Madame Marcelle was a marvelous individual. Tall, big-boned, with wide hips and a big bosom and a personality bigger than any *chef de cuisine*. She'd say to me, *Cherie, you are who you are. Do not try to be someone else. You are not one of those straws we see on the television.*" I spoke with an exaggerated French accent. "*Those straws are thin on the outside and empty on the inside. You, mon Cherie, are a luscious glass of wine, a good, solid sip of life. But you must make sure you care for yourself so you can live your life to the fullest. Too thin or too heavy, both are bad for the heart and the soul. Find yourself and free yourself.*"

"That was all it took?" he asked.

"No, but it was the start. I knew it was more important to be healthy than be thin. I was fat, and that affected my life and my work. I needed to do something to change it."

Dallas nodded. "I know what you mean."

I doubted he did, but it was nice of him to say it. "I ate more because I was depressed and I knew I was ugly. When I finally got a job, it was hard to work because of my weight. I was always sweaty and exhausted. That only made me feel uglier. It seemed impossible. I needed to lose two hundred pounds." I shook my head. "Where should I even start? Plus I was working in kitchens and food was everywhere."

"What did you do?" Dallas asked.

"I tried everything. Any popular diet? I tried it. I counted carbs, counted calories, counted fat. Things worked at first, and I was skinny and pretty and damn hungry." I sighed, remembering those heady days of size eight dresses. "Then I'd fall off the wagon and eat and eat and gain the weight back."

"It sounds like a curse."

"It's a curse most women face because we see these beautiful people in magazines. I had an image in my head about who I should be. I wanted to eat food and enjoy pastries and wine, and I wanted to be thin. I wanted to be tall and one-hundred-twenty pounds with a flat belly and long legs and long hair. I wanted to be beautiful. But it wasn't possible."

"Tall?" His brown eyes twinkled with mischief. "Vastly overrated."

"Spoken by a man who's six-feet tall and never has to get a stepstool to get anything from the top cabinet."

"Good point."

"I needed to rethink what the best version of me was. I was focusing on my appearance. I needed to focus on being healthy. I started an exercise program I'd follow. I used to love to swim, but I got away from it because I was afraid of what people would think of me—a fat person, at the pool." My face got hot, remembering my swimming adventure with him.

"Tugboat," he murmured.

"Yep. I decided I didn't care what people thought of me. I wanted to swim, and by God, I would do it. I got an exercise tracker—" I raised my hand, "I bought a swimsuit, and I joined a gym with a pool. I went swimming every morning, first thing."

Dallas raised his head, looking like he might speak. When he didn't, I continued. "I didn't want to live a life of crackers and diet cola. I came up with a routine that I could follow without much effort. I eat small portion sizes. I exercise every day, and I lost two hundred pounds over the course of many years. Here I am, owning a bakery and still swimming every morning. At the park in summer, at the gym in winter."

"That's a hell of a story." He finished the sandwich with two large bites and pushed the plate away.

There was more angst I wasn't saying, but he didn't need to know about that. It was tough to date anyone when you needed to be asleep by six at night in order to be in the kitchen at two in the morning. And it was tough to date, period, when you were overweight with a stocky physique and boring brown hair and a slightly too-big nose. No, Mr. Sexiest Man Alive didn't need to know about that.

"What about you?" I asked. "I know you were in the movies for a while, right?"

"Yeah, but it didn't feel right to me. I forgot what I wanted to do. When you're in the movie business, you get shoved into this character and that character, and before you know it, you sort of lose track of who the characters are. It was fun at first but later…" He shrugged. "Later it was only a job. That's when I decided maybe I'd try my hand at cooking again. I always loved being in the kitchen."

I doubted if he was in the kitchen now, and my skepticism must have shown because he said, "I work with the chefs at my restaurants. Sometimes they even let me cook." He sounded wistful.

"I'd like to see that," I said with a small laugh. "As I recall, you weren't the clumsiest student, but it was close."

Dallas shot me an admonishing look. "I remember someone who almost cut off her finger trying to show off her knife skills."

I raised my left hand and wiggled it. "And I have the scar to prove it." I grinned at him. "I try to offload as much as I can anymore. I don't DIY. I WTC."

"What?"

"I write the check. I don't have time for the daily grind."

"It's not a grind. It's a channel for our creativity."

"Spoken by the man who hires everything done for him."

"Not all."

"Yeah, right."

"You don't believe me? I'll show you."

"Show me what?"

"Help me design a mural at the restaurant, and I'll cook you a meal."

"What kind of mural?"

"Something with a lake theme. I have a mural done in every restaurant that's local. Something about the local scene. I usually design it and paint at least part of it."

I pointed a finger at him. "You see what I mean? You have a mural done. You don't do the murals."

Dallas made a grab for my hand, but I evaded him. "I'll bet you forgot how to chef."

He grinned. "I haven't heard chef used as a verb since Mr. Hans' class."

I wrinkled my nose. Old Mr. Hans taught Meat Fabrication. It was not my favorite class. "I'll bet you haven't spatchcocked a chicken since your butchering days."

"I haven't forgotten how," he said. "I'll tell you what. You help me with the mural, and I'll show you I haven't forgotten Meat Management."

I considered his challenge. What did I have to lose? "Okay. I'll do painting, you do chefing."

"Deal." He drained his lemonade glass in one long gulp. "I'll show you I still know my way around a stove."

"We'll see. Here." I pulled a business card from my coat pocket and jotted my cell phone number on it. "Give me a call when you're ready to start painting."

He pocketed it. "Will do. It's good to see you, Tug."

"You, too. I'm glad to see that you and Lily are still together."

He fumbled the glass, dropping it on the table where it took a bounce. I caught it before it tumbled to the floor. "Lily and me? What about us?"

"You guys were together during school. And it looks like you're still together." I wasn't sure how to gauge his reaction. He appeared almost panicked by my assumption.

"Lily works with me. In fact, she works for Sirena. You remember her, don't you? Our guidance counselor from school? Sirena runs a company that helps people handle the business side of the restaurant business."

I did remember Sirena, and the memory wasn't a fond one. She was young at the time, in her mid-twenties, and she really didn't have the aptitude or the empathy to be a guidance counselor. She certainly never gave me the time of day the few times I talked to her. "I didn't know that. I lost track of most folks when I left school."

"Lily and I were together briefly, then I went west and went into acting. We got together a few years ago on that stupid dancing show." He looked sidelong at me.

"Sorry. I go to bed early, remember? I don't have time for T.V."

"I'm glad you never saw it. Lily tried to make a go of it in New York when I was there, and that didn't work out. Then I left, and I guess she kind of fell on hard times. She was in Vegas, and they were doing auditions for that dumb TV show. That's how she found me again. My agent wanted me to do the show."

From his tone of voice, Lily finding him wasn't exactly a fortuitous occurrence. "What a happy accident," I murmured.

"She was hoping that might get her dancing jobs, but it didn't. Then Sirena got in touch with Lily with an idea to go into restaurant management. Lily works for her." Dallas tapped the table as he spoke, a staccato rhythm punctuated now and then by one heavy thump. "When I decided to leave acting it was natural to go back to the restaurant business. I always wanted to try it." He frowned, his eyes fixed on something in the distance.

"I guess I assumed you and she were together all this time. You're well matched."

"Really?" He shifted his attention to me. "Why?"

"I don't know. You're both attractive, both come from rich families—you have a lot in common, I suppose."

"A lot in common. I suppose it looks that way. I suppose it's always looked that way."

There wasn't any answer to that. He seemed sad or maybe in a funk. "Hey, whatever happened to Ricky— you know the guy, the one who made that lewd cake and nearly gave Mrs. Anderson heart failure." I don't know what recess of memory housed that incident, but it was suddenly vivid.

That did the trick. We launched into a few minutes of 'I wonder what he's doing now', getting caught up on our old classmates. Dallas had stayed in touch with a surprising number of them, and I gradually realized that many of them hit him up for help now and then. "The Alumni office has been after me to do promotion for them," he said. "Maybe you and I can team up and do something for them—you know, a photo spread or something."

"I think they'd rather have you in their promotional materials," I pointed out. "You're the successful restaurateur. I'm a lowly baker."

"This isn't the digs of a lowly baker. You've done well for yourself, Tug." He shook his head. "I can't get past that name."

"Jamie and I were talking about that earlier today. It's been so long since anybody called me Theresa, I doubt I'd remember it's my name."

"Theresa." The syllables rolled off his lips.

I shivered at the sound of it. The way he said it was sensual. The mood was broken by the cat, who meowed at us from the patio door, pawing at something on the doormat. "What's that creature doing now?" I went to the door, prepared to shoo the beast away. "Oh, for heaven's sake."

"What is it?" Dallas joined me to view a mouse, squished under the cat's paw. "Look, he brought you a present."

"I don't need a dead mouse," I muttered. "I run a bakery. That's all I need—a health code violation."

"It's not dead," Dallas pointed out.

I did a doubletake. The poor rodent was squirming under the cat's toes. "You dumb cat." I went to open the door, but Dallas put his hand on mine on the door handle.

"If you do that, he's liable to sneak past us and drop it in here." Dallas glanced behind us to the door to the bakery. "Close everything up before you do anything."

"Good thinking." I hurried to the door and secured it. As soon as I did, Dallas opened the patio door and scooped up the cat, hooking one hand under the big feline's belly. The mouse stumbled away while the cat dangled in Dallas' grip.

It purred loudly, and I suspected this was his end game—*give them mouse, get picked up.* "It's not a bad thing to have a mouser around," Dallas said, going outside to set the cat in the grass edging around the steps. The cat promptly stropped Dallas' legs, purring madly.

"Maybe," I said, knowing full well I'd never encourage it.

"I'd better be going." Dallas paused at the top of the steps until I joined him, then we descended them together. The cat, mission accomplished, vanished into the shrubbery near the path. "Listen, thanks for the heads-up about that senator."

"What?"

"You know, the bigoted one. I want to make sure to be inclusive at my restaurant. Lily tends to steer me toward what she thinks are safe clients to work with, but I think it's more fun when I branch out." He got to the runabout and unhooked the guideline from the stanchion. "If somebody wants to rent my restaurant for their wedding, gay or not, I'm all for it."

"I'm glad to hear you say that. I know what it's like to be on the outside, looking in. I hate to imagine planning my big wedding then finding nobody wants to host it or make a cake for it." I shook my head. "It's unfair."

"You're a good person, Tug."

"Nah. I just like to stick to the Man every now and then." He laughed. "Can you find your way home?" I asked.

"I've navigated this lake hundreds of times," he assured me, jumping into the boat. "Some things never change. Unlike you, Tug. You changed."

"Not really. I'm still the girl with the world's best buttercream frosting."

He grinned. "That you are. Good night."

"Hey, Dallas?"

He looked up.

"Don't worry if you don't want to do the bakery thing at your restaurant. I won't hold it against you."

"Are you kidding? I'm looking forward to it." He undid the rear mooring line and let the boat drift away from the dockside.

"Will you be okay on the lake?"

"What, you don't trust my navigation ability?"

"It's a big lake. And it's getting dark."

"I'll be fine." He started the engine and backed away from the dock, waving before he headed out. I watched him, reassured when I saw how capably he piloted the small boat. I went back up to the lighthouse, pausing to check for any mouse bodies near the porch. Thankfully there were none. I tidied up Dallas' dishes then went upstairs.

I was surprised by how easily he and I talked. It was like old times, hanging at the test kitchens, chatting over recipes and batter. I went upstairs to my bedroom, going on the deck to watch the boat go across the bay then southward, out of sight.

How odd that he and Lily were back here, together but not together, if Dallas was to be believed. Well, if anyone would know, he would, I thought. I changed into my sleep T-shirt and nestled into my covers, bits and pieces of conversation rattling around in my head. Dallas and Lily weren't a couple and hadn't been for years and years. He was interested in using my desserts at his restaurants, which might mean I'd need to consider increasing my output. If I did that, I might need more help.

I mulled around a few ideas, then sleep finally took me. I had developed the habit of allowing myself a few minutes of worry-time at night, but I learned early on in my bakery career that I needed to shelve worry in favor of grabbing what sleep I could. Within fifteen minutes I was settling into a light doze.

I was in that first foggy phase of sleep where I was drifting into semi-consciousness when I heard the fireworks. It was a series of distant booms, heard through the open window across the room. Somebody always set off fireworks at one of the lake homes. This one sounded close. I sat up to peer through the north windows above the staircase, expecting to see a shimmer of light. Those windows were made of glass block, and I never got a clear view of any fireworks.

Instead, the glass of the window exploded.

Chapter Three

"What the hell?" I swung my feet over the side of the bed but stopped myself in time. There might be glass, and I was barefoot. Not a good idea.

I leaned out perilously, placing one hand on the wooden floor gingerly. My slippers were somewhere under the bed. I groped about and finally found them, jamming them on my feet before stepping cautiously onto the floor.

My bed was at an angle in the southeast corner, and the bathroom was opposite me. On the south and east side of the room were the doors to the deck. I checked each of those and breathed a sigh of relief. Thank God those hadn't broken. The doors were six-feet wide and tall and expensive to replace. I knew how expensive they were because I had them specially made when I bought the lighthouse.

It was one of the two windows at the top of the north wall that now had a halo of broken glass around a hole. I approached it, moonlight and the nightlight from the bathroom showing me the way. I couldn't get close to the window because the downward stairs were between me and it. But from what I saw, there was a small hole with discoloration around it.

I considered trying to cover the hole then reasoned that it was small enough I didn't need to worry about it. I'd take a closer look in the morning. Those windows were thick, and any damage would be minimal. I shuffled back to bed and was asleep in a few minutes.

I came downstairs at five the next morning and tackled the day's quota of decorating. I made the frosting for Thursday's cake and the fondant for one of Saturday's cakes. The tiers for the Thursday cake were made and cooling. Plus six small four-inch cakes awaited me for piping as well as several dozen cupcakes. The night shift had already handled the turnovers and cookies, which required less work.

I enjoyed this time of day. Windows were on each side of my lighthouse, plus the patio door led to the catwalk connecting the lighthouse and keeper's house next door where the Jolt was situated. The east sun peeked in above the couch to highlight my working island off the kitchen. I heard the morning crew downstairs getting ready to open at six. We always had a steady stream of early customers. It would slow in mid-morning and pick up again at lunch when people bought their afternoon snacks.

I finished in an hour then went downstairs, waving to the girls behind the counter before slipping out the main door. Morning was my time to swim and, in the summertime, that meant swimming in the lake. I followed the path at the edge of the bluff, the rocky lake shore below me, as much as a hundred feet in spots. My only company were the two cats who prowled through the flowers, tails flicking while they stalked an unsuspecting creature.

When I first bought the property, this was a weedy and overgrown piece of turf, with bare patches of dirt showing where the wind off the lake scoured the land. I worked with local Master Gardeners to rehabilitate the six-acre property, installing shrubs as windbreaks and planting the terrain with pollinator-friendly plants. The result was a flower-lined path that buzzed and bloomed happily.

I walked along the pebbled path in the dawning sunlight, the tall oaks and maples bordering the property in sharp relief from the rising sun. About two hundred yards from the lighthouse, I came to the spot where my land intersected the adjoining park occupying the rest of Hardscrabble Point, a narrow peninsula of land jutting eastward into Church Bay. The bluff here was more of a slope, the land easing downward to meet the shore.

I followed the path to the sandy beach. It was lightly pebbled with a diving platform about a hundred yards from the shore with a smaller, 'resting' platform at about fifty yards. I kicked off my Crocs and shed my baker's jacket and shorts. My swimsuit was the first item of clothing I pulled on in the morning, winter or summer. It reminded me to get off my butt and exercise, which was a key component in me losing weight gradually without the unsightly gathering of loose skin that often accompanied a big drop in poundage.

I also changed the band on my exercise tracker daily, another reminder to stay fit. It was my only "jewelry", and I liked to change it up. Today's was a pink flowered one which matched my swimsuit, a demure two-piece, with a pink flowered blousy top and a pair of black boy-short bottoms. I walked to the water's edge, gazing at the bay where a few lazy boats puttered toward me. We often got hometown folks— known as lakers—in the morning. They'd hop in their boats and come over to load up on treats for their houseguests. A couple of the B-and-Bs in the area had a standing arrangement with us for pies, cakes, or breads.

I walked into the water, the cool liquid lapping against my shins. Minnesota lakes were always cool, if not icy. This year the ice didn't go out on the lake until the first part of May, plus we had a cool spring so the water was still chilly. Now we were smack in the middle of June, and summer had descended on us with high temperatures and choking humidity.

Freeze or burn, I thought as I dove in. I swam through the lapping water, following my usual routine. Freestyle to the resting platform, backstroke to the bigger one. Rest a minute or two then sidestroke back to the shore and repeat it one more time.

By the time I finished, kayakers were on the shore, getting ready to launch. I left the water and stretched out on my beach towel, catching my breath and basking in the morning sunlight. A light breeze always eddied on the beach, and for the time being, at least, I was cool and comfortable.

I flipped onto my stomach and resumed the thread of my contemplations from the night before. If I got work from Dallas for his restaurant, I would need to consider an auxiliary location. We had converted the lightkeeper's house into the Jolt, and half of the one-story building was used for my bakery. It was adequate to supply the shop, but if I wanted to produce products for a restaurant, I'd need more room.

Jamie and I had discussed adding an addition to the Jolt, but we weren't anxious to incur debt if we weren't assured of a quick way to pay it off. This deal with Dallas might be the answer we were looking for.

The idea energized me. I dried off with my other towel and dragged on my clothes, hurrying back to the lighthouse. To avoid the morning shoppers, I went into the back door of the bakery at the Jolt and up the steps to access the second-floor catwalk connecting the two structures. I entered my kitchen through the sliding door next to the stove.

When I passed the sitting area, I noticed the light blinking on my phone. I pressed the Play button on the answering machine.

"You think you can do whatever you want, and decent people won't care. You wait and see. We have ways to get you and those perverts off the lake. If you're not careful, you might have a nasty accident. You might even fall off that deck of yours at night when you're sitting and having a drink. Or maybe when you go for a swim. You're there alone. Who knows what might happen? Your rich celebrity friends can't help you. You'll never know when it will happen, but it will. We don't want your kind of people here."

The voice was calm and low. I think it was a woman. I sank onto the couch, my knees rubbery. Was someone watching me? I touched the button to play it again then I stopped. I didn't want to repeat it.

I sat there for a few minutes, shaking. When I was obese, I grew accustomed to the sidelong looks, the faintly accusing way people evaluated me. This was far, far worse. This was a direct threat. I needed to call the police. Even if they didn't care what happened to me, the caller was threatening my place of business, and that meant innocent civilians might be put at risk. I sprang to my feet and raced upstairs. I showered and changed into clean capris and a fresh baker's jacket over a polo shirt with my logo.

I brushed my hair, thankful that it required no upkeep on my part other than washing and going. I tried a variety of styles through the years and always came back to chin-length hair, parted in the middle and held back with a headband. My straight-as-a-rail hair seemed to prefer that.

I started down the steps but then I remembered the window. I would need to get someone to look at that. I went on the deck to examine the damaged glass. I saw it better in the morning light. It was a small, round hole with a tiny bit of crackling surrounding it. I turned to go back inside when I noticed other round holes in the concrete of the lighthouse structure. I reached up, trying to see how deep the pitting went. What could have caused that pattern of holes? This was too high up to be subject to rocks or other debris from the shore. I shelved that worry for later. Right now, I needed to call the police.

Call or visit? I considered that on my walk downstairs. Maybe a visit might carry more weight. I paused at the answering machine, wondering if I dared disconnect it and take it with me. It was part of the entire phone, though, and I might erase everything if I did that. In the end, I called the Denmark PD and left a message for Detective Usher, the young policeman who came to see me when I got the first of the nasty letters.

I went to the shop, pausing to chat with a couple of my regular customers before going next door to check in with Jamie. He was busy behind the counter whipping up customized coffee drinks, but he soon shook free and joined me on the front porch. "I talked to Lily and Dallas last night," I said, pulling him to one side to talk in private.

"Are you kidding? You said you weren't calling them." He dabbed at his sweaty face with the bar towel tucked into his back pocket. The coffee shop was often hot because the northerly breezes were blocked by the lighthouse, and the western side was where the bakery was housed so it was always warm. "That's great. Did you mention our idea about being featured in the restaurant?"

"They came to me. They must be staying on Turfmoor Peninsula or one of the hotels on Anderson's Point. Dallas was using a boat from Pride of the Sea. A guy we know owns it now."

"What guy?"

"Nate something or other. I vaguely remember him. He was taking marine mechanics while we were in school. He and Dallas hung out together. Anyway, Dallas and Lily came and asked to talk to Theresa Gallant." I waited expectantly.

Jamie dabbed his face again. "Wait a minute. They didn't know who you were?" I nodded. "Man, that's sweet. They came to see you on reputation alone. Did you make a deal? Are we serving up coffee and dessert?"

"Nothing's in writing yet. Lily is supposed to get me a business proposal. She's Dallas' business manager or restaurant manager." I frowned. "I'm not sure what she is. I got the impression from her that she's his main squeeze, but last night he ditched her and had Nate come and get her. He stayed and we talked."

Jamie grinned at me. "You sly fox, you. Look at you, slim and svelte, seducing the local celebrity. You go, girl."

I waved his innuendos away. "It wasn't like that. It was more like two old friends, hanging out and shooting the breeze."

"How could it be two old friends shooting the breeze when one of them is voted Sexiest Man Alive and was up for an Oscar nomination a few years ago?"

"That's the weird thing." I leaned against the railing of the Jolt's front porch. "It was like two old school friends getting caught up. I don't see him as a celebrity."

"What's not to see? He's rich, he's famous, and he's handsome with a capital H. How can you not see that?"

"I see it. But it doesn't matter. He's just Dallas Prinze, a guy I know." Years of being on the outside looking in had made me learn to evaluate people, not the appearance of people. When you're obese, you're automatically labeled and often dismissed as weak-willed or ineffective or over-indulgent. Because of that, I was sensitive to making assumptions about people based on their physical appearance. "He's a nice guy, and he's handsome with a capital H. I think the first is more important than the second."

"Well, I don't care if he's lame, halt, and blind. If he'll give you a contract for baked goods that means we can make improvements to the Jolt and maybe build you a proper bakery with real air conditioning and a kitchen you don't have to share with my baristas."

"As soon as I see the business proposal, I'll share it with you," I promised. "But first, I need to bring you up to speed on something that's not as pleasant." I quickly filled him in on my nasty phone call and the latest threatening mail. "I called the police and reported it, but I doubt they'll do anything. I did point out that they were threatening my business, though, which means their constituents might be at risk. If they don't give a shit about me, they might care about the mayor, who comes in every day for coffee and a cookie."

"If they don't do anything, you let me know. A couple of local cops come in now and again for a coffee to go. I'll ask them if there's anything we need to do to light a fire under the local constabulary." He walked with me back to the Jolt's front door. "I'd better get back. Keep me posted on our new business front, and make sure you mention that my coffee's the best around the lake. Maybe we can do a coupon, like buy a cupcake and get a free cup of coffee."

"Sounds good. I'll keep you in the loop." I left him at the Jolt and walked back to the lighthouse, going in through the shop and upstairs. No matter what threats might be percolating, I had wedding cakes to finish. The one due on Thursday was easy to decorate, and I tackled it first. I always asked bridal parties to give me their reception playlist, and that played in the background while I cut, smoothed, and swirled.

Odd how things work out. Here I was, happy and successful with my little business, and the Big Man on Campus approaches me. The guy whose life I saved, except he didn't know it. I suppose I was to blame for bringing Lily and Dallas together, in a very odd way.

I always loved to swim. When I was obese, I felt light and free when I was in the water. My weight fell away, and I was me, the Real Me, the one buried under the flesh. I grew up around water and learned to swim when I was a child. My father insisted on it.

"Maybe you'll need to save me someday," he'd joke because he never learned how to swim. I went through swimming lessons and on to learn Red Cross Lifesaving, which is, I suppose, why I saved Dallas Prinze's life. It was automatic for me to help.

It was late at night, and that's the only time I'd go swimming at the beach near school. The kids made fun of me otherwise. I was nineteen years old, and I weighed more than two hundred pounds. I was only five feet tall, so you can imagine what I looked like. I hated being teased but I loved to swim.

The beach was lit only by moonlight and lights from the two boats anchored in the bay. There was a party going on earlier on one of the boats, a big cabin cruiser. I saw guys laughing and fooling around, obviously drinking. Some girls were with them, but I couldn't see who was who at that distance. I stayed on the shore, lurking behind the lifeguard's chair until it got quiet on the boats. They were probably drunk and passed out, or maybe below deck, having sex. Whatever they were doing, I hoped they wouldn't notice me.

It was a hot night, and I longed for a swim to wash away the sweat from the day's work in the kitchens. I moved away from the tall platform and went down the beach, out of the range of the lights that still shone on the boats. I pulled off my chef uniform and waded into the water, striking out to the right, away from the boats. I knew this stretch of beach, and I could paddle around and circle back in a dozen yards away from my clothes.

I heard him before I saw him. Someone was gasping and splashing on my left. It took a minute for my eyes to adjust to the faint light reflected on the waves from the moon. I saw a head, bobbing in the water. Well, not bobbing but more like ducking and floundering. "Hey," I called softly. "Are you okay?"

A strangled gasp was my answer. "Help," he managed. "I can't—"

I swam toward him. I couldn't see who it was. It was too dark for that. It was a guy, though, and a tall one. I saw because he bobbed up and down and when he was up, he was big and broad-shouldered. "Are you okay?" I asked when I neared him.

"Can't find shore," he gasped.

"Come on." I held out my hand and he flailed for it. I was wearing one of those friendship bracelets, a flimsy thing woven from nylon cord. He grabbed it, and it snapped off in his hand.

"Don't panic." I reached him and saw his face. His hair was plastered to his scalp, and I wasn't sure who he was. "Look, lay back. Relax. I'll pull you to shore."

"You—can't—" He swallowed a mouthful of water and gagged, hands slapping the water.

"I can if you'll shut up and lay back." I hooked an arm under his chest and began a sidestroke, pulling him with me. "Don't fight me," I said into his face, which rested against my breasts. "Let me do it."

He went limp in my grasp, and for a second I was sure he was drowning. I had visions of him and me sinking to the bottom. They'd find me, naked, with a guy, and nobody would be able to figure out the mystery. Then his feet began to flutter, his supine body sliding against mine. That's when I realized he was naked, too. It was hard to be sure in the dim light, but I didn't see anything like a suit, and I did see what looked like boy-parts, or at least what I guessed were boy-parts. At that point in my life, I had no first-hand experience.

I struggled with him to the shallows, his breathing raspy and harsh. I fought to stay afloat and fight the waves, which thank God were relatively calm at this time of night. I finally sensed the bottom under us, and I touched down, digging my feet into the muck and sand. He rolled over, and that's when I saw it was Dallas.

"Are you okay? What happened?" Someone waved at us from the shore.

I gave him a shove, and he managed to stand, water lapping around his stomach. The person on shore plunged into the water and swam toward us with a strong overhand stroke. I backed away, kicking into the deeper water when Lily reached Dallas, her arms going around him. She was like a sea goddess, tanned and voluptuous in her tiny bikini that revealed as much as it hid.

"What happened? Did you fall over?" Lily clung to him, large boobs pressed against him and his boy-parts mashing up against her girl-parts.

He swayed, his arms around her. "You saved me," he said, staggering forward. "You were on the boat. Did you jump in?"

I swam back into deeper water, not anxious to watch. His hands were on her breasts and his face was lowered to hers. I imagined passionate action on the beach, and I didn't want to be around to witness it. I could barely manage to get back to my part of the beach without drowning myself. I was exhausted from hauling Dallas to shore. I finally got to my clothes and dressed, hurrying into the night lest I be seen by the party boys on the boat.

The next day all people talked about in class was how Lily saved Dallas' life. She acted humble and waved it off, but Dallas stuck close to her, his arm around her.

"I was stupid and drunk," he said. We were in one of the Hospitality classes, maybe Hospitality Accounting. Lily was in that class with us, and she and Dallas were always 'studying' together. "I remember being on the deck, and I fell down. I hit my head on something, and I pitched over the side."

"You're lucky you didn't drown," someone said.

"If Lily hadn't jumped in and saved me, I would have." Dallas regarded her with a look of such gratitude I longed to leap up and slap both of them. Instead I kept my mouth shut. Who would believe me?

Ah, memories. I straightened up, stepping back to eye the cake in front of me. The bridal couple were both gardeners and birdwatchers. The two-tier cake would have a bride on top standing amongst a replica of the bride's bouquet. A 'garden path' would wind along the tiers, lined with flowers and birds, ending at a tiny groom who peeked from a small door cut into the bottom of the cake.

I wasn't that far along, of course. It was only Tuesday, and I needed to add the second coating of buttercream. I would do the third coat later today then decorate the cake tomorrow.

My intercom from the shop buzzed. I set aside my bowl and went to the wall. "What's up?"

"A woman here would like to talk to you. Are you expecting anybody?"

"No, I'm not." I wondered if it was Lily, bringing me a business plan. Somehow, I doubted she worked that fast. Or, God forbid, it was the old bitch from yesterday. "Is she old and angry?"

"She said her name is Sirena Winchell. She works with Dallas Prinze." Saul Temple, the morning clerk, sounded excited. "Did you hear that he's building a new restaurant in town?"

"Yeah, I heard. She can come up." I set the cake on the staging table and tidied up my tools. I'd tackle another cake later in the day. I discovered that I could do only so much standing and piping before my quality suffered.

The door at the bottom of the stairs opened, and I heard someone ascending the steps. The stairs were a bit steep, which I suppose accounted for the huffing and puffing I heard. I hadn't seen her in thirty years but, somehow, she hadn't changed. The word that popped into my head when I saw Sirena was 'overblown', from her overly coiffed hairstyle, red hair color out of a bottle, the heavy makeup, and the clothes that were a tad too snug to be attractive. Her boxy silhouette was mannish with her broad shoulders and heavy middle. Everything about Sirena shouted 'notice me' in a loud voice. Unlike Lily, with her sleek stylishness, Sirena was a woman who strove to be sophisticated but instead appeared tacky.

"I haven't seen you in a long time." I crossed the room and extended my hand. "How are you doing?"

Sirena smiled, blood-red lips parting to reveal perfect white teeth. "Theresa, it's good to see you again. When Lily said you were here, I was surprised." She gave my hand a good shake then brushed past me to look around the room. "What an odd place to live. Interesting, but odd. Why did you set up shop here?"

It was the only thing I could afford, but I wouldn't tell her that. "It's a great location. I get lake traffic as well as people on the way to the park. I don't need much space for myself, so it works well to combine my work and my home." I gestured to the couch and the armchairs opposite the kitchen. "Can I get you something to drink? Water? Lemonade?"

"No, I'm fine." She went to the armchairs, walking cautiously on her stiletto heels. Sirena was big-boned and heavy. The dark blue pantsuit she wore looked tight enough to be uncomfortable. "Lily mentioned that you and she chatted last night. She asked me to drop by and have preliminary discussions about a possible limited partnership." Sirena sat, setting a bulky black bag on the floor next to the chair.

I considered calling Jamie then decided it was too early in the game to bring him in. "I'm happy to discuss an opportunity with Dallas' restaurant." I settled onto the couch opposite her.

"You've done well for yourself, Theresa." Sirena's gaze swept over me, head to toe. "This is a nice little store. We'll need to inspect the facilities, of course, before we can commit to any agreements. Lily and I like to talk to the shareholders in our businesses in order to ensure that we're providing a quality product."

Something about the way she said it made a little red flag go up in my head. "I believe Dallas has the last word on shareholders, doesn't he?"

She waved a hand, her red fingernails slashing through the air like talons. "He has input, certainly, but he's far too busy to bother with small details."

I remembered yesterday and Dallas saying it was up to Lily to handle details. "I'd be happy to have you and Lily come to the bakery at any time. It's offsite, in the coffee shop next door. We converted it when we bought—"

"I'm sure it's adequate for your storefront, but I'm not sure it will do for a high-end restaurant." She glanced to the left at the staging counter. "Your cakes are whimsical, but that's not what we're looking for. We need bigger and bolder, something to match the other items on our menus."

She was starting to annoy me. I always dislike it when someone uses the royal 'we', as though that implies importance. "I'm sure I can work with you on some signature desserts. I have several recipes that I don't use in town that might be perfect for—"

"We normally start by trying products two days a month. If they appear to be acceptable to the public, then we'll expand to one or two a week."

Two days a month? That wouldn't be worth the effort. "I'm not sure that will work."

"In what way? Is that too much?" She watched me, her narrow green eyes suspicious.

I remembered now why I didn't like her. I always had the feeling she was subtly undercutting me. I felt it back in school, and I was feeling it now. "Too much? No, it isn't. I was under the impression you wanted far more stock than that. When Dallas and I talked last night, he said that—"

"Please. You can't take what he said seriously. Dallas doesn't understand the day-to-day minutiae of running a restaurant. He likes to putter around in the kitchen now and then, but it's Lily who actually runs things."

I leaned back, her condescending tone grating on my nerves. "That wasn't the impression he gave me. He told me that Lily manages only a portion of his business interests. I got the feeling he likes to get in and get his hands dirty now and then."

"It's a hobby, nothing else. If you want to do business with us, you'll need to do it with Lily and me." She reached into the black bag and rummaged a bit, finally pulling out a sheaf of papers. "This is a sample contract that we've used in other locations. Please review it, and we'll meet to discuss in a day or two. Let's see." She extracted a calendar planner and opened it. I saw various appointments noted throughout what was apparently the week. "Today's Tuesday. How about Thursday? We have time at three in the afternoon. You can meet us at our office." She regarded me expectantly.

I was tempted to say that wouldn't work, but I wouldn't blow this chance. "Let me get back to you. I have several cakes to do this week. I need to see how many I can get done before I can commit to a time on Thursday."

Her red lips thinned. "I'll pencil you in," she said, doing just that. "We don't have much time in our schedule."

The threat was implied but there. *Come see us or lose this chance.* "I'm sure I'll be able to get there," I said, hoping I didn't sound as pissed off as I felt.

"Good." She handed me a business card then stood. "It was nice chatting with you. Please call me if you have any questions."

I stood, too. As I did my cell phone rang. I didn't recognize the number. "Excuse me. I need to check this. I'm expecting a call from a bride." I wasn't, but I liked making her wait on me. I moved to one side. "It's Tug."

"Hey, you. Are you busy? Can you talk?" I heard noise in the background and Dallas' voice was loud.

"I'm surprised to hear from you."

"Why? Did you think I can't find my way across the lake?"

"Oh, no. I had confidence in you. I meant that I wasn't sure if you were serious about our project."

"You bet I'm serious. I'm already planning the menu."

Sirena must have heard him because she stared at me, her eyes wide with surprise. "Is that Dallas?" she demanded.

None of your damn business. Then I remembered the contract. "Yes, it is. Hey, Dallas. Let me call you back. I'm in the middle of something."

"Okay. I'm at the restaurant. Call me when you can."

"Will do." I ended the call and tucked the phone back in my pocket.

"What did he want?" Sirena asked.

"I don't know if that concerns you," I said. "Thank you for giving me the business information. I'll look through it and plan to meet with you and Lily on Thursday."

She nodded once, her head jerking, then she went to the stairs where she paused at the top. "Listen, Theresa, let me give you some advice. I know you and Dallas were classmates, but he and Lily have been together for a long time. Don't think you can come between them. Other women have tried and haven't been successful."

She was getting on my nerves, but I forced myself to be civil. "He's an old friend, and that's it. I don't care if he and Lily are together. But if you ask him, he'd deny it."

"Why? What did he say?" Sirena spoke quickly, her words slurred into one long string.

"That's not your concern. Your business is business. What Dallas and I discussed has nothing to do with that." I stood at the steps, and she took the hint, putting her hand on the bannister. "Thank you for stopping by. I'll go through that contract and be ready to talk to you on Thursday."

She walked downstairs but stopped mid-way to look back at me. "Don't believe what Dallas tells you, Theresa. You can't trust him. If you interfere between him and Lily, you might regret what happens." She hurried down the remainder of the stairs and left.

I watched her, not sure if I'd been threatened or not. I think I had been.

Chapter Four

I didn't have time to worry about Sirena and her accusations. My shop phone rang, and it was the detective I contacted earlier. He wanted to listen to the phone message himself. I had a brief moment of panic when I visualized a police car pulling up to the coffee shop parking lot. Then I reasoned it might add a bit of interest to a sleepy June day, so why not? I assured him I'd be home and was anxious to talk with him. He promised to be there within the hour.

While I waited for him to arrive, I returned Dallas' phone call. "I was surprised to hear from you," I said when he answered. "I figured you were blowing smoke last night."

"I know a dare when I hear one," he said, a laugh in his voice. The background noise wasn't as loud as before, and I heard him clearly. "I need to prove I've still got what it takes in the kitchen."

"You don't have to prove anything to me," I said.

"Ah, come on. Give me a chance. Hang on." I heard him say in the background, "I'm surprised to see you here. You told me you had meetings today." Then he came back on the line. "How about tomorrow night? Is that too soon for you?"

"I have something tomorrow night that I can't miss. It starts at five-thirty, and we usually wrap up by six-thirty or so. I can go after our meeting."

"What kind of meeting?"

"I host a support group for women with weight issues. We meet on Wednesday nights at the bakery."

There was a pause then Dallas said, "Isn't that tempting fate? I mean, there's a bunch of good food around them."

"It's a challenge," I admitted. "But that's part of the learning process. Just because you see food, you don't have to indulge."

"I suppose," he said dubiously. "Maybe I could come there, and we can talk about the mural design."

I imagined Dallas Prinze walking into a room where five or six ladies were discussing self-image issues and their struggles with weight loss. "Why don't I call you later today? I have a cake to frost, and I want to work on gum paste flowers this afternoon for a cake on Saturday. Then I have another cake to finish tomorrow night for Thursday. I doubt if I'll have time."

"I can help. I can frost and pipe with the best of them."

"Bullshit," I said, flopping on the couch and relaxing. "You hated cake decorating. Your daisies were awful."

"But my roses were great. Even you said they were great."

I considered his offer. Cake layers were worked separately, depending on the design. I had the two-tier cake due on Thursday morning and two three-tier cakes for Saturday morning. That meant I needed to get the flowers and decorations done early. Then I could assemble at the right time. If he finished my prep for the Thursday cake, then I'd continue work on the embellishments for the Saturday cakes, which were more elaborate.

"You're thinking about it, aren't you? Come on, it'll be like old times."

I laughed. "Old times? Are you going to squirt frosting down my smock? You did that once, as I recall."

"I've grown up. Really. You can trust me. Why don't I help with the decorating, and we can discuss the mural at the same time? How's this afternoon work for you? We'll see how far you get with the cakes and can decide about tomorrow evening for painting."

"Well, I have the cakes cooling now. I suppose you can help me level the layers and crumb coat the Thursday layers but—"

"Hold on." Once again, I heard him talking to someone nearby. This time he sounded angry. It was a woman with him. Her voice was higher pitched, and she sounded upset, too.

"Listen, give me a call back when you can," I said. "I know you're busy."

"I'll be there at three, is that okay?"

"Yeah, sure."

"Okay. See you later." He hung up fast, and I knew he was sure I'd change my mind. I went to the table to review the designs I tacked up. If he'd prep for me, I'd focus on the mermaid and the flowers. That meant Saturday's cakes could be started by my interns. The kids were proficient enough to apply the fondant. I would only need to do the trickier flowers and final piping. Wow. I might have a bit of free time this week.

It was too early to pull out materials to bring to room temperature, so I set an alarm on my fitness tracker to remind me to do that in an hour. As I was setting the alarm the intercom buzzed, letting me know the detective was downstairs.

Detective Usher was a bland, unassuming man with sad-looking gray eyes and a shock of unruly red hair that sat atop his head like the Muppet character Beeker. He listened to the answering machine and wrote the message verbatim in a small memo book pulled from his jeans pocket. "You didn't listen to this until this morning?" he asked.

I gestured to one of the armchairs, and he settled down. I sat across from him. "I heard it come in last night when I was upstairs, but I forgot about it. I had company and by the time they left, I was tired, and I went to sleep. I didn't notice the light blinking on the machine until this morning when I came in after swimming."

"You swim every day?" He jotted a note in that little book with his equally small pen.

"Yes, every morning. I do icing and cake work, then I go to the park and swim to the diving platforms and back a few times."

"That's a lot of exercise."

"I work in a bakery. I need to keep the pounds away. And I enjoy it," I added.

"Who's the celebrity friend they're talking about?" he asked.

"I suppose Dallas Prinze. He was here last night. That's why I didn't listen to this immediately. Dallas and Lily came here, and I was talking to them. Lily Monroe. She's his restaurant manager. I talked to him. Lily didn't stay long. She had a business meeting."

"You know Dallas Prinze?" His eyes widened as though I was a celebrity, too.

"Oh, he's a passing acquaintance. He and I went to school together."

Usher nodded ponderously, jotting another note. "That's right. You graduated from the tech school."

"Yes, I did. Then I worked at various spots and came back here." Because it was cheap, I knew I'd get a start without much working capital, and people would cut me slack because I was local.

"What did you and Mr. Prinze talk about?"

"A possible business arrangement. We chatted about that last night, then he left before it got dark." That reminded me. I still needed to call someone about the window. "You wouldn't happen to know a good window repair person in town, would you? Something happened to one of my bedroom windows, and I need to get it fixed." I smiled apologetically. "The company I used when we fixed up this place has changed hands, and I'm not sure if they'd want to work on it anymore."

"What happened to it?"

"Debris or something must have been thrown last night. One of the windows cracked."

"Do you mind if I look at it?"

"Why? It's not a police thing. It was..." My voice trailed away when he shook his head.

"Some other folks in town have had problems. Why don't I check it?" He stood, pocketing the little memo book.

"Who? What kind of problems?"

"I'd rather not say. You understand. Things are under investigation." He regarded me with polite insistence. "Can I see it?"

I jumped to my feet. "Sure. This way." I led the way up the steps to my bedroom, now bathed in soft morning light. "You can see it best from the deck." I went outside and he followed, going to the pitted area under the window. To my surprise, he used his phone to take pictures, jotting notes in his book then looking at the opposite shore.

"What is it?" I asked. "Gravel or something?"

"I'll need to get somebody here to do a closer examination. Do you have a stepstool or ladder handy?"

I went into the bedroom and the attached bathroom. I kept a small three-step folding stool there to reach the top shelves in my closet. I brought it to him, and he ascended, putting his phone close to the holes to snap pictures. "It's the window that's broken," I pointed out. "I think there might fragments or something inside the block."

He examined the window, too, taking pictures, then he cautiously descended, staring at his phone. "Not debris," he said. "Bullets."

"What?" I peeked at his phone then up at the holes. I started up the stepstool, but he put a restraining hand on my arm.

"Let's leave it as it is. I'll have one of our technicians come and retrieve the evidence."

"Evidence? Of what?" I touched the concrete wall. "Did someone shoot at my lighthouse?"

"Like I said. Other folks in town who are—" He hesitated as though searching for a word, "tolerant have had problems. A broken window here, trash cans dumped on the lawn, graffiti sprayed on the side of a garage."

"But gunshots? Bullets? Who would do such a thing? It's the law, damn it. People deserve to be treated fairly regardless of their race or—"

Usher raised a hand, halting my diatribe. "I understand, ma'am. A few folks don't see things that way, though, and change comes hard to them." He folded the stepstool and carried it into the bedroom, leaning it against the wall. "We're short-handed right now. It might be tomorrow before our tech can do a more thorough examination. Please try not to disturb anything until he can get here."

My anger was cooled somewhat by his obvious desire to take this seriously. "I'll be here when he wants to check it. I have several cakes to work on for weddings this weekend. One of which is a gay wedding," I added. "Do I need to have somebody guard my shop or something? Do you think somebody would try to disrupt my business?"

He went downstairs, speaking over his shoulder while we descended. "It might be a good idea to ask your staff people to keep an eye out for anyone that seems suspicious. If anything seems unusual, you give us a call." He extracted a business card from his shirt pocket and handed it to me. "That has my direct number and my mobile number. I live nearby, down the road. You call me if anything like that happens again. I can be here in minutes." He gestured up the steps to my bedroom. "Make sure to lock your doors and windows, and don't hesitate to call if anything bothers you. Anything at all."

I was reassured by his insistence but irked by it, nonetheless. "Who's doing this? Do you have any idea?" I put the business card in my pocket and went with him to the shop.

"I can't say, ma'am. It's an investigation, and we don't like to talk about things while they're in progress." The steps ended at the front door, and I walked outside with him. "Just take precautions until we get this thing handled." Usher moved away from the door and a customer coming in. "I'll be in touch," he said, then he left.

I went into the shop, which was bustling with activity. I stayed out of the way of my staff, who had things well in hand. I chatted with a couple of the customers and went onto the veranda. It wrapped around the lighthouse on the lake side. You reached it from an outside entry door, which I kept locked at night, or from the inside through a door that opened onto a small, screened porch, accessed from the shop.

I spied the two cats on the veranda, lounging in the sun. I had often seen them there when the entry door was supposedly closed and prohibiting their presence. Obviously, a closed door held no worries for them. The customers at the tables didn't appear bothered by the feline company, so I decided to let them stay. I went back inside and up to the kitchen, ready to tackle my cake chores.

Most people don't know how long it takes to put together a wedding cake. I blamed those stupid cake competitions on TV. It made it look like you baked, frosted, and decorated in a day. It took a minimum of three days to get a cake ready. I prepped many of the sugar flowers and embellishments a week or two early, but most of the work was done during the three days prior to delivery.

My alarm reminded me to take the cakes and frosting from the fridge to bring them to room temperature. I fixed a small salad for lunch then experimented with crafting a mermaid for the Saturday cake. Before I knew it, midday had flown past and Marty, who'd come on duty at noon, was buzzing me on the intercom. "Dallas Prinze is here," he said excitedly. "He's already signed a bunch of autographs."

"Damn. I should have told him to come in through the Jolt." I didn't mind the notoriety, but I wondered how Dallas felt about it. "Tell him to come upstairs."

"You know him?"

"Yes, I do. Have him come upstairs when he can shake loose from his fans." I turned to the pink and pale purple colored gum paste, pressing it into the molds for the peonies to decorate the lower tier. I examined the photographs of the flowers tacked up next my station, then I cued a playlist and put on my red reading glasses, essential to help me add the tiny details to the flowers. Robert Palmer's *Bad Case of Loving You* began to play, and it was almost finished before I heard footsteps on the stairs. "Up here," I called.

Dallas' head emerged from the stairwell. "Am I interrupting? Is now a good time?" He came into the room, dressed today in brown shorts, pale gray deck shoes, and a dark brown T-shirt. The clothing showed off his tan and his toned body to good advantage.

"Sure. I'm doing flowers, but there's frosting to do." I held up a spatula. "You said you'd help."

He crossed the room. "Do you trust me?"

"That's the good thing about frosting. I can always scrape it off and re-do if it if I have to." I waggled the spatula at him.

"Thanks for that vote of confidence." He looked around the room. "I didn't know you lived here, too."

"Yep. Living room and kitchen here, bedroom upstairs. If you're helping, you need to wash your hands." I pointed the spatula at the sink. "Aprons are on a hook there."

Dallas took a clean white apron and pulled it over his head then approached the sink. The voice intoned, "Prepare to scrub your hands, minion," then the Preamble to the Constitution appeared on the mirror. "What's this?"

"Recite it and soap," I said.

"Seriously?"

"No soap, no work."

"The Constitution?"

"It changes daily. You got history. Tomorrow you might get the Rolling Stones." I focused on the flower I was crafting, pressing the delicate gum paste into the mold. I heard the water start to run.

"We the people of the United States…" He soaped and spoke, his voice deep and carrying. Dallas saw me in the mirror and stuck out his tongue. I grinned and went back to peony creation.

He finished his recitation and joined me, drying his hands on a paper towel. "You changed your tracker band."

I was surprised he noticed. "I change it most days to match my mood."

"How come?"

I shrugged. "I don't wear earrings. I guess this is my attempt at style."

His lips twitched. "Stylin'. That's you, Tug. Is that one of the ones you can wear in the water?"

"Yep." I extended my arm so he could see it. "It keeps me on track."

He examined the flowered band. "What does pink flowers mean?"

I pointed to the cakes on the counter. "It means wedding time. I have two due on Saturday and one on Thursday."

He straightened. "I like the music." Rod Stewart was singing *Ooh La La* and Dallas sang with him. "I wish that I knew what I know now, when I was younger." Dallas waggled his eyebrows at me.

"Ain't it the truth?" I pointed to the cake. "Do you remember how to do a crumb coat?"

"Please. You offend me. That was drilled into me during Intro to Baking." He eyed the six cooled layers that would comprise the two tiers for the Thursday cake. "Do you want me to level them first?"

"Bonus points to the actor. Yes, please level them." I laughed aloud at his pleased look. I pointed to the leveler. "You can use that or a serrated knife. Your choice."

"You trust me with a knife?" He lifted the razor-thin knife I used for leveling, which was lying next to the layers.

"It depends. How much do you remember?" I paused in my pressing to watch him. Dallas splayed one hand lightly on the top of the layer and ran the knife parallel to the counter, making a wafer-thin incision. Then he spun the cake gently on its paper doily and repeated the process four more times to peel off the lumpy outer layer.

He wrapped the finished layer in plastic wrap. "Does it pass inspection?"

I was impressed. "It does. Leveling is harder than it looks."

"Piece of cake." He winked and put the wrapped layer in the fridge, then he did the other layers, leveling and wrapping them as quickly as I could. When he finished, he cleaned the knife before coming to watch me create flowers. "What do you want me to do while we wait for them to chill?"

"Listen to you. If I didn't know better, I'd say you had culinary training." I finished another layer of petals and set the partially done flower into the bag to keep moist.

"Tell me about this group meeting you have. How long have you been meeting?" He watched me start another flower, leaning against the counter next to me.

"A year or so. We get together and talk, mainly about self-image issues."

"Can I join you?"

I lowered my head and shot him a disbelieving stare above my dime store cheaters. "Are you crazy?"

"Why?"

Where to start? "It's not an open group. You don't walk in. You need an invitation."

"Well? Invite me." He took one of the larger petal molds and began shaping.

I sighed theatrically. "You can't come. You'll intimidate people."

"What?" He straightened, his eyebrows drawn together in confusion. "Why?"

"Oh, for heaven's sake. You were voted Sexiest Man in the World for the third time. You'll make everybody self-conscious. Besides—" I barreled ahead, cutting off his response. "Why do you care?"

He blinked widely. "Because you care. And I care about you."

I gaped at him. "What? Why?"

"Why do I care about you?" He ducked his head and regarded me from under his lashes. "You know why, Tug. It's your buttercream frosting. I'm after your recipe."

I laughed.

"No, seriously. I'd like to, you know, maybe help if I can."

"Help how?"

"I don't know. I worked in Hollywood for years. I know about self-image issues."

He had a point. And I had the feeling if I didn't acquiesce, he might show up anyway, and that might be disastrous. I aimed one of the peony leaves at him. "Seriously. You're too attractive. You'll make people nervous."

"You think I'm attractive?" He fluttered his long eyelashes at me.

"You dork. You know you are."

He was quiet for a minute, shaping leaves, then he said, "I was an actor. I can make myself look not like me."

I considered his proposal. It was always useful to get another point of view. And a male point of view might be interesting. "Okay. You can join us but only if you do something to make yourself less noticeable. Promise me."

"Promise. Easy as pie. Or cake." He finished several petals then went to the fridge and removed the leveled layers. "Crumb coat, right?"

"Yep. Frosting is there and cake boards." I pointed to the bowl that I'd set on the counter and the cardboard bases. "Don't forget the wax paper." I watched covertly while Dallas prepped the bases with wax paper, got one cooled layer, and added a fine layer of frosting. He put it back in the fridge to chill and took another layer.

We worked in companionable silence, humming to songs on the playlist. He finished the crumb coats and washed his spatula before removing the first level for a buttercream coating. When he came back to the counter, he noticed the sheaf of papers on the coffee table.

"That's one of our contracts, isn't it?"

"Yes. Sirena stopped by this morning."

"We don't need six pages of legal bullshit to come to an agreement. We're friends. I trust you."

"Maybe that's why we need it, so we can stay friends." I hurried on before he spoke. "As long as we understand who does what, it'll be fine."

"Lily was talking to her grandmother," he commented. "It seems the old lady has a beef with you."

"What? Do I know her?"

"She knows you. She was here yesterday and complained about the bathroom."

I rolled my eyes. "That old biddy. I suppose she told Lily I'm a raving liberal. Which isn't far from the truth, I suppose."

"Something like that." He spread frosting for a minute then he said, "Lily seems to have fun dissolving friendships."

"What?"

Dallas' head was lowered, and I didn't see his face, but his shoulders were tense. He'd have a neck ache later if he didn't relax a bit. I was going to suggest that when he said, "When I opened the restaurant in Kansas City, I struck up a friendship with a lady whose specialty was barbeque sauces and rubs. I wanted to feature them in the restaurant. Everything was fine, then all of a sudden she said she wouldn't work with me anymore. I asked her what was wrong, and she said that Lily was too hard to work with." Dallas raised his head to shoot me a perplexed look. "She didn't have to deal with Lily after the initial contract was signed, but I guess Lily kept micro-managing everything Sylvia did. She kept nagging Sylvia about the color of the rub and the consistency of the sauce and—" Dallas sighed. "I don't know why Lily was doing it."

I could well imagine why Lily did that. Simple jealousy. "Was Sylvia single?"

"Yeah, but what's that got to do with anything?"

Oh, you silly man. "How big a friend were you and Sylvia?"

"Friends. You know."

I returned to peony-crafting, focusing on adding more layers of the delicate petals. I slipped little bits of paper in between the petals to make the flower look opened. "Can't you fire Lily? I mean, you and she are in business together, right? If she's not handling your business the way you want, can you do anything?"

Dallas frowned. "It might be weird. We've got the whole past thing together."

"Oh, yeah. The drowning."

"The drowning? No, I meant— Yeah, sure. The drowning."

I hazarded a glance at him. His face was red. What the hell was making him blush? Oh, wait a minute. That's right. He and Lily had a thing at one time. "Because you and she were a couple? Is that it? Are you still together?"

"Not really." He straightened, twisting his neck and setting down his frosting spatula. I was glad to see that. A tense cake decorator was one who made errors. "I mean, yeah, we were together in New York, and after that she followed me to California, but it didn't last long. Then I got involved in the movie stuff and I was never home. We sort of drifted apart."

"But you still worked together." I kept my voice non-committal although I was hard pressed to do so. Talk about weird. He and Lily had a relationship, then he drifted away and she was still— "Wait a minute. You said she followed you to California? Didn't she get in touch with you after she and Sirena started the business?"

"Sirena got in touch with her. Lily was sort of between jobs, and I was helping her out. I suggested her for that dancing gig and volunteered to partner with her." He grimaced. "I hate those stupid shows. Sirena told her about the idea of the restaurant management thing, and I got them in touch with people I know who needed help. Then when I decided to get into the business, it made sense to use their company." He picked up the spatula again. "I have talked to Lily about how she's handled our partnerships. She doesn't seem to see the problem."

I finished assembling the final layer of the flower and hung it on the rack to dry overnight. "She doesn't see the problem because you and she aren't seeing the same problem."

"Huh?"

I shook my head. For such a smart guy, he sure was dense. I waited until he paused to turn the cake then I said, "She's still in love with you and she doesn't want to share you."

To his credit, he raised his hand, thus preserving the work he'd done from any inadvertent mishaps. Maybe he did still remember how to be a chef. "What?"

"Put down the spatula," I said when I saw his hand wavering, frosting poised on the tip. "I don't allow any negative vibes around my cakes."

"What?" He looked at the cake then at me.

"You heard me. Negative vibes when you're decorating get into the final product. I won't have my cakes promoting bad luck."

He eyed me skeptically. "You're not serious, right?"

"I'm dead serious. Step away from the cake. If someone works on a cake when they're pissed off or upset, it carries into the decorating." I waited until he did as I asked, moving back a step, then I said, "You know what I meant. She still loves you."

"She never loved me. It was a brief thing, you know, nothing serious. Then we kind of hooked up again when she was in California. She was directionless, and I think she felt if she had somebody, that would give her the direction she needed." He turned away, wiping off the spatula with the damp towel he kept on the counter.

"A lot of women are that way. Men, too," I conceded. "They think they need to be part of a pair in order to be complete. I suppose she was raised that way. I know I was."

"You were?"

I began a new flower, pressing petals then moving them back into the plastic bag to keep them flexible. "My father was a minister, and his expectation was that I'd get married, settle down, and have a family. Then he and Mom were killed, and I had to go to work. But to be honest, I don't think I'd be happy with the typical three kids and a house and a husband who goes off to work every day."

"How come?"

"For one thing, I don't particularly like kids, so that's kind of a showstopper." I focused on the bigger sized petals, pressing and shaping them.

"Yeah, I know what you mean. Some of my friends have kids, and it seems like it takes over their lives."

"Plus I like working. Well, most of the time at least. I like setting my own hours and designing cakes and working with the public." I put the bigger petals back into the bag and focused on curling the smaller ones, putting them on my foam board and rolling them with my ball tool. This was delicate work, but I'd done it a million times before, and I knew how much pressure to apply.

"It might be nice to have somebody special, though." Dallas was staring at the design for the mermaid wedding cake tacked on the wall.

"You have somebody. Lily. She probably thinks you love her, especially because you've never been married."

"What's that got to do with anything?"

I finished curling the smaller petals and traded them for the larger ones. "I'll tell you how it looks to an outsider. You've had a close association of one kind or another, off and on, with the same woman for years. From what I've read in the gossip magazines, any other relationships you've had don't seem to work out. Therefore, you must be carrying the torch for her because you've known her for such a long time."

His face seemed to freeze, a muscle twitching at his chin. The lack of emotion only made him more handsome, like a statue. "You're making a lot of assumptions for somebody who doesn't know anything about the two people involved." He raised his spatula then stepped back. "I can't do this anymore. I'll make mistakes."

"Thanks for knowing that. And thanks for the work you did. I appreciate the help." He was obviously upset, and I didn't pursue the Lily topic anymore. "We didn't talk about your mural, though. You wanted to do that this afternoon."

"Yeah, well, I guess time got away from us." He put the layer into the fridge, slamming the door.

"Yeah, I guess it did." His pissy mood was starting to rub off on me. "Give me a call when you've got the time and we can talk about it."

He pulled off the apron and laid it on the counter. "I was glad to help out. And I meant what I said about the contract. I don't think we need too much legalese."

I put down the peony leaf I held. "I don't want to get into a tug of war with Lily. Maybe it's best that I don't provide any bakery items for you." I hated to say it because I knew I was throwing away good money, but I didn't want to be a punching bag for a jealous woman.

"You won't," he snapped. "I'll handle Lily."

"Are you sure?"

"Of course—" He stopped then shook his head. "No, I'm not sure. I've talked to her in the past, but she doesn't seem to get it. And you're right. I don't want you to get messed up because of her."

"To be fair, I think any partnership you come up with that involves any woman would have problems." He nodded glumly. I felt sorry for him. That's what prompted me to say, "I don't think you have much to worry about, though."

"Really?"

"Yeah. I'm not jealous material. I think you'll be okay. If you want my desserts, I'm willing to try it for a few weeks and see how it works."

He appeared relieved, and I knew I'd said the right thing. "Maybe you're right. I'm sorry I didn't finish the frosting."

"No worries. Thanks for what you did. It helps." I returned to the peony petals, working quickly so the gum paste didn't soften too much. I needed to start forming them around the center I'd already crafted, and too much handling made them malleable.

Dallas headed for the stairs, then stopped. "You're wrong."

"About what?" I asked, not looking up.

"You are."

"Are what?"

"Romantic material."

My head jerked up, and the gum paste petal split in half. "What?"

"See you tomorrow."

"Tomorrow?"

"Support group, remember? Five-thirty."

"You can't—I can't—"

"I want your desserts in my restaurant, and I won't take no for an answer." He winked. "Plus, I want your buttercream recipe." He dashed down the steps.

Chapter Five

I went to the Sanitation Station and stared at myself in the mirror, ignoring the admonishment to wash my hands. What I saw did not jive with 'romantic material.' Straight black hair streaked with gray, tucked behind my ears. A triangular face with a pointed chin. Wide mouth and good teeth. High cheekbones. Blue eyes that were too large for my face. One former lover called me girl-next-door pretty, and I suppose I was, but I sure wasn't in the same league as the Sexiest Man Alive. Dallas was teasing me. He always used to do that and, apparently, he hadn't changed.

I went back to the counter to tackle the last of the flowers. I'd have to deal with Lily if she got a misguided notion. I'd nip it in the bud. I wanted that contract. Visions of a larger bakery were dancing in my head, and they continued to dance as I wrapped up the flowers and turned my attention to finishing the initial coat of buttercream frosting on the Thursday cake.

I took my time with the frosting then studied my Cake Checklist, a detailed step-by-step I compiled for every cake I made. I was on track for Thursday, and tomorrow I would start work on Saturday's cakes. I went downstairs to check in with Marty. We'd had a good day, and I took a few minutes to chat with customers.

"The cats are cute," one woman gushed, pointing to King Fisher, who was chasing Shrimp among the rocks near the beach below the porch. "They're unafraid of anything. I even saw that big one go into the water."

He was probably trolling for fish. "Yeah, they showed up one day and adopted me."

"Well, they're adorable. And I'm sure they're worth their weight in gold. A bakery out here, so isolated, must be a magnet for mice. I know my brother has trouble with mice, and he's only a quarter-mile along the road toward town."

I mulled that over while I took a stroll around the veranda. Dallas mentioned the same thing last night, and King proved his worth by bringing me a mouse. Maybe it wasn't too silly to have them around.

I went back into the store. "I'm going to town for supplies," I told Marty. "Lock up if I'm not back before closing."

"Will do. Hey, Dallas Prinze is nice. He acted like a regular person. He signed autographs and talked with people and was friendly."

"He is just a regular person."

"You know what I mean. He's a celebrity. And he's putting down roots here."

"What?"

"He said he's got a house on the lake."

"Well, he can afford Turfmoor prices."

"No, he said he was remodeling a place over on Storybook."

That didn't make sense. Storybook Cove was northeast of us. If he built there he'd be directly across from the lighthouse, about a half-mile as the crow flies. "Talk is cheap," I said. "I'll believe it when I see it."

"He said he liked being back here. People weren't treating him like a big celebrity."

"Yeah, right. That's why he was busy signing autographs."

"He was being nice."

"Well, like I said. I'll believe it when I see it." I left the shop and took the road into Denmark. Main Street held a dozen stores, three of them geared to tourists. I went to the supermarket and stocked up on groceries, adding a bag of cat food and kitty dishes to my usual purchases of salad fixings, deli meat, cheese, and pickles. Dry supplies for the bakery came from the local organic Co-op where I was a member. I swung by the farm where I got eggs, milk, and butter to top up our supplies then returned to the lighthouse for the evening.

As I expected, all was quiet. King lounged on the top step of the dock stairs, tail flicking while he watched Shrimp, who was stalking a bird in the shrubs nearby. I approached the big animal and he regarded me warily.

I set down my cloth shopping bags and rummaged inside, looking for the bowls I bought. I went to the back of the lighthouse under the catwalk connecting the lighthouse to the Jolt. It was out of the way and protected from the elements by the overhead walk. No one would be using it until morning when the bakers would bring the day's wares to the lighthouse from the kitchen at the Jolt.

I unlocked the back door of the Jolt and filled one cat dish with fresh water then dumped kibble bits into the other dish. I set them under the overhang then returned to the Jolt pantry to tuck the food bag onto a shelf. When I came back outside, the two cats were already sniffing at the bowls.

I watched them test the food. I apparently chose well because they dug into it with single-minded determination. Satisfied with my Good Samaritan deed for the day, I relocked the Jolt and returned to my purchases. I'd forgotten I bought dairy products for the bakery, but I was lazy and put those into the downstairs cooler at the store in the lighthouse. We had enough dairy supplies on hand in the Jolt's bakery for the morning.

I hauled the rest of my food up to my kitchen-living room, setting bags on the counter. The light was blinking on the answering machine, and I approached it cautiously. Instead of another vicious message I heard Lily's icy voice.

"Hello, Theresa. I wanted to let you know that I talked to Dallas and he's insistent that we develop a business partnership with you. I suggested we might want to evaluate your bakery to make sure it can accommodate our needs, but he was adamant. We plan to open in one month. I hope you can meet our schedule. Call me as soon as possible, and we can discuss the terms of our agreement." She recited a number, and I was hard-pressed to jot it down. I replayed the message in order to make sure it was right.

Well, maybe Dallas put his foot down. I considered calling her, but I was hungry and a bit pissed off at her sharp tone. I considered going up to my deck for a pre-dinner drink. It felt creepy, though, now that I knew I was being watched. Instead I sat at the kitchen counter eating leftover spaghetti. I worked on a few more embellishments for one of Saturday's cakes and did the second layer of buttercream on the Thursday cake then put it in the fridge to chill. By then I was less annoyed at Lily and I returned her call only to be sent immediately to her voice mail. I asked her to call me then I went to bed.

I kept the lights off in the bedroom, undressing in the dark. I went to the deck doors and peeked out. I saw nothing worrisome, but would I even see a shooter if one were there? I made a mental note to check in with Detective Usher in the morning. Surely if they had any news he'd share it, wouldn't he? I peeked again and saw lights on the opposite shore. Dangerous? Not?

I decided I didn't want to know. Ignorance was bliss, or in my case, reassuring. I fell into a light sleep only to be awakened almost immediately by my ringing phone. I heard Lily's voice below me. I leapt from bed and raced downstairs, not anxious to give her a reason to nix our budding partnership. I lifted the receiver as she was saying, "… on Friday. If you can, that might be a good start to working with us."

"Hi, Lily. Sorry, I just picked up." I was breathless but coherent. Barely.

"Oh, good. You're there. As I was saying, we're having a private dinner for thirty or forty people on Friday. It's investors and their spouses and other people from town who support the restaurant. We need you to provide dessert. It will be a good way for you to show us what you can do. A three or four tier cake would be acceptable. Something with a Hollywood theme, to play up Dallas' career."

"I beg your pardon?" Was she asking what it sounded like? A major cake in forty-eight hours?

"Can you do that? It won't be too much a problem for you, will it? This is the kind of work we'll have you doing in the future, you know. A special client may call at the last minute and need a customized dessert for an event or a party. Surely you do those kinds of things, don't you?"

I didn't, and for good reason. Trying to do a detailed and customized cake, pie, or cupcakes was time-consuming and required planning, not to mention it required bakery time that was better spent on creating items to sell in the shop.

"If you can't do it, that's fine. I'll explain to Dallas that you aren't up to the task, and we'll look at having a modified business arrangement with your bakery for—"

"No problem," I said with more assurance than I felt. "I think a two-tier cake would be best. Anything more than that and it'll look ostentatious. We want something classy, not overdone."

"Good. Please make sure it's delivered by four o'clock on Friday. Cocktails are at five and dinner at six. We need it in place and the staff out of the way by four-thirty."

Staff. She meant me. *Drop off the cake and disappear.* Granted, I did that at most weddings, but I usually had at least some schmooze time with the bride or groom before I vanished. I loved seeing their reaction when I delivered the goods. "I'll make a note of that," I said. "Do I need to be concerned with any allergies or restraints?"

"Not that I'm aware of. I'll make certain and let you know by the end of the day tomorrow."

"That will be too late. I need to bake the cake in the morning."

"Oh, well, we'll post a little sign telling people about the cake and they can decide whether to have any or not. And you might want to make five dozen cupcakes for people to take home with them. The same frosting and theme, of course."

A cake and five dozen cupcakes. Why not ask for the moon while you're at it? "Of course. I'll have those boxed up and ready to go when I deliver the cake."

"We'll use our packaging."

"No, I'll use my packaging. If Dallas would like to include a personal note or other branding, he can add it to my boxes." I would *not* miss an opportunity to put one of my cupcake boxes with my logo and address into the hands of the wealthiest people in the area.

"I'll discuss it with Dallas. Can you come to the restaurant tomorrow with your design? I'll need to approve it well in advance."

Now she was seriously pissing me off. "Let's have it be a surprise," I said. "I'll run my ideas by Dallas when I see him tomorrow."

"What?" Her voice took on a shrill note.

"He and I are getting together tomorrow night to discuss his mural. I'll discuss my design then. Thanks for the call, Lily. I look forward to working with you." I hung up before she pissed me off any further.

Sleep would be impossible. I fumed for an hour, sketching ideas for a Hollywood themed cake and throwing them away. At eleven I trudged upstairs to bed again, my mind devising schedules for baking and decorating. I fell asleep, exhausted by the knowledge that I'd have many long days ahead of me.

The intercom near my bed buzzed, yanking me out of a dream where I chased Lily with an offset spatula on the rocks near the lighthouse. I fumbled for the lever that activated the connection to the Jolt. "Yeah?" I mumbled, nearly falling from the bed to see the clock. Twelve-thirty. What the hell?

"Tug, I hate to bother you, but something's wrong. This is Daria. I'm at the bakery."

I sat up in bed. Daria was one of my most dependable student bakers, the leader of the midnight-to-morning shift. "What's wrong?"

"I got to the Jolt and the door wasn't locked. And those cats are here."

I rubbed my forehead where a headache was forming. "Yeah, I fed the cats near that door tonight. I went into the Jolt but I'm sure I locked it when I left."

"No, they're off to one side and I think the little one is sick. The big one won't let us get near her. He looks sick, too. And the door isn't locked. It's weird."

Okay, now I was awake. Daria was one of the most common sense, down-to-earth people I knew. If she said it was weird, it was weird. I swung my legs to the floor. "I'll be there in five minutes. Wait for me."

"Okay. We'll wait under the overhang at the catwalk. It looks like it'll rain. What should I do about the kitty? I think it's sick."

"I'll be there in a minute." I was already dragging on shorts and a polo shirt. I ran down the stairs, grabbed a chef's coat, and jammed my feet into my Crocs. I went into the attached catwalk to the Jolt as lightning split the air outside.

It was a few yards to the Jolt's upper level. Jamie always left dim lights on at the back of the coffee shop where the steps led down. The kitchen entrance was straight ahead on the right. I went inside and flipped on the lights. This used to be two rooms at the back of the lighthouse keeper's house. We removed the wall and now we had a large rectangular space.

The inner and outer doors were in the center of the workspace. The pan rack, cabinets, and two industrial-sized mixers were on my left. Ahead against the outside wall on the left were the two big refrigerators. Straight ahead of me was the outside door, the light showing me the crack of darkness where it was ajar.

On my right were the tables, more pan racks, stoves, range, and sinks. I paused in the doorway. It seemed like it always did, stainless steel countertops gleaming in the light. I began walking across the white tile floor, making for the back door then stopped. Something was wrong. Something was out of place. Something was odd.

Thunder grumbled in the distance. What was wrong? I examined each piece of equipment, my eyes scanning the surfaces to see—

The cabinet. The big steel framed cabinet where we stored flour, sugar, salt, baking soda, and other dry goods. The door to the cabinet was wrong. Thunder rumbled again, louder this time. I went through the back door to the right, under the overhang that protected bakers when they brought goods from the Jolt to the lighthouse. Daria, Pete, and Doug, today's bakers, were there. They all had their phones out, looking at Lord-knows-what at one o'clock in the morning.

"Come on in," I said, gesturing to them. "Check the cabinets and the fridge, would you? Something doesn't look right."

"Somebody should check that cat. I think it's hurt or something." Doug jammed his phone into his back pocket and jerked a thumb over his shoulder before following the others to the back door.

The two cats were shadows at the far end of the building. I suppose when the humans showed up, they ran away. I approached them cautiously, lightning giving me enough illumination to see Shrimp facing me, hunched and swaying, touching the shrubs along the Jolt. King had a similar position to the little cat's side, blocking the light rain that began to fall.

"What's the deal, guys?" I asked softly, moving forward. "Where's your food? What's up? Didn't it agree with you?"

Shrimp peered up at me, its green eyes groggy and unfocused. I didn't know much about animals, but something was definitely not right. I reached them and knelt down, extending my hand. The big cat tried to intervene, but he seemed wobbly, too. That's when I saw a pile of brown bits under the shrub. "What the hell?" It looked like undigested kibble.

Rain began to fall, big, fat drops. I took a chance and scooped up Shrimp. "Come on, guys. Let's find a dry spot." King hissed at me, but I ignored him, deciding he was all talk and no action. Clutching the small cat, I hurried around the building to the back door and passed it, going to the small storage shed tucked against the back of the building. Shrimp was quiescent in my arms, struggling feebly but without any real energy.

I opened the shed and set the little cat inside. "Hang on. I'll get a box or something." I left the door open and as I expected, King staggered past me into the shed. I found the flashlight on its hook and shone it around the interior. Garden tools, a few rags and—yep, there it was. I remembered an old cardboard apple crate tucked back in the corner.

I dashed into the bakery and snatched an apron from a hook near the door then came back outside and put the apron and my baker's jacket into the crate. I put Shrimp in it then set it off to the side, away from the partially open door and the rain sheeting down. King took up position not far from Shrimp, facing the door. He seemed exhausted or maybe sick. He sure didn't look like the big burly mouser from the previous evening. I decided I'd done what I could for now. I ducked back into the bakery, my shoulders soaked.

"What's the damage?" I asked, shaking water off my hair.

"The eggs are broken." Doug's voice echoed because he was waist-deep into the fridge. "It looks like they took the box of eggs and slammed it on a rack."

"The butter's smooshed," Pete said from the opposite side of the room. He was near the counter where we set butter to soften for the night's work.

"What?"

"See." He held the one-pound block of butter in his hand. It had a sharp indentation in the middle, as though someone karate-chopped it. The wrapping was loose and butter oozed from one end.

"Damn it. We can't use butter that might be contaminated." I pointed to the counter's surface. "Look at that." There were butter smears everywhere, blobs and gobs of it making the normally shiny surface greasy. "Shit. We'll need to sanitize before we can do anything."

"It'll take work to get this fridge in shape," Doug said. "It looks like at least three dozen eggs are everywhere. Milk's spilled, too. It's a mess."

Daria was examining the dry good cabinet. "Check the flour," I said. "Sift through it. Make sure nothing was put in. And check the sugar." I had a special sugar that I created myself, milled raw sugar with raw processed sugar that I ran through a special blender to create powdered sugar. That was one of the secrets to my buttercream frosting. If my supply was ruined, I had a long night ahead of me.

"They didn't get in," Daria said. "That's why the door was weird. Somebody tried to jimmy the lock." She tried her key in the handle but it wouldn't turn. "They screwed up the handle when they tried to get in."

I breathed a sigh of relief. "We'll have to buy a new one," I said. "Break into it however you can."

"It's a good thing we lock that," Pete said. "As it is, we'll have to chuck the eggs and butter. And the milk."

"I bought some tonight," I said. "It's in the cooler in the lighthouse."

"Enough for tomorrow's baking?"

I mentally reviewed my recipes. "We'll need to make a run to the Cities. There are all-night grocery stores there. We have enough to get cupcakes and cookies done for the shop for tomorrow, but I need more for the cakes I'm doing." Damn. If I sent one of them on a food run, I'd be short-handed. I'd have to do it. "What about the ovens? Are they okay? And the mixers?"

Daria scurried to the mixers and Pete inspected the two ovens, pulling doors open to check inside. I held my breath, waiting for the verdict. If either of those were impacted, we were out of business for the foreseeable future.

"Mixers are okay," Daria said. "They're clean." She started one, and the comforting sound of the motor filled the room.

"The old oven is good," Pete said a minute later. "Nothing inside. Still looks clean. The new one is, too. The stovetop is iffy, though. I think they smeared butter there."

"That's first priority," I said. "Get it cleaned up. Who the hell did this? And how did they do it? I know I locked up behind me." Actually, I had a sinking feeling that maybe I didn't. I went to the door to check it while the kids went to the supply closet, talking excitedly.

I examined the deadbolt lock. Everything seemed okay until I opened the door wider and bent to examine the mechanism. That's when I saw scratches in the hole where the key went. "Somebody jimmied this." I straightened, remembering when we installed the locks. The locksmith warned us that somebody could pick a deadbolt with only a few simple tools, but we hadn't been worried. Why would anyone want to break into a bakery?

Why would anyone take a shot at me? This was related, wasn't it? Then I remembered the cats. "I wonder…" I grabbed a wad of paper towels and went outside, making my way along the side of the building to where the abandoned cat dishes sat. The kibble dish wasn't where I left it earlier. Somebody had pushed it away from the overhang. I picked it up and then used the paper towel to pick up a handful of the vomited bits

I saw earlier. They were wet but not too soggy from the rain.

I came back into the shop and took a plastic bag from the box under the counter. "Let's start cleaning up," I said, stuffing the soggy bits into the bag. I took it and the bowl into the Jolt, away from the kitchen area. "I'll make a run to the Cities and buy supplies."

"I can call Skip and Roger," Pete volunteered. "They'll come in and help."

I tried to map out a strategy, visualizing and rejecting ideas. "If they'll come in, have them work on cleanup here. You guys can use my kitchen to do the baking. We'll do mini-muffins and drop cookies. Forget any cutouts and rolled ones. Dairy is in the cooler in the shop." I surveyed the pan racks. "Is the equipment okay? They didn't mess with them, did they?"

"I think they're good." Daria rifled through the racks, inspecting the sheets.

"Good. Here's what we'll do. Daria, you and Pete use my kitchen to prepare ingredients. Come here to the Jolt kitchen to use the mixers and bake. Take goods back to my place to decorate and cool while the other guys clean up. I'll get supplies, come back, and by then it'll be clean enough for me to make cakes in my kitchen while you finish the shop goods here."

"Shouldn't we call the police?" Doug asked. "Report it?"

I hesitated. If I did that, I'd be delayed getting supplies. And the cops might want to inspect the premises, which meant we wouldn't get cleaned up and ready for the morning.

"They won't do anything," Pete said with assurance. "It's only vandalism. They don't take that kind of thing seriously. You're not going to file an insurance claim, are you?" he asked me.

I shook my head. "It's an inconvenience. There wasn't anything major broken."

"We should still take pictures," Doug insisted. "That way we'll have proof if we need it." He took his phone and began prowling around the kitchen, snapping photos.

"That's a good idea. Let's take pictures. That way if the police want proof, they can't claim that one person made it up." Daria got her phone and went to the fridge.

I left them to it and went back outside. The rain had morphed to a steady drizzle. I went to the shed and checked the cats. They were both in the box, the little one nestled against King, who peered woozily at me. What to do? I didn't know any vets and certainly not any who were open in the early hours of morning.

"You can take them to the school," Pete said behind me.

"What?" I scurried back to join him at the door.

"There's an emergency clinic at the school. They're open all night. It's on the south side of campus, up the road from Baker's Hall."

'Baker's Hall' was the term culinary students used for Seacliff Hall, where most of the hospitality and culinary classes were taught.

"They look weird. You can drop them off. The techs will take care of them, then you can pick them up when you come back." He looked doubtfully at the shed. "Maybe."

"They're not my cats." I brushed by him to go into the kitchen.

"They live here."

"Yes, but—" I stopped protesting. Granted, these weren't my pets, but I wasn't about to let any innocent creature be injured simply because somebody was pissed off about me baking a cake for a gay couple. I remembered the way Lily nudged-kicked the cat. What was it with people? "Okay, okay. I'll take them to the clinic. Come on. I'll get you set up in my kitchen then I'll leave."

I led the way into the Jolt and up to the catwalk and back to my kitchen. I showed them the equipment and saw them start the night's work. I ran upstairs, changed clothes, snatched my purse, and was out the door by two o'clock. I went back to the bakery and tucked the bag of kitty vomit and the bowl of kibble in my car then went to the shed and lifted the crate, staggering under the weight of two limp cats. King tried to hiss and raised a paw at me, but he didn't have the energy to do anything more than that. I took them to my car, parked next to the Jolt, and put the crate on the front seat, reasoning that I needed to keep an eye on them in case they decided to run.

I didn't need to worry about that. Both of them were pathetic. I drove as fast as I dared through the rain and went to campus, driving past Baker's Hall until I saw the lights in a low rectangular building. I went in and explained my situation to the clerk. She took the cats, the bag, and the bowl into a back room. I left my credit card information on file and promised to return soon.

I raced to the southern metro and found a 24-hour grocery store. Two hundred dollars later I had a car full of fridge goods, cat dishes, and a fresh bag of cat food, reasoning that perhaps the one I bought was tainted, either by accident or on purpose. I sped back to campus, frantically evaluating a bakery schedule in my head. I returned to the clinic where a harassed looking vet took me into an exam room. "Your cats were poisoned," he said, crossing his arms. "Rat poison from the look of it. Luckily, they're cats so it didn't work well."

"What? Poisoned? What do you mean?" Damn it. My hunch was right.

"Cats are efficient eaters. If they eat something that doesn't agree with them, they immediately throw it up. The small one was affected more because of his weight, but the female was able to shake off the effects quickly."

"Female? King?"

His mouth twitched. "King is a queen. Neutered, too. She had a bad surgery. There are scars. Where do you live?"

"In the lighthouse, on Hardscrabble Point."

"Somebody probably dumped them. They may be a mother and son. He needs to be neutered in a month or so. He's almost ready."

My already low opinion of the human race sank lower. Then the vet's words soaked into my beleaguered brain. "Rat poison? What kind? Is it a powder or liquid?" What if somebody put something in the bakery? Good Lord, lawsuits were on the horizon.

"Maybe a powder, sprinkled on the food. I couldn't tell."

Damn. I needed to get back to the bakery. Then I remembered that the dry goods cabinet was locked. We were safe. Maybe. "Will you keep them here?"

He shook his head. "No, we're emergency only. Have your regular vet check them if they're not back to normal. We pumped the stomachs and gave them liquids. They'll sleep for the rest of the night."

Back to normal? I had no idea what was normal for a cat. "I don't have a vet. Can you recommend somebody?"

He took a brochure from a cabinet and gave it to me. "These are vets in the area. The top two aren't far from the Point."

Double damn. Now I had two cats to take care of on top of everything else. I thanked him, winced when I saw the four-hundred-dollar bill, and put the sleeping cats in their apple crate back in the car.

It was now five o'clock. The bakery would open in an hour. I drove as fast as I dared to the lighthouse, screeching to a halt next to the Jolt. I unloaded the cats, who were still drowsing, and tucked them into the shed. I'd figure a better solution later. Maybe.

The bakery was abuzz with activity. Pete and Doug brought in supplies from my car while Daria updated me on the status. We were almost back to full capacity after an intense two hours of cleaning and baking. "The sweet goods are mostly done, but I decided not to bake the bread we had proofing," she said. "That chest isn't locked, and I was afraid the rat-fink did something to the dough."

"Rat-fink? That's a mild word for what I'm thinking. Thank you, Daria. That makes perfect sense."

"We're making quick bread instead. Nut bread and lemon-poppy seed and cinnamon bread. I hope that's okay. I called Saul, and he's setting up the shop now."

"Perfect. I couldn't have done better myself. Thank you all," I said, lifting my arms to encompass them. "You saved the day!"

"It's good experience," someone called back. "Make sure you tell our teachers about it, okay? Maybe we'll get extra credit."

Everyone laughed, but I made a mental note to do just that. These kids deserved an A for everything they did. I still had cakes to make and decorate, but at least the shop would be open for another day. I left the bakery, my exhaustion tempered by optimism. I was even getting an idea for Dallas' cake. What if I did something like the other cake I was doing but in reverse? I'd have a Hollywood sign on the top of two tiers with a city skyline. A path on the side of it would wind around, showing an escape route. Then I'd have a half-sheet cake at the bottom that was like a lake. Dallas would be poised to jump in.

The air was rich with the smell of damp earth and vegetation. The night's rain was passing, and the sun rising on the lake cast long streaks across the bay, adding inspiration for my idea. I walked to the steps overlooking the lake, wanting to imprint the sight into my mind to sketch it later. The rocks below glistened from the night's rain, their rough and tumble shapes softened by the light.

Instead of a beautiful sunrise, though, I saw a body sprawled on the dock below me.

Chapter Six

Even from this distance I recognized her. It was the old lady who argued with me.

She lay like a discarded doll on her back, her face angled toward the lake and her body twisted where she fell. At first it looked like she must have fallen from the rocks, which formed a wall near the steps. Kids occasionally liked to poke around the boulders, looking for Lord knows what.

This wasn't a kid, though. This was an elderly lady, and she wasn't capable of scrambling around boulders that were nearly vertical in spots. Her pale blue slacks and patterned blouse were twisted on her body, like she fell then maybe rolled a bit. Her white deck shoes stood out in sharp relief on the red of the dock. Odd that she was wearing deck shoes. Those seemed way too common-sense for someone like her. Of course, she was also lying on her back on the dock, which wasn't very common-sensical. Maybe the two balanced out.

I raced down the wooden steps. "Hello? Are you okay?"

"Tug!"

I stopped at the bottom, looking around at the faint sound of my name. I didn't see anyone. All I saw was that body, sprawled on my bright red dock like some kind of sad puppet left behind when the puppet master dropped it. I took a step forward when someone called my name again. I turned.

Dallas stood at the top of the steps. He looked like he'd been at a photo shoot at GQ magazine or Vanity Fair or one of those classy publications. He wore pale blue swim shorts, a royal blue shirt open on a sleeveless white T-shirt, and sandals. It wasn't the clothes, though, that made him stunning. It was his tan and his long, lean muscles, and his chiseled features and white-flecked steel-gray hair and his tanned face and eyes and goatee—

And everything that made him the Sexiest Man Alive, standing at the top of my dock steps. "What's going on?" he called. "You said you swim every day. I was waiting to surprise you." He started down the steps.

"Something happened." I hurried forward but slowed when I approached the woman. Now that I was closer, I saw she was wet, her clothes clinging to her body. The patterned blouse was weird, like it was stained or torn. Why would she lie here on the dock in the rain? Why not come up to the lighthouse or the Jolt?

I stopped in my tracks, and a second later Dallas joined me, walking up behind me. "What is it? What are—" He must have seen it, too. "What happened? How long has she been here?"

"I don't know." I gestured behind me. "I was busy at the bakery. We had a break-in."

Dallas knelt next to her on one knee. "A break-in?" He tentatively touched the old lady's shoulder. "She's cold. I think she's dead." He leaned near her then sat back on his heels abruptly. "She's dead, Tug. It looks like there's blood on her side."

"Who did it? When—" Then it hit me. Damn it. The police will have to come here, and nobody will be able to use the dock. It's bad enough somebody tried to poison the cats and trash my bakery but now—

Wait a minute. I fumbled for my phone. Rat poison, a trashed business, and now a dead body. Add that to bullet holes the night before, and business be damned. Somebody was after me. I managed to find Detective Usher's phone number, which I'd added to my contact list. I dialed it, ducking my head and avoiding looking at the lifeless body. "There's been a break-in, and somebody got killed," I babbled when he answered. "I'm at the dock at the lighthouse. Is this part of it? Did the person who shot at me come back and now somebody's dead?"

"Somebody shot at you? When?" Dallas demanded.

"Miss Gallant, please calm down. Who's hurt?" Usher said something in the background, and I heard another voice.

"I'm on the dock. It's an old lady. I think she's related to Lily Malone. They both work for Dallas Prinze. He's here. He said she's dead."

"Why is he there?" Usher's voice faded in and out. I wondered if he was getting dressed, pulling on clothes while holding the phone. "When did he arrive? Was he there when you found the body?"

"He wasn't here. He was at the park, and he came here. I was at the bakery because somebody broke in and they ruined some of my inventory. I drove to the Cities to buy more." The words just kept pouring out of me. "I don't know how long she's been here, but she's wet. I suppose she was here when it rained. Whoever killed her must have poisoned my cats. Well, they aren't my cats but they live here. I took them to the vet, and the vet said somebody tried to kill them with rat poison." I lowered the phone, unable to make sense of anything around me. My knees gave way, and I dropped with a thump on the dock.

I sucked in air, struggling to stop the panic that threatened. Somebody wanted to either put me out of business or— What if the old lady wasn't the intended victim? What if I was? What if somebody killed her by mistake?

"Tug, are you okay?" Dallas knelt in front of me, his hands cupping my face. "Take a deep breath. You're hyperventilating. Come on, honey, take a breath."

I stared into his concerned brown eyes. "How did you get here?" I gasped. "Where were you?"

"I boated. I'm docked at the public slip at the park. I came to swim today." He squeezed my arm. "Relax, Tug. It'll be okay."

"No, it won't," I wheezed. "My shop was burgled, and the cats were poisoned, and Lily's grandmother is killed. Who's doing this to me?"

His eyes widened and, for one sliver of an instant, I glimpsed something in their depths, knowledge or an idea quickly hidden when he pulled me into his arms. "It's okay," he whispered against my face. "Don't worry. It'll be okay."

A distant voice reminded me I was still holding my phone. I drew away from Dallas, leaning on him while I talked. "I'm here," I said. "What do we do? Should we cover her up?"

"No. Leave the body and go back to your shop. Wait for me there. I'll be there in a few minutes. I've called the BCA, and they'll boat to your dock. Leave everything exactly as you found it." The line went silent.

"We're supposed to go up and wait. He called somebody, and they're coming across the lake." I put a hand on the dock to help myself up but before I could stand, Dallas put his arms around me and hauled me to my feet. For an instant we were pressed against each other. I was shaking, my legs rubbery, and it was marvelous to lean into his warm, solid body. I enjoyed it for a brief second, then I caught a glimpse of the dead body and reality returned. "Come on," I said, heading for the steps. "What's a BCA? That's who he called."

"Bureau of Criminal Apprehension," Dallas said. "This is a small town. They probably don't have a big forensic team. They'll call in the state guys."

It was all I could do to put one foot in front of the other. Dallas half-dragged, half-pushed me up the thirty steps to the landing outside the porch. "How do you know about that?"

"I used to hang with Billy Newkirk. He was in the Criminal Justice degree program. I heard way too much about how criminal investigations work. Are you sure it's Lily's grandmother? Did you know her?"

"No, I didn't. But she came into the store, and you said I talked to Lily's grandma. I figured it was her." Lights were on in the shop, and I had a moment of panic. "Will they make me close for the day? The kids put in so much hard work after the break-in."

"What happened? You said something about supplies?"

"The night shift called me. Somebody broke in and trashed the place. I had to make a run to the Cities to get more supplies. And the cats were sick, and I needed to find a vet and—" An approaching police siren made me jump. "Damn, he said he lived close and I didn't believe him. Who's doing this? Is it because I made cakes for gay people? The nasty phone calls and letters were bad enough, but this is too much."

Dallas' hands clamped on my arms, pinning me in place. "What phone calls? Have you been threatened?"

"It's some asshole who thinks I'm a pervert because I'm helping gay people have a nice wedding cake." I struggled feebly. "Let go of me."

"Damn it, Tug. You're not invincible. You're here alone. Somebody can hurt you."

"I know." I wiggled from his grasp and put my arms around him for a brief hug. "Thanks for worrying about me. It's nice." Then the siren got louder. Usher must have driven onto the road to the Jolt and the bakery.

I walked around the lighthouse to meet them, Dallas behind me. Usher drove a dark sedan, rolling to a stop when he saw me. "You can park there," I said, pointing to the gravel road around the Jolt. "That's where the bakery break-in was. You can get to the dock from there, too."

"More cars will be coming," he said. "Is there room there for an ambulance and a couple of squad cars?"

"I think so. That's where the staff parks. Most of them are going home because they've finished their shift."

"I want to talk to them before they leave."

"I'll go tell them. I'll meet you back there." I turned to Dallas. "Can you stay here and show the other cars where to go? This is Dallas Prinze," I said to Usher. "He was with me when I found the lady."

"I'll want to talk to you, too, Mr. Prinze. Please come with us now. I'll radio to the others following me about where to park." Usher let the car idle at a crawl, raising a phone to talk into it while he steered.

"I wonder why he wants to talk to you," I said, hurrying after the slow-moving car.

"I'm probably a suspect."

I stopped, and Dallas bumped into me. I whirled and ended up in his arms. "What? Why would you be a—"

"I showed up here early in the morning, and I don't have any alibi." He released me, draping one arm on my shoulders and pulling me after the sedan.

"What? Alibi?"

"Come on. You need to be there when he questions your staff." Dallas gave me a little shove, and I scurried ahead of him, rounding the corner of the Jolt to the back of the building.

"The cats are here," I said to Usher, who was getting out of the car. I went to the shed and peeked inside. Shrimp and King were still in the apple crate. They peered drowsily at us then resumed napping. "They were poisoned. That's what the vet said."

"Shouldn't you be checking on the dock?" Dallas asked.

Usher regarded him with an impenetrable calmness. "There's a forensic crew on their way by boat. They'll do a complete examination of the scene.

I'm here to secure the land-side part of it." He faced me. "When did you find the cats were ill?"

"The kids called me at midnight or so. They said the bakery door was open and the cats were sick. You won't close the shop, will you?" I demanded.

"We'll need to block access to the porch and the back of the lighthouse for the day. We'll do a preliminary investigation of the store. If we see anything that needs closer examination, we might need to close it for the morning. And I want the tech to examine those bullet holes outside your bedroom." Usher went to meet two squad cars driving into the parking lot. Five men, some in police uniform, got out. He gave three of them instructions, and they went to the lighthouse, disappearing inside. The others waited near the cars.

"Why didn't you tell me about the bullet holes?" Dallas asked.

"It never came up, I guess." I struggled to process everything, but a lack of sleep and shock was making it tough.

"Sir, it might be best if you give us your statement then leave," Usher said to Dallas. "The press will be anxious to connect you to this incident."

"Incident?" I blinked in surprise at this understatement. "There's a dead body and somebody broke in and there was rat poison and—"

"And he's right," Dallas stated. "It'll be sensational as it is. If they get wind I'm here, it'll be blown out of proportion. I'll be at my restaurant or my rental for the rest of the day in case you need to get in touch with me further," he said to Usher. "I have plans to come back here tonight for a meeting."

"Tonight?" I dug my fingers into my hair, massaging my head and trying to massage intelligence into my beleaguered brain.

"Group meeting, remember?"

"Oh, yeah. Right." I was losing track of my days.

"I'll have an officer escort you to your boat. He'll take your statement on the way." Usher gestured, and a young man in a police uniform hurried to join us.

Dallas turned to go but paused. "Are you sure I can't help, Tug? You can use my restaurant if you need to get your work done."

I shook my head. "Thanks, Dallas, but I can't shift my whole operation across the lake. I'll figure out something." I had no idea what I'd figure out, but it sounded good.

He hesitated. "I mean it. You can use my equipment. Just say the word."

"I'll keep that in mind. Thanks." I shooed him away when it looked like he'd hesitate. "Go before the paparazzi shows up."

"In Denmark?" Dallas smiled but it was strained. "I'll call you later."

I waved an acknowledgement and went with Usher to the bakery. "The kids should still be here."

He stopped at the door. "You and Mr. Prinze are good friends."

"Yeah, Dallas and I went to school together. He touched base with me when he got back to town. He's the hometown kid who made good."

Usher tilted his head, his face puzzled. "That wasn't exactly what I meant."

I pulled open the door and went into the kitchen. Daria and Pete were wiping down the counters. "Hey, guys. There's been a—" I stopped, not sure what to say.

"A police incident," Usher said. "We need to talk to you. Miss Gallant, please go outside and wait for me. I need to talk to them separately."

"Uh, no, that won't work. They're my staff, and they're students, and I won't leave them alone with police. Not that I think you'll bully them or anything," I hastened to add when Usher leveled a stare at me. "It's a good employment policy." That sounded lame even to me, but I wouldn't let a bunch of kids face a police investigation without at least offering moral support.

Usher regarded the gleaming countertops. "I'm sorry to see you're so tidy. There isn't anything to show what happened."

"We took pictures." Pete dug his phone from his back pocket. "See? We figured we'd document what was done."

"We all did." Daria wiped her hands on the towel she held then retrieved her phone. "Doug took pictures, too. He already left. He has a test this morning."

"Good thinking." Usher pulled a notepad from his pocket. "Let me get your names and contact information." He went to one of the counters, and the students followed him.

"Tug? What's going on?" Jamie peeked in from the door to the Jolt.

"Oh, crap. I should have called you." I joined him at the door, pushing him away from the kitchen. "We had a break-in. And somebody died."

"What? Where? Who?"

"Who are you, sir?" Usher asked, notebook in hand.

"Jamie Priest. I'm co-owner of this coffee shop. I need to open for business in a few minutes. Is that a problem?"

Usher looked like he'd object, then he nodded. "Please keep your people away from this area until we give you the all-clear. And keep people away from the back of the lighthouse and the dock. We have it marked off with tape."

"No problem." Jamie pulled me to the side when Usher rejoined the students in the kitchen. "What the hell happened?"

I filled him in on the events of the night, including my visit to the emergency vet clinic at the school. "And King is a queen."

"He's gay? How does a vet know that?"

I shot him a long-suffering glare. "No joke. He's a she."

"Wow. That's a big girl."

"Who would do this, Jamie? Is it because I baked cakes for a few gay people? That old woman had nothing to do with that."

He put a comforting arm around me. "If they're trying to put you out of business, it'll backfire. This will give us so much publicity, we'll have to add more staff."

"Not if the cops put my kitchen off-limits," I griped. "What if they call it a crime scene? I need to finish the cake for tomorrow. And I have a new one due on Friday and two of them due on Saturday. That's not counting the regular baking we need to do." I sighed, trying to calculate in my addled brain how I would do it. "Dallas offered to let me use his restaurant. I may need to take him up on it."

"Dallas? Was he here?" Jamie gave me a little shake. "What are you up to, Tug? Do you have a not-so-secret admirer?"

"Yeah, right. He said he came to swim." Now that I considered it, that sounded a bit weird. I did mention to him that I swam every day at the beach, but why would he come to join me? I shelved that thought for the moment. "I wonder if he'll tell Lily. I think it was her grandmother. I suppose I need to tell the police about that."

"Yeah, you'd better tell 'em. Do you want help to get your baking done? Is there anything I can do?"

"I don't know." I tallied up what I needed to accomplish. "I need to make at least one sheet cake and a dozen layers for the cakes on Friday and Saturday. I have to decorate the cake for tomorrow and finish the design for the one on Saturday. I need to come up with a design for the one due on Friday. I need to make frosting and fondant for the cakes. Most of the embellishments are done, but I may need to make more for the Friday cake." The Friday cake. The one for the restaurant. It was essential that I knock that one out of the ballpark.

"Maybe you'll need to take Mr. Sexy up on his offer of a kitchen." Jamie headed to the Jolt. "I'll go up front and handle customers. Let me know if I can do anything."

Do anything, like make my life normal? "Thanks, Jamie. I'll keep you posted on developments." I left him and went back to the kitchen.

Usher was still talking with the students, rehashing what was done and how they did it. He jotted notes in the little notepad while they spoke, his questions simple and direct. I was impressed by his calm professionalism, then I gave myself a mental slap for being impressed. Just because he was a cop in Small Town, Midwest, that didn't mean he wasn't a professional.

As he was wrapping up his talk with the students a man came in, handing Usher some photographs and huddling with him to talk for a few minutes. The newcomer wore a polo shirt with an insignia on it and BCA on the back.

I joined the kids while we waited for him. "I'm sorry to keep you guys here. I hope it won't be too much longer."

"It's okay," Pete said. "It's not every day we get to participate in a murder investigation."

I winced. Daria patted my arm in sympathy. "Don't worry. He swore us to secrecy. If anybody finds out about it, it won't be from us."

I had little hope that 'no one would find out about it'. Denmark was a sleepy resort town, and a murder would make the news not only here but in the Twin Cities as well.

A few minutes later the man left, and Usher rejoined us. "Do you have any knives here?"

"Of course. It's a kitchen." Then I realized what he was asking. "Oh."

"Can you show me where they're kept?"

"I have a custom set that I don't use much. I had it made when I graduated from school. I keep them here." I looked around the room. "In the drawer there." I pointed to the large stainless-steel island in the middle of the oven side of the space. "Do you think—was she—"

"Stabbed?" Pete prompted.

I swallowed hard.

Usher frowned at Pete as though he'd committed a faux pas. "We're not sure. Can you show me where you keep your knives?"

I led the way to the island. "What's her name? Who is she?"

"Her name is Mrs. Adella Dronning. She lived in town." Usher followed me, the two students trailing behind us.

I went to the knife drawer and opened it. Six of the knives in the collection were nestled into their custom-made slots. The big butcher knife was missing. Usher examined the drawer, inside and out. "You don't keep this locked, but you keep the cabinet locked where you store flour?"

"Dry goods can be easily contaminated by humidity or insects or smells in the air. I seldom use these knives here in the bakery. Like I said, I bought them when I graduated. It was a splurge, I guess. I wanted to be an executive chef. I didn't plan to do bakery work."

"Why does that matter?" he asked.

"We don't use knives like these much in a bakery. Our equipment is specialized. Spatulas and the thin knives we use for leveling. Those kinds of knives are too delicate to be used for—" I gulped. "They're thin and flexible. They'd break if someone tried—" I gave up on an explanation.

"Who used this drawer today?"

I looked at Daria and Pete. They both shook their heads. "I didn't use it. I doubt if Doug did. Our bakery equipment is kept separate. We seldom need to get into this drawer."

"Where are those bakery knives kept?"

"I have some in my personal kitchen, and we have some here."

"There are a couple in the dishwasher, too," Daria volunteered. "I saw them when I loaded it. They're in the top tray with the piping nibs in the mesh bag."

"The what?" Usher waited, pen poised above his notebook.

I went to another drawer and opened it, showing him the different sized tips used for piping frosting onto cakes. "We usually clean the nibs by hand to remove most of the frosting, then we put them into the dishwasher to sterilize them."

We all eyed the industrial-sized machine, humming and gurgling in the corner. Usher sighed. "You're very efficient."

"It's a bakery," I said through clenched teeth. "We have to be clean. It's part of our process. We clean up after every shift because we start baking at midnight, and everything has to be ready to go, otherwise we'd be delayed and wouldn't be ready by six in the morning for opening. Believe me, we're not trying to hide any evidence or anything."

"I know that," Usher said mildly. "It's inconvenient." Three men came through the door carrying large leather bags, suitcase sized. "Please wait outside," Usher said, steering me and the students toward the exit. "This will take some time."

"What are they doing?" I asked, trying to look around him.

"Fingerprints," Pete said. "The fridge and the drawers, I bet."

"Indeed. We'll need to get your fingerprints before you leave. The officers outside will handle that." Usher pushed me toward the door and closed it firmly behind me.

The minute we stepped outside a police officer swooped in and led us to the squad cars. He placed our fingers, one by one, on a device that reminded me of an old Blackberry phone. A light flashed and then we were done. The kids hopped in their cars and left, promising to return if I needed them for more work that night.

Usher emerged while they were leaving. "Can I go to work now?" I asked, looking past him to the kitchen.

"Not here. They'll be busy in there for a while."

"Can I use my private kitchen?"

He regarded me then the lighthouse. "Let me check." He hurried away.

I peeked around the corner of the Jolt, assessing the parking lot and the foot traffic. It seemed like a regular day, with people going to and from the Jolt to the lighthouse under the blue-and-white striped awning connecting the two structures. No one seemed to notice the police presence, or if they did, they weren't gawking. Most of the action was on the back side of the lighthouse, and as long as someone wasn't on the porch, they might not even be aware of it. I wasn't sure whether to be relieved or annoyed that no one was noticing.

I went to the shed to check on the cats. King-who-was-Queen was gone, probably out hunting. Shrimp appeared perkier, but still a bit tired. I suppose having your stomach pumped was a pretty nasty experience. I went to my car for the cat dishes and filled one with water from the outside faucet and one with the new kitty kibbles.

Usher returned. "Are they okay?" he asked, peering into the shed.

"I have no idea," I admitted. "I've never had pets. I'm not sure what's normal for them." Shrimp chose that moment to inspect the food, taking a mouthful. He didn't spit it out, so I suppose that meant it was okay.

"I need the name of the vet you contacted."

I dug into my jeans pocket and handed him the business card I got at the emergency vet office. "Can I use my kitchen?"

"Yes. The BCA doesn't need access to it for their investigation."

"Why not?"

He copied the information from the business card into his notebook. I had the impression he was trying to avoid looking at me. "We don't think the lighthouse has anything to do with the crime. We'll need to keep it partially blocked off, though, until we wrap up our investigation." He handed me the card.

"What about the bullet holes?"

"You'll be in the lighthouse kitchen working for the next hour or so?" he asked.

"I'll be there most of the afternoon."

"I'll have a tech come to take photos and samples."

"Have them come in through the Jolt," I said, gesturing to the door to the kitchen. "I'd rather not have police people coming in through the shop carrying God knows what kind of equipment."

"Understood. I'll make sure of it. Thank you for your cooperation." He tucked the notepad into his jeans pocket and held out his hand.

I gave it a brisk shake. "Let me know if there's anything else I need to do."

"We'll be done at the dock by afternoon. Someone will let you know when you can open the porch again." He hesitated then said, "Make sure your employees stay alert for anyone who might seem unusual or overly curious about what happened."

Holy crap. Did he think the murderer would be visiting my shop? I considered asking him, but one of the men in the kitchen poked his head out, and Usher hurried to talk to him. I decided I'd had enough of the police for one day and went to the lighthouse, slipping in the front door and waving to Saul behind the counter. *Upstairs*, I mouthed then escaped up the stairs to my kitchen.

I breathed a sigh of relief when silence surrounded me. Too much had happened. A murder investigation. I couldn't wrap my head around it, and I didn't even try. It was now mid-morning, and I had cakes to make.

The first thing I needed to do was restock my supplies. I made several calls to my local dairy person, and they promised to bring butter, eggs, and milk to replace that which was despoiled. Then I called the local locksmith. He assured me he'd be there that morning and get me a new deadbolt, working with Jamie at the Jolt.

I had cake work to do. The students had left my kitchen tidy but not exactly the way I liked it. I busied myself with cleaning up before beginning the process of measuring, mixing, and baking. I've always been able to compartmentalize work, pushing distractions to one side to focus on the work at hand. A baker needed to do that because our goods required advance planning. You don't just whip up a batch of bread. You need time for it to proof and rise and rise again. The same was true with cakes. It took days to get an event cake ready, and if a baker couldn't work to that schedule, that baker didn't stay in business long.

I focused on the marital couples as I worked, remembering their happy excitement when we discussed what to have for their wedding. I'd never been in love like that, not enough to consider making a commitment to anyone. I drew on the interviews to recreate the euphoric feeling. I read through my notes from our talks to reacquaint myself with their personalities, using that to drive away the bad vibes from the morning.

I soon had their layers baked and done. I started to work on the cake for Dallas' party, making an extra layer in case I wanted it for the decorating. I was reviewing my checklist for the Saturday cakes when my phone rang. I took my checklist with me and dropped onto the couch. "Tug's Treats," I answered.

"Theresa, this is Lily Monroe. I wanted to verify with you that you'll have a special dessert ready for us on Friday." Lily's voice was brisk, efficient, and cool. "It was rather late last night when we talked."

"I—do you know—will you still have the dinner?" I asked.

"Why wouldn't we?"

Oh, Lord. She doesn't know. I hesitated, not sure how much to say.

"Oh, you mean my grandmother." She paused. "That won't affect our plans, I assure you. If I'm busy, Sirena will handle the details."

"Oh. That's good," I managed to say. It wouldn't affect their plans? That was a cold-hearted response to someone's death.

"We do need to have a signed contractual agreement. I know Dallas thinks we can operate on a handshake, but that's not how businesses manage things. I'll create a revised contract and get it to you as soon as I can. I wanted to make sure you'll be able to fulfill your obligation. The police are on your premises, and it might prevent you from working."

She sounded absolutely delighted by the idea. "I'll be fine," I snapped. Then a little devil made me say, "In fact, I may take Dallas up on his offer."

"What offer?" she demanded.

"He suggested I use his restaurant kitchen for my baking. I may do that."

"He needs to check with me before he makes those kinds of offers." Her voice was now definitely icy. "I doubt if we can accommodate you and still have the kind of dinner I'm planning."

"Well, maybe you and he need to work that out." I slammed down the phone, any sympathy I had for her evaporating. What a bitch. Then I began to smile, my sour mood lightened. Before I could change my mind, I called Dallas.

Chapter Seven

"Of course you can," Dallas said when I explained I wanted to decorate his cake at his restaurant.

"It'll be easier to build it on-site," I said glibly. "That way I don't have to transport it." *And I'll piss off Lily Monroe in the bargain. Win!*

"You can make the cake here, too," he urged. "You don't have to only decorate."

"Sorry, it's already in the oven. I'll cool it this afternoon, and tonight we can do the crumb coat and leveling. I'll come early tomorrow and do the first buttercream frosting layer." I mentally visualized the tasks to do. "Then tomorrow afternoon I can do the final buttercream layer, and I'll start assembling tomorrow night. It needs time to rest overnight before I do final decorating on Friday."

"I should warn you. We have bakery equipment, but it may not be good enough for what you need."

"It's a simple design." I chuckled. "Sort of. I'll bring what I need."

"Now I'm intrigued. What is it?"

"Oh, no you don't. It's a secret. I have an idea for something special."

"What kind of special?"

"I was thinking about a cake Madame Marcelle made once. She made it for—" I blinked, realizing what I almost said. *Her lover.* "For someone she knew, a friend. She did something special for the frosting. I'm afraid we'll have to put our bet on hold. I won't have time to help you with your mural."

"No worries. I've been working on it already because I know exactly what I want to do. I'll unveil the mural on Friday."

"Wow. You work fast."

"It's easy once you have the right idea."

I hesitated then plunged ahead. "Look, I spoke with Lily. I mentioned I may need to use your kitchen, and she didn't sound happy about it. Are you sure it's okay with your chef that I be working in his space while he's whipping up your fancy Friday meal?" The hierarchy in a high-end kitchen was firm and fixed. I would be infringing on someone's territory, and I wanted to make sure there were no hard feelings both in back of the house and in the front of the house.

"I'll explain the circumstances. I'm sure we can make it happen. I'm glad you're taking me up on my offer to help, Tug. It's the least I can do for you."

"Huh? Why?"

There was a pause. "Being at school together and stuff like that." He chuckled, but it sounded a bit strangled. "Hometown kids helping each other, you know?"

"That's nice of you. Thanks." I glanced at the clock. "Speaking of which, I need to get working on the cake that's due tomorrow. I'll gather the supplies I need for tonight and be ready to go when you are."

"We can come after the meeting. I'll drive, and we can load up my car."

"Damn. I forgot about that." I considered canceling it then decided against it. I hated to let the Wednesday

Night Gabby Girls down. "Sure, we can do that. But I can drive over. That way you don't have to make an extra trip to bring me back here."

"I don't mind. I think the kitchen staff would be glad to have me out from underfoot. They're in the final stages of testing the menu for Friday. I can't taste-test another appetizer without barfing."

I laughed. "God forbid. Thanks, Dallas. I appreciate the help."

"I'm glad to do it. Hey, listen. I have to go. Lily came in. I'll tell her about our arrangement."

"Good luck." I hung up then jumped to my feet. I had cakes to decorate and not much time to do it. I got the Thursday cake from the cooler and began assembling it. I prepped the cake board, dusting it with powdered sugar and then decorating it with pale pink paper doilies. I doweled the layers before cutting in the design for the garden path and the groom's doorway. Once I was satisfied with that, I began piping the rosettes and embellishments.

The colors on this cake were muted pastels—pale green, mauve, delicate yellows, and creams. The faux bouquet at the top seemed to trail around the cake, hiding the garden path leading the bride to her groom. I added the delicate peony flowers I made the other day, mixing up several different piping bags with different colors to accent the layers.

As I was moving around the cake, I spied two men walking toward me through the catwalk. They showed me their police identification, and I went with them upstairs, pointing to the holes in the wall. They assured me I didn't need to hang around, so I went back to the kitchen and resumed piping.

The cakes in the oven were soon done, and I let them cool while I put another batch in to bake. The kitchen was specially vented to keep the oven's heat from infringing on my decorating counter. There was nothing worse than trying to prep a cake when it got too warm from oven overflow.

The two men came as the last batch of cake layers were leaving the oven. I walked with the men to the door, then I took a break, flexing overused muscles that were tense and tight. I went upstairs and onto the deck, letting the warm breeze wash over me. It was still cloudy but not as humid. Last night's rain had pushed away the soggy air, at least for now. I didn't have much hope it would stay away. It was June, after all.

The only evidence I saw of the visit from the police technicians were scuff marks near the holes. Activity continued on the dock. Several boats were tied up, and three people, two women and a man, stood near where I found Mrs. Dronning, deep in conversation. They all wore the BCA polo shirts, and one of the women had a toolbelt with various things hanging off it. What would that job be like? To be called out at any hour of the day or night to various locations and often to view extremely unsavory things.

I shuddered. The dead woman's face had been startled, her eyes wide, and her gaze fixed at a point in the distance. Who would do such a thing? Hell, who would break into my shop? I couldn't imagine breaking into a business much less killing someone. I didn't have the nerve to do such a thing. Why that old woman? What was she doing on my dock early in the morning— or late at night? How would the police even start to investigate that?

I whirled and raced down the steps in sudden panic, bursting through the kitchen and into the shop. Marty was behind the counter, chatting with a customer. Two of the four tables were occupied but otherwise the shop was empty. I waited until the customer left then I went to Marty. "How's it going?" I asked in a low voice.

"Great. Word got out about the excitement. I think half the town came to find out what happened and, in the process, we're about sold out." He checked the clock. "A new record. Three o'clock."

"We need to take precautions," I whispered. "Look for anybody suspicious or acting weird. I need to talk to the night shift and make sure they're alert."

"Oh, they'll be alert," Marty said. "That cop put the fear of God into 'em."

I sighed. "I'll be lucky if they come back tonight."

"Are you kidding? It's a crime scene. You'll have more volunteers than you know what to do with."

He was probably right. I told him to close up at three-thirty, then I went to the Jolt. Jamie was getting ready to close. "Here's your new keys," he said, handing me a set. "I put the duplicate set on the shelf in the shed. Your night shift can get them tonight."

"I'll meet them," I said. "I want to make sure everything goes okay."

"You're already working on less sleep than usual," he pointed out.

"I'll drop in on them and make sure they have what they need." And hopefully scare away anybody who lurked around.

"There's lots of speculation about what happened." Jamie went to the kitchen door, and I followed.

"When did the police leave?" I checked around the bakery. If the police did any fingerprinting stuff, it didn't show. The surfaces still gleamed in the fading afternoon light. That was a relief. I didn't have time to sterilize the work environment.

"It was after lunch. I was getting worried that we might be kept out longer."

"I'm using Dallas' kitchen at the restaurant to do the cake Lily wanted for their party on Friday. It makes sense to do the final decorating there. That's one less thing to worry about, at least." I went to the fridge and checked the contents. We were completely restocked. I silently blessed my local sources for coming to my rescue.

Jamie leaned against a counter and crossed his arms. "Are you sure that's wise?"

"Why not?"

"I heard that his girlfriend is the jealous type."

"You heard?"

"I have my finger on the pulse of the community. I heard they've been together for years."

"That's not what I heard from Dallas."

Jamie shrugged. "I'm only repeating what I heard." He checked his watch. "I'm off to pick up the kiddo. Are you making your cupcakes here, or should I lock up?"

"Oh, shit. I forgot." I always made a special cupcake for the ladies in the support group. "I'll do them at my place. I'll talk to you tomorrow." I went to the shed and grabbed the keys from the coffee can on the shelf. I didn't see the two cats, which I took to be a Good Thing. I debated whether to close the shed or not but, in the end, I left the door ajar in case King Queen and Shrimp needed shelter.

I raced back into the Jolt and up the steps to the catwalk. I threw together the cupcakes in my kitchen and got them into the oven, then I showered, changed clothes, and removed the finished cupcakes. I put them into the fridge to cool, a shortcut I disliked using. But sometimes it was needed.

I set an alarm on my fitness band to wake me at eleven that night before the bakery staff arrived. I gathered what I would need for cake work at the restaurant, then I whipped up a batch of buttercream frosting. I piped a big rosette on each cupcake, putting them into their individual boxes, the way I always did. I split the remaining frosting between two glass containers, one colored a pale blue and the other a pale gray. I'd use that for the crumb coat and first buttercream coating that night. I put the cupcakes on a tray, put the cakes and equipment I'd need at the restaurant into two bags, then juggled it in my arms and went downstairs to the now-quiet shop.

I checked the porch, thinking we might sit there. But the humidity had returned, and I decided the air-conditioned store might be better. I got the five tablet computers I kept in the closet and loaded the coloring app on each one. The Girls would each do coloring while we talked. I found that keeping them busy was one way to keep them talking. I'd get them going on a mandala pattern that was reasonably difficult but not annoyingly so. Mandalas were repetitive, colorful, and usually intricate enough to occupy someone for the entire hour, especially when someone was talking while they colored.

I took a minute to prepare myself for the evening's meeting. The four ladies—the Gabby Girls—had come to chat every week for more than a year. Two were married and two were single. All were in their thirties and facing various medical issues because of their weight. I met them at a local health fair and became a sounding board for them, giving them a place to air their gripes and maybe—just maybe—learn what might help them become the best person they could be. That might or might not mean they'd lose weight.

Boisterous laughter heralded their arrival. They entered the shop and greeted me then made a beeline for the tablets lined up on the counter. Nobody wanted to use the old Kindle Fire, and everybody loved the newer iPads, which I bought secondhand on eBay.

"Save one of the iPads for our guest," I said when I saw Coral head for it. She hated using the older tablets and always aimed for the newer ones.

"Guest? Who? A newbie?" She took an Android tablet and went to the table where I had their cupcakes sitting.

"He's new to town, yes. And he asked if—"

"He?" Fleur interrupted. "What does a guy care about eating problems?" She flopped into a chair across from Coral.

"I know a few guys who should care." Coral mimed a beer gut, patting her ample belly.

"Men can have the same kind of insecurities as women." I prayed that Dallas had taken me seriously. He knew how handsome he was. He *had* to tone down his appearance.

"I doubt that." Brooke took the smaller Android tablet and joined the others. Unlike Coral and Fleur who both wore dark slacks and attractive blouses, she was in leggings and a tunic top that billowed around her when she plopped into a chair. "Most guys just care about getting enough to eat, not how it affects them."

"Perhaps he's different." Pearl, always the peacekeeper, came in and shot me a long-suffering look when she saw that one of the iPads and the Kindle Fire remained. I took pity on her and handed her my personal iPad. She nodded gratefully and joined the Girls, her flowered summer dress swirling around her like a cloud.

I glimpsed a silhouette outside, and I hurried to the door, prepared to intercept Dallas and stop him if needed. He was too fast, though, and swung open the door, stepping into the small entry foyer.

I barely recognized him. It wasn't only the clothing, although that was surprising enough. Baggy, faded jeans, a worn, blue-flowered shirt misbuttoned on a white T-shirt, and tattered-appearing sandals. It was everything else. His hair was parted in the middle and combed to reveal a receding hairline. Horn-rimmed glasses accented the lines around his eyes, giving him a haunted, sad appearance. And he slumped. He was round-shouldered and paunchy and somehow...faded. Gone was the laughing, confident jokester. Instead I saw a hesitant, anxious man whose worries appeared etched on his face. He reminded me of my father's parishioners, people whose lives had taken a turn and were now lost.

Then I realized what I was doing. I was assessing a person based on appearance. Here I was, trying to help women get past their concern about their looks and I made a judgement about a person based on his looks. How deeply ingrained that habit was!

I remembered my mother, of all people, pulling me aside one day after church. My father was speaking with a woman who appeared small, frail, weak. My mother said, "Never blame anyone for your mistakes. If you make a choice, then own it. And if it's a bad choice, then face the consequences." She watched the woman, and her face was cold and harsh. "Don't try to blame others for what you chose to do."

I was young and didn't know the story, but later I found that the parishioner cheated on her husband because he cheated on her. It was a sordid affair and one that caught my father in its drama. I heard him and my mother argue about it at night, when I was supposed to be asleep.

Dallas smiled tentatively at me. "Am I early? Can I use this door?"

I shook myself away from memories. Good heavens, I was gawking at him. "That's fine." I had an immediate impulse to help him, to put him at his ease, as though he was as insecure as everyone else in the room. "We're just getting set up. Come in." I stepped to one side and he saw the four women watching him with varying expressions of wary curiosity. He hesitated, then came in.

I led him to the counter. "Group, this is our visitor." I suddenly realized I didn't know how to introduce him.

Dallas saw my panic. "I'm Bruce," he said in a shy, tremulous voice. "Thanks for letting me sit in."

"You don't look like you have an eating problem." Brooke eyed him balefully.

"That's not fair," Pearl said. "You know that problems don't always show in the way we look." She smiled encouragingly at Dallas, the welcoming look of a librarian helping a patron, which is what she did in real life. "Take a computer and take a seat. We always work on coloring programs while we talk."

"Coloring?" Dallas took the remaining iPad then took the seat between Coral and Brooke, who raised her tablet. "How come?"

"It's nice to have something to focus on. That way you don't always have to talk directly at somebody," Brooke whispered loudly. "It makes it easier to say things sometimes."

I stared at her in astonishment. That was why I chose the coloring apps for them to use. Was my purpose so transparent?

"I still say he doesn't have a problem," Fleur muttered.

"He asked if he could sit in, and I didn't pry into why." I picked up the sad old Kindle and joined the group around the table. "We don't have a set agenda or anything," I told Dallas. "I usually get the conversation going, then we chat about what's been happening in our lives." I leaned back in my chair and pointed to the tablets. "I loaded tonight's assignment."

They activated the tablets. "Ooh, that's a nice one," Pearl said. "I like the lacy ones."

Dallas stared at the tablet on the table. "I don't understand."

"Here." Fleur slid a stylus pen to him. "Here's how you do it." She demonstrated, and I nodded encouragement. She wiggled her eyebrows, proving to me that she didn't hold any grudges against the thin guy.

Talk turned to everyone's week and their struggles. Each of them were trying, in their own way, to improve their health, but I knew from bitter experience what a difficult road it was. We talked about various tips and tricks to change habits, and I shared a few of the things I tried when I was on my weight-loss journey. As they talked, they colored, each with a different approach to the app. Coral often did all of one color then did the next one. Pearl worked on one part of the design, while Fleur treated it like a contest, tapping impatiently at the smaller areas with rapid little pecks. Brooke often seemed to get lost in the artwork, tracing lines that had nothing to do with the coloring.

People took turns hashing over their peeves, then Brooke said, "I have this Facebook friend who's always traveling. She's in France now. Her husband pays for everything. She doesn't work."

"Nice job if you can get it," Fleur said.

"She went to Peru and saw that big thing there, that macho thing."

"Machu Pichu?" I asked, struggling not to grin. Dallas ducked his head to examine his screen, and I saw his shoulders twitch.

"Yeah, the one with the steps." Brooke shifted the design on her screen. "I couldn't do any of that stuff because I'm fat. And I'm not rich," she added morosely, her dark blonde hair dangling around her face and hiding her expression.

"Do you want to do that stuff?" Dallas asked. "I mean, I see friends who post stuff, too, but when I think about it, I don't want to spend my time tramping around with a bunch of tourists." He peeked at her with a sidelong look. "I figure I'll let them spend the money and the sweat and I'll enjoy the pictures."

"It's FOMO," Pearl stated. "Fear of missing out." I was surprised she spoke up. She seldom contributed much to our conversations. "It looks like somebody's leading a glamourous life but maybe they'd like to be sitting, talking with friends and relaxing."

Coral snorted. "Denmark, Minnesota versus Paris, France? I think I know which one is more fun."

Dallas lifted his gaze to me. "It depends on who's sharing the experience." I wasn't sure what I saw in his dark brown eyes. Hope? Sadness? He lowered his head. "If the right person isn't there to share it, why bother?"

"That's where I disagree. Our society assumes people need to be part of a pair to enjoy things. There's nothing wrong with being single." I spoke with assurance, hoping the two single ladies heard my message.

"That's not what I meant." He kept his gaze on the tablet, tapping colors. "Sometimes it's good to have friends, and if it changes to be more than friends, well, you had the friend thing to start with. You know it's solid. It's not only superficial stuff like looks or money."

"Well, that's not going to happen if you're fat," Coral declared. "Nobody looks past the fat to see the person."

"It can't be that bad," Dallas protested mildly.

Everyone there raised their head and stared at him.

Fleur laughed, but it was a sad, croaking sound. "I've heard it too many times. *You'd be pretty if you'd only lose some weight.*"

"I know, right?" I looked around the small circle. "Haven't we heard that? Like our beauty is tied to our weight."

"Guys don't think about that kind of stuff. We're pretty basic." Dallas peeked at Brooke's tablet. "Where does that pink color go?"

"There used to be a ton of get-em-up advertising," Coral said. "Is that the problem that guys focus on?"

"You bet. Of course, it depends on the guy." He had a wicked grin. "And the incentive."

Coral laughed. "There's no pill substitute for a bit of slap-and-tickle excitement."

"You had a bunch of excitement today, and it wasn't the in-the-sheet kind," Fleur said, glancing sidelong at me.

"It's excitement I can do without."

"Well, come on. What happened?" Brooke pecked impatiently at the tablet, filling in colors. "The Dowager Queen died on your dock."

"The Dowager Queen?" I asked.

"The old bitch who owns our dress shop. I work at the Mermaid Couture dress shop," Brooke explained to Dallas. "On South Main Street. Old Mrs. Dronning owned it. This brown-root blonde came in and acted all high and mighty." She pursed her lips, looking sour while hunching. "You should know it was my grandmother who passed away this morning. I'll be handling the store from now on," she said in a high-pitched voice.

"Handling the store?" Coral asked. "You already have a store manager."

"We do. The old bitch didn't bother with us for at least the last ten years. Maybe this new one will let us get updated inventory. I'm tired of selling old lady clothes."

"I heard they were shopping local, but Manny told me they brought in their tables and linens from Chicago." Pearl frowned at her tablet. "They should at least buy a few decorations from people in town. The Crabby Cove has nice hand-carved wooden pieces made by local folks. They need to put a few of those in their restaurant."

"And paintings," Coral said. "Ship's Rest Gallery has nice artwork from local artists. I heard they got their artwork from some place out west."

"It's probably one of those chain restaurants," Fleur said. "You know the kind. You eat at one in Chicago, and it looks the same as the one in Vegas. Like those Hard Rock ones."

"Maybe they're getting started," Dallas ventured. "You know, just getting stuff set up. Maybe they'll add local things later."

"Not if Skinny Bitch has her way," Brooke said. "She made it very clear that this is a cute little town but it's not her idea of a good place for a business. Apparently, the actor guy got it in his head that he wanted to help his hometown by putting a restaurant here, and she's going along with him." She snorted. "Like we need his help. We're doing fine without him. There's all kinds of good places to eat."

"Like Tug's Treats," Pearl said, tapping the cupcake box next to her.

"Maybe he wanted to come back to a place that's real," Dallas said. "From what I've heard, life in La La Land can be pretty weird."

"So he left L.A. for Denmark, Minnesota?" Fleur shook her head. "It can't be that weird. No, I think he came here to lord it over the locals. The rich folks will suck up to him, and he'll be a big fish in a little pond. Or lake."

"The way that little bitch talked, nothing she saw was good enough for their high-class place. We were too quaint for them."

Dallas was bent above his tablet, focused on tapping the colors.

"Maybe she's not used to shopping in a small town," I said.

"And maybe she's a snob." Fleur put down her stylus. "It's too bad that old witch died on the dock. I hope it won't hurt your business. And I hope that new restaurant doesn't hurt you, too."

"I'll manage." I checked my fitness tracker, which lit when I lifted my wrist. "Speaking of which, I have cakes to work on tonight. I'm shooing you girls out early."

"I'm always surprised that an hour goes by fast," Coral said, setting her tablet on the table, a fully colored mandala displayed. "Why can't work go by this fast?"

"Then it wouldn't be work. It would be fun, and you wouldn't get paid for it." Brooke tucked her cupcake box into the voluminous bag she always carried. "Good to meet you," she said to Dallas, sticking out her hand.

He shook it. "Good to meet you, too. If I need to shop for ladies clothing, I know where to go and who to ask for."

"You do that." She beamed at him then slung the bag on her shoulder, leading the other Girls from the shop. They each left the tablets on the counter when they went.

I followed them to the door then shut off each tablet. "I told you it was a pretty low-key meeting."

"It was interesting. Why do you use the coloring program?" Dallas joined me at the counter, handing me his tablet.

"It tells me a lot about a person. Some are methodical. Some get impatient. Some like to flit around and do a bit here and there."

"Flit?" He grinned.

I slapped him on the arm. "You know what I mean."

"Flitters. I like it."

I stared at him, examining his face. "How did you do it? I mean, I knew you were an actor, but I almost didn't recognize you."

He ran a hand through his hair, pawing it back into place with a part on the right. "I hate showing off my thinning hair," he said with a self-deprecating frown. "It's a matter of attitude. If you think you're successful, you can make others believe it." As he spoke, he rebuttoned his shirt, tucking it into the jeans which didn't look baggy, somehow. They appeared softly casual, well worn. In just a few minutes, he'd transformed back into the man on the pages of *Vanity Fair*.

"I'm not sure that works if you're fat." I lifted one of the bags of bakery goods. "Are you ready to do cake work?"

"I sure am." He followed me, waiting while I locked up. We walked to the parking lot at the Jolt. "What are you going to do about the cats?"

"Do about them?"

"It's like that Chinese proverb. If you save someone's life, you're responsible for it." He gestured to the shed when we passed it. "Or something like that."

"I suppose I'll feed them," I conceded. "They must have someplace to sleep. They've survived this long without my help. They'll be fine."

"I have an idea for a house." He chuckled. "A cat house. That's my car. I'm renting one until I get moved here, then I'll buy a car." He led the way to a bronze-colored Subaru Outback.

"You're moving here?" I stowed the cakes in the back seat, and he set the bag with the cake tools next to it.

"I was thinking I might build a house." He slid behind the steering whee,l and I hopped into the passenger seat.

"Where?"

"Out here. You know. On the lake."

"Why?'

"Why not? I need to live somewhere."

I suppose he was right, but it was odd to think of him, a movie star, in a house here.

"Just think. I might be across the bay from you."

I shook my head. "That's not high-rent turf. You'll want to be at Turfmoor."

Now he shook his head. "No way. I don't need to be in the high rent district."

"Says the millionaire movie star."

He drove through the lane to the town street. "I wish people would forget that I'm an actor. I'd like to just be the guy who came home."

I considered that while he turned onto the highway that would eventually wind around the lake and take us to the Richers. "It's hard to see that, I guess. Many people here have never experienced the life you've led."

"Or you." Dallas stared at the road ahead, his profile highlighted by the setting sun. "You've been to Europe and big cities and you came home."

I wasn't in show business. I wasn't voted Sexiest anything in a national magazine. "Give it time. Once you've been here awhile, people will see you as only another business owner." I doubted it, but he seemed bothered by his notoriety. "Look at that." I leaned forward, peering past him at the sun slanting on the lake, making the sailboats look like a well-regulated regatta. Then one cut in front of the other, spoiling the illusion.

Dallas hazarded a glance out his window. "Those idiots. They're too close to the rocks on that side. Don't they know how shallow the lake is there? It looks safe but it's not."

"Maybe it's Darwinism at work. Trust Mother Nature to winnow the herd. What else would you expect from an entity who created bugs with little butts that light up. What kind of method of communication is that?"

He laughed. "It must work because we keep getting more little bugs with lighted butts."

"Damned inefficient, if you ask me."

"Ask the bugs."

I laughed, too, and the mood in the car lifted. Whatever depression had caught him seemed to dissipate in the summer sunlight.

We got to the restaurant. It sat on a promontory east of the lighthouse, which I spied across the bay. The customer parking lot was in front, several cars sitting there. That was on the landward side, which meant most of the building would have a lakeside view.

Dallas drove around the building and down a hill, behind the restaurant. "This is staff parking. The kitchen is on the lower level, and the restaurant is above. We have a cool dumb waiter system to bring the food upstairs. The wait staff doesn't have to go to the kitchen at all." He parked in a graveled area near an enormous double door. "We can load and unload directly into the kitchen."

"That's a tricky drive for a delivery truck." I hopped from the car and grabbed my bag.

"We don't have any big ones, just small ones. Despite what your friends said tonight, we are buying from local producers, and that means small deliveries." Dallas came around the car and joined me, reaching past me to get the other bag. "Tug?"

"Hmm?" I looked at the lake in the distance.

"What those ladies talked about. You know you were always beautiful. You still are. In a different way."

I patted his arm. "Thanks, Dallas. But I was fat."

"And you were beautiful." He brushed a kiss against my lips.

I turned away from him, and that's when I saw Lily standing in the doorway at the restaurant.

Chapter Eight

One glimpse of her face confirmed those rumors Jamie heard. "Oops."

Dallas turned to see what I was staring at. "What's she doing here? She said she had a meeting in town tonight."

"Hey, Lily," I called. She didn't seem inclined to join us, so I walked toward her, holding the bag in my arms, careful not to jostle the cakes too much. Then I worried that she might hit me and that would jeopardize the cakes. I let the bag dangle from my arm, just in case.

"Hello, Theresa. Dallas mentioned you needed to use our facility." Lily shifted to one side but didn't open the door. She wore chic pink capris that were molded to her long legs and a form-fitting top that emphasized her slender arms and large breasts. Her gaze went past me. "Dallas, we need to chat. I checked with Chef Le Mer, and he's concerned about the fish we plan to serve on Friday."

"What's the problem?" Dallas hurried forward, opening the door for me.

"I'm sure Theresa is busy and would prefer not to be delayed." Lily nodded at me while I walked past her. "The bakery area is ahead and on the left."

I inched by her and into a spacious receiving area, an open space where tradesmen would bring in

141

supplies. The main refrigeration unit was on my left, and two smaller ones were on the right, one labeled Fish and the other Meat/Poultry. Smart. Fish would be a major part of the menu, and it made sense to keep it separate from other carnivorous choices.

Straight ahead was the main kitchen. I walked into the gleaming, bright space. I'd worked in many a commercial kitchen in my day, but I never saw one pristine and new, before it was used. This was a wonder. Everything gleamed, utensils were in their places, there weren't any smells of food or humidity from the dishwashers or sweat. It was like paradise.

I passed the large dry storage locker and the main prep counter, which was wide and long. It stretched at least ten feet ahead, running half the length of the center of the kitchen. It was four feet wide, which meant two people could work on either side of it simultaneously. I ogled the copper and stainless-steel pots dangling overhead and the crisp towels hanging on their hooks. The meat prep area was on the left, knives lined up like soldiers in their slots. On the opposite wall was the dishwashing unit and pot sinks.

Beyond the meat prep section was the pastry section, an area about 8-by-8 feet. It had a dedicated stove and small cooler, with a large industrial oven across from it in the center cooking area. I counted four ranges, two more ovens, and a rotisserie. In the corner past the pastry area was a pizza oven, brick-faced and deep.

All along the back wall were prep counters, sinks, and more prep space. I peeked around the corner. Stairs led upward, and a small elevator was next to them, big enough for large orders. Everywhere I turned there were handwashing stations, sinks at each section.

"Good heavens," I whispered, setting my cake bag on the gleaming metal surface in the bakery division. "When he builds a restaurant, he doesn't scrimp." A rack of shelving separated this area from the ones next to it, and I glimpsed Dallas and Lily through the mesh backing. He seemed annoyed and Lily was sad, maybe, or beleaguered. I suppose she had a bazillion things to do now that her grandmother was dead. I considered suggesting that Dallas help her instead of me but, before I could, she left him and strode through the kitchen to me, her stylish sandals clicking a sharp rhythm on the white tile floor.

"I'll have a contract ready for you in the morning," she said. "What time can I come to your shop?"

"Whatever time is convenient." I busied myself with the cakes, avoiding looking at her. "I'll be up at five to work at the bakery, and I usually swim as soon as it gets light. Any time after seven or eight is fine."

"Is that for Friday's dinner?" She nodded at the cakes I pulled from the bag.

"Yes, it is. I'll do a two-tier main cake with a sheet cake." I hazarded a look at her. She appeared confused, not angry, as I expected. "It's part of the design."

Lily studied the pale golden cakes for a second then said, "I suppose you know what you're doing. I'll come to your shop at eight in the morning." She spun on her heel and strode away from me, almost running over Dallas, who waited by the door. He said something to her. She didn't pause, brushing past him. Dallas watched her, my cake tools dangling from his hand. Then he seemed to shake it off and strode to me. "Do you think you can work here?" he asked, gesturing to the gleaming counters.

"Oh, I'll manage," I said with an attempt at a chuckle. I took the bag he handed me, pulling out my leveling knife and cake boards. "I'm sorry Lily's unhappy with this working arrangement. I was afraid that might happen. It's stress on top of her grandmother's death."

"Yeah, I guess I should've listened to you. I thought she understood." He watched me work, a confused look in his dark eyes.

"Understood what?" I went to a sink and washed my hands, mentally humming a tune as I did so.

He leaned against the cooling rack, his arms crossed. "She and Sirena and I talked last night. I told them I was done opening restaurants. I want to focus on this one. I told them I'd sell the one in Vegas to them if they wanted it. I already have a buyer for the ones in L.A. and Kansas City."

"Why?" I unwrapped the cake board from its plastic covering then dusted it with powdered sugar I'd colored pale blue. I placed the lower cake on the board, eyeing it to make sure I had it where I wanted. "Why sell them?"

"I'm tired. I want to stay in one place and not go from town to town every week. I told them they can keep the name. I'd show up now and then, but I wanted them to have total ownership and responsibility."

"But what if they did something to damage your reputation? You know, what if the quality changed?"

"That's written into the contract. I suggested reasonable terms for the sale. I think Sirena was interested but Lily isn't."

"Lily is interested in you, not your business." I removed my leveling knife from the carry carton and went to work on the bottom layer.

"What we had was over a long time ago. It's only business between us."

"That's not how she sees it. Or that's how it appears, at least." I worked on leveling the layer, slicing off the tiniest sliver of cake before doing the same to the other layers, putting them on cake boards on the counter to protect them from the cool temperatures. "From what you've told me, she's tried to sabotage relationships you've had."

He was quiet, his hands dug into his pockets while he watched me. "You know, I think if I really cared about someone or if they cared about me, she couldn't sabotage it. She failed with you, didn't she?"

I wasn't sure what he was saying. My confusion must have shown because Dallas laughed. "Oh, Tug. You're priceless."

"What do you mean?" I pulled out the buttercream and opened the jar, checking the consistency. It was maybe a little too warm for a crumb coat but usable.

"Nothing. Everything." He shook his head. "I'm not sure."

"Okay. When you figure it out, share with me, okay?"

He smiled. "Oh, I will."

"Now on to bigger issues. Your cake."

"I'll help."

"No, I need to do this myself."

"Should I be offended?" He leaned on the counter and regarded me with big, innocent eyes. "Don't you trust me?"

I stuck my knife into the frosting and dished up a large dollop. "I trust you. But I want this to be a surprise."

"Okay. Challenge accepted." Dallas straightened and tapped the tip of my nose then turned, going back to the entryway. "I'll be in the office if you need me. It's outside near the loading dock."

"You don't have to stay here. Oh, damn. I guess you do, don't you? I'm sorry. I didn't think it through. You're stuck here while I work, aren't you?"

"That's okay. I have stuff to do. Owner stuff. Yell if you need anything." He left before I could protest.

I silently berated myself. I should have taken him up on his offer to help. That way we'd finish faster. Oh, well. I worked quickly, leveling the layers then starting in on the crumb coating. The cakes and the frosting were a bit too warm and it went slower than I liked. I put the tiers in the cooler to chill as I worked. Once again, I marveled at how well equipped and well designed the kitchen was.

I was working on the first buttercream coat on the bottom layers when I heard footsteps coming from the doorway near the dishwasher, opposite me.

I looked up, expecting to see Lily. But it was Sirena at the serving counter. "Lily said you were coming here. I heard what happened at your bakery today." She came around the tall counter and approached, walking between the big stoves and the long prep counter. Today she wore casual denim capris and a loose knit top with blue sandals—a far more casual look than I'd ever seen her wear. It was also far more flattering than the business suit. The looser clothing softened her plumpness.

"I needed to work on the cake for Friday, and it made sense to do the decorating here," I said. "I appreciate Dallas giving me the space to work."

She came closer, watching me apply the frosting in smooth, even strokes. "You make it look easy."

"I've been doing it for years." She stopped near the cooling rack that separated the baking section from the rest of the room, a foot or two away from where I worked. I smelled her perfume, and I wondered if I should protect the cake lest it absorb her odor.

"Lily is extremely upset about her grandmother's death. She's taking it hard." Sirena opened a towel then refolded it and put it back on the rack. "Her father was difficult. He had extremely rigid ideas about how to raise her. Lily's grandmother often intervened and was actually her only friend. After Lily's mother left, Lily was lonely."

I kept my face averted so Sirena wouldn't see my disbelief. I had heard stories growing up about "King" Monroe, his wayward wife, and his wild-spirited daughter. If her old man did anything to prohibit Lily, I never heard about it. "I'm sure she is upset." I finished another layer and swapped it for the final layer to frost.

"Lily is very business-minded. She cares a great deal about Dallas and making sure his restaurants are a success."

"I'm sure the success is important, especially if you and she buy the restaurant he wants to sell."

Her eyes widened, and she took a step backward. That brought her under the bright overhead lights. Her skin was as gray as the frosting on the cake layer I just finished. "Did Dallas tell you about that?"

"Yes, he did. It makes sense, I guess. You guys know how those sites are being run, and he doesn't want to do it anymore."

Sirena was quiet for a moment then she said, "I'm sure Lily won't be able to make any decisions until her grandmother's estate is processed. She's the only relative Adella had. The only living relative, that is."

"Adella?" I finished the last layer and put it in the cooler before going to the sink to clean my tools.

"Mrs. Dronning. She and Lily were close. Adella was happy when Lily told her that she'd be here to work on the restaurant." Sirena regarded me with hawk-like closeness. I wasn't sure why, and it made me nervous.

"That's nice," I said inanely. I hated it when people watched me work, and here she was, a few inches away, eyeing everything I did. "I'm surprised Lily didn't go into entertainment work. Didn't she want to be a dancer or a singer?"

Sirena froze, her green eyes wide like a deer in the headlights. "She was a dancer in New York, then she went to Vegas and was in a show there. The TV people were looking for dancers for their show, and Dallas recommended her. That brought them back together again."

Hmm. That wasn't the story that Dallas told me. Oh, well. Perhaps Lily spun it differently for her business partner. "Could you move, please?" I asked. "It makes me nervous when people watch me work."

"I like to see how you do things. After all, the cake is for our investors. I want to make sure it's well done."

You wouldn't know if it was properly made unless someone diagrammed it and shoved it down your

148

throat, I almost said. "This isn't a big part of the process. I'm doing the initial frosting coats tonight. The real decorating comes tomorrow night."

"Oh." She eyed the sheet cake. "We ordered a tiered cake."

"You did. It's not unusual to have a sheet cake as part of a tiered cake." It was damn unusual, but I wouldn't tell her that.

She watched me level the sheet cake, thankfully not asking any questions about that process. If she had, I might have attacked her with the knife. I set aside the thin upper crust I removed and put the cake back in the cooler.

"What time did you discover the break-in at your bakery?"

"Why do you care?" I checked the consistency of the blue buttercream and put it in the cooler.

"I was curious what you might have seen. I suppose the police know that you and Adella argued."

"We didn't argue. We had a polite discussion about religion." Sirena was definitely getting on my nerves. Didn't she have anything to do? That gave me an idea. "Hey, I wondered if Lily mentioned a revised contract to you. If you have a copy, can you get it for me? I can review it before I sign it."

"She did mention it, but I don't know if I can find a copy." Sirena reluctantly left her place near the shelving unit.

"Can you look? I'd appreciate it." I removed the bottom cake layers. "I need to get these frosted tonight, then I can assemble the cake tomorrow. If I could review that contract in the morning, it would sure save me some time."

"I'll see if I can find it." She headed toward the exit but paused. "You didn't mention when you got to the bakery last night."

Holy cupcakes, why did it matter? "I think it was midnight or thereabouts. That's about the time the students arrive to do the baking, and they called me."

She stood near the group of ovens, frowning. The red of her hair appeared to frizz and crackle around her face, a trick of lighting from the bright overheads. "I'll see if I can find that for you."

I watched her scurry away, going back the way she came. Thank heaven she was gone. If I had to make small talk with her for one more minute, death by buttercream was a real possibility.

I quickly finished the frosting, getting two layers of buttercream on top of the crumb coat. I didn't like pushing it this fast, but I had no choice. If I had time tomorrow morning, I'd do the final buttercream coating, then tomorrow night I'd decorate. I still had only a vague idea of what I'd do. I would need to spend tonight on that.

Dallas came into the kitchen while I was staring into space, visualizing the design. "If you want, you can leave your tools here," he said. "We don't have any bakery work being done until next week. The dinner on Friday is special. The real cooking starts on Monday. That whole bakery space is yours to use if you need it."

"Thanks. I'll take you up on that." I pointed to the cooler. "The layers are in here getting chilled. I'll be back tomorrow morning and do the final buttercream coat, then tomorrow night I'll try to get here and do the dowels. I have two wedding cakes to do, though. It may have to wait until Friday." I yawned and headed for the sink.

"You didn't change your exercise band."

"I'm tired. And busy." I yawned again.

"Somebody sounds grumpy."

I leveled my frosting spatula at him. "One more crack like that, and you'll have buttercream in your beard."

"It's a goatee." He ran his fingers over his whiskers.

"Whatever."

"Can I help?"

"Not unless you can bake me a hundred cupcakes and frost them for the wedding on Saturday."

"Okay. What flavor?"

"Get serious." I leaned over the sink to wash my tools.

"I am serious. I can bake the cupcakes tomorrow and frost them tomorrow night or Friday morning. If you don't trust me, loan me a couple of students from the school."

I cleaned my tools and considered his offer. Cupcakes were simple. The bride had requested fifty yellow ones and fifty chocolate. White cream cheese frosting on all. Easy. "I'm not sure—"

"Oh, come on. I have a bit of free time tomorrow afternoon. Loan me two students, and we'll have those cupcakes knocked out in no time."

Oh, it was tempting. "Let me think about it." I tucked my bag of tools into the cabinet next to the cooler. "I'm done here. Can you drive me back to the lighthouse? Or boat me?"

"Boat you?" He laughed. "Sure, come on. I'm leasing a few boats to have on hand for guests. We can take one of those."

"Oh, wait. I asked Sirena to get me a copy of the contract."

"She left." Dallas headed for the door, and I followed him, slinging my purse onto my shoulder. He flipped off the master light switch, leaving dim overhead lights on behind us. "She was parked in back, and her car's gone now. I think I saw her leave about ten minutes ago."

"So much for getting a copy to review tonight," I muttered.

Dallas held the exterior door open for me. "There shouldn't be much to review. I told them to simplify it as much as possible." He came behind me, slamming the door and checking it was locked. "The boats are here."

We walked past the covered concrete slab where trucks would pull in. "What about your car?" I asked when we passed it.

"I'll come back tonight. It can stay parked here until I get back." Dallas went past the graveled parking area to a wooden platform. When I reached it, I saw it was the top of a short flight of steps at a dock. Four runabouts were tied up below.

Above and behind us the restaurant's windows gleamed in the setting set. "The façade is impressive," I said. "It looks like a ship's prow."

"There'll be great lake sights in the winter and summer. My other restaurants are in urban settings without any kind of a view. I'm glad I was able to buy this piece of land." He led the way to the dock and the boats, hopping into one runabout.

I followed more sedately. I've lived on a lake most of my life, and I knew that one bad misstep could bring a person to serious grief. I settled in the prow, half-turned to face forward.

"You look like a ship's figurehead," Dallas said. "A mermaid staring at the sea."

I glanced back at him while he piloted us away from the shallow bay and into the lake. "Not me. I don't long to live somewhere else. I'm happy where I am." I faced the lake, angling my face to feel the setting sun through the light mist of lake water.

"You always seemed happy to be in school. Most of the kids were only there to make their parents happy. You seemed glad to be learning."

"I was glad to have a chance to go to school. My parents had died, and I was broke. I was grateful for the opportunity."

He was silent for a time, steering us into the channel. The lighthouse was ahead, a tall shape in the distance. "I always had the feeling you weren't too impressed by Lily or me when we were in school."

I twisted on the seat to regard him. "Impressed?"

"Other kids sucked up to us because our parents were rich. You never did."

"That didn't matter to me." What I didn't say was that I knew it wouldn't make any difference. I wasn't in his league and I knew it.

"You always acted like I was just a regular guy."

I wasn't sure what he was getting at. "You were, Dallas. You never acted like one of the snobby rich kids." I peered at our destination and spied someone or something near the base of the lighthouse. "What's that?" I shaded my eyes with my hand, trying to see past the glare of sun on the waves.

"Where?"

"I'm sure I saw somebody moving around the steps." I leaned forward, but whoever or whatever it was had vanished.

"Maybe your partner is there. Or maybe one of the students is there early." Dallas piloted the boat with sure competence, angling it so we didn't bump against any of the wakes from the other boats returning to home base at the end of the day.

"Maybe. Although I doubt it's Jamie. He's never around at night." I considered it then remembered. "It might be the police, too."

"Police? Why?"

His voice was sharp. I turned to look at him, but Dallas shifted the boat, moving it to approach at an angle to the lighthouse. I held on to the seat to keep my balance. "The police might be there to collect more evidence or something."

"I suppose that's possible."

The boat bounced on waves, and I had a hard time focusing on the lighthouse. Then it got closer, and I saw that I wasn't wrong. Someone was on the rocks near the steps. "Who is that?" I leaned forward, unconsciously willing the boat to go faster.

"Do you have your phone? Maybe you can call the police and see if they have somebody there."

I reached for my purse but hesitated, visualizing an expensive iPhone slipping from my hands and ending up at the bottom of Spirit Lake. I stared at the lighthouse, trying to figure out who might be there.

Whoever it was, they were dressed in dark clothing and maybe wearing a hoodie. I didn't see any hair or face, but for all I knew, the person had his or her back to me.

Dallas cut the engine back to an idle. "What are you doing?" I asked. "We need to get there and see who's mucking around my lighthouse."

He glanced to the starboard. "Boat traffic. We need to wait."

I spied the speedboat heading our way, and I subsided. The rule on the water was that boats on that side had the right of way. Dallas let our boat rock forward, assessing the speedboat as it neared. The driver of that boat waved an acknowledgement when he passed then Dallas shifted the gears, and we were moving again.

Within minutes we were close enough that I saw the person scrambling on the rocks. I still didn't see any features, but he/she was moving up. Why the hell would anyone go down the rockface that way? What was so important someone risked life and limb on wet and slippery rocks?

"I'll go after him while you tie up the boat," Dallas said when we neared the lighthouse dock.

"What?"

"You heard me. You jump out. I'll toss you the bowline and you tie up the boat, and I'll go after whoever's poking around your house." He headed for the dock, barely slowing.

"You shouldn't do that. Who knows who it might be? Or what they're doing? You might get into trouble or—"

"Get ready." He aimed at the side of the dock, cutting the motor and letting the boat bump against the dock. "Get out, Tug. Now!"

I jumped to my feet and used the sway of the boat to help propel me up to the dock. I grabbed the line Dallas tossed me but almost lost it when he leapt from the boat, pushing it away from me. I dug in with all my might and managed to get the boat close enough to loop the line around a stanchion.

I took a precious few minutes to get the boat hook I kept near the steps. Dallas was already at the top, running like crazy. "Dallas, wait!"

He paused, looked back at me, then he took off running along the bluff on the path that led to the park. "You stupid asshole," I wheezed while I raced back to the boat, pulling it nearer to me. I flailed about with the boat hook and snagged another line, which I used to tie up the stern, thus keeping the boat securely against the side of the dock and not drifting about.

I headed for the steps, ascending as fast as I dared on the wooden planks. When I got to the top, I ran to the path but saw no sign of Dallas or the mysterious figure. Now that I was on stable ground and away from the water, I used my phone to dial Detective Usher.

"This is Theresa Gallant," I panted, my words tumbling over each other. "We were boating across the lake and saw somebody at the lighthouse. Do you have anybody working here?"

"At this time of night? No, of course not. Who was it? Did you get a good luck at the person?"

I shook my head then realized he wouldn't see me. "No, we were on the lake. As we got closer to the lighthouse, we saw somebody on the rocks near the dock."

"Where at on the rocks?" Usher's voice was calm but insistent.

"You know. On the rocks. By the steps."

"You said 'we'. Who's with you?"

"Nobody now. Dallas took off running after whoever was here. I think they went toward the park ,but I needed to tie up the damn boat. I didn't see where they went."

"Where are you now?"

"I'm at the lighthouse. At the top of the steps."

"Don't leave that spot. I'll be there in a few minutes."

I ended the call and stuck the phone back in my bag. I began walking along the path, thinking I might spy Dallas, but Usher said to stay put. I reluctantly returned to the steps. The sun was low in the sky, long shadows from the lighthouse and the bluff putting the rocks and the nearby lake in darkness. Then the breeze went through the trees lining the bluff and I saw sunlight glint off something in the rocks.

King Queen appeared a few yards away from me at the top of the bluff. She hesitated when she saw me, then she apparently decided I was boring because she began a tortuous descent down the rocks, stepping onto various boulders and sandy patches with a clear intent.

"What are you doing?" I approached the edge of the bluff to watch.

The cat picked her way along a path only she could see. She was heading for the glinting spot I saw a moment earlier. I dropped my bag and went to the bluff, sliding to the topmost boulder. I'd climbed these rocks many times in the years since I bought the lighthouse, and I had a healthy respect for their slippery, smooth surfaces.

The cat was below me, about twenty feet away. I shifted position, and at that moment the sun shone through the shadows covering me. I saw something shiny in among the moss and debris of the rocks. Most of them were smooth, worn away by years of water washing against them. There were a few jagged ones, the sharpness caused when ice coated the rock in the winter then a sudden thaw or cold snap would expand the mineral.

I inched my way downward, facing the bluff and feeling my way with my foot to test each step before I took it. I went slowly, but I was lucky. Most of the rocks were dry with only a few that were slick. I scrambled to the rock below me. It was one of the slick ones, and I had to be careful to keep my balance on the slimy surface. King Queen was dancing ahead of me, tail flicking as though to say, "come on, puny human. Keep up with me."

I lost sight of the shiny object when I got lower, the sunlight no longer highlighting it. I peered around the area, looking for anything that might be unusual.

When I saw the blue handle of my butcher knife, I knew I'd found what I was looking for.

Chapter Nine

King Queen leapt onto the rock above me then whirled, pivoting to glare at the top of the bluff. I followed her gaze.

Detective Usher stared down at me. "I told you to stay put," he called. With his dark polo shirt and pants, he blended into the shadows at the top of the rock-strewn bluff.

"I meant to. Then I saw what she was doing so I followed her." I pointed below me, to the knife still lying among the debris. "My knife is here."

"The forensic team is on its way. Please stay there until they arrive."

Stay here? Balanced on a rock? I started to protest, but he left the edge, phone to his ear.

"What the hell am I supposed to do?" I asked the cat, who was poised on the rock above me, still staring at Usher.

The cat's attention came back to me. She regarded me calmly for a moment, then she sagged on the rock in the classic Cat Loaf pose, paws tucked under her chest. The sunlight angled on us, and she blinked sleepily.

"Look for Dallas," I called. "He ran after that person. He might be in trouble."

Usher appeared again at the top. "We're handling it, Miss Gallant."

"You don't appear to be handling anything," I mumbled under my breath. I climbed up a foot or two and sat on a relatively flat rock, my legs dangling. "He doesn't seem surprised my knife is here," I said to the cat, who was perched on my right. "How did they miss it? Good heavens, they must have searched these rocks, didn't they?"

King Queen yawned then regarded me through sleepy gold eyes. Her black-on-gray stripes matched in front, making her paws appear to disappear into her fur. She blinked at me, head tilted to one side.

"Oh, you're right. They did search. I saw them earlier. That means the person who was here put the knife here. I wonder if there's fingerprints." I leaned forward but didn't see if anything was smeared on the knife handle. "Whoever took it might have had butter on their hands. Maybe they left fingerprints." I shook my head. "Or else they washed it thoroughly and left it here to make it look bad for me."

I heard voices above me. I craned my neck, nearly toppling off my perch when I tried to see who was talking. Then Usher's head poked over the edge. "I told you not to move."

"I got tired of standing. What's he going to do?" I asked King Queen. "Arrest me?"

"I might," Usher called down. "Wait there."

"I'm not going anywhere," I told the cat. "And it appears you aren't, either."

Small clumps of dirt began dribbling past me on my left. I twisted and saw a young Black man in polo shirt and khaki pants poised at the top. "You may want a rope," I called. "These rocks are slippery."

"You don't have a rope," the guy said as he began inching down the cliff, his brown work boots scuffing along the rock surface.

"I've climbed these rocks a bazillion times. Well, maybe only a million or so. It's not hard as long as you look where you're going."

He didn't answer, just kept moving downward, a thick rope around his middle and looped through his legs in a harness contraption. His shirt was taut against his chest, which was impressively large as were his arms. The guy was definitely in good shape.

"Are you the forensic person?" I asked when he neared me. "Detective Usher said a forensic person would be coming."

"Yep. My name is Tommy." He landed on the rock next to me on my left. Now that he was close, he was younger than I originally guessed, only in his twenties, with close-cut hair and pretty blue eyes. A toolbelt was hooked around his waist. "You're right. It's not a hard climb."

"It's a tricky climb. It's not hard." I pointed at the knife. "It's there."

"How did you find it?"

"The cat found it." I gestured but King Queen was gone, vanished like a Cheshire Cat. I saw her tail flicking among the rocks, several feet below us. "Somebody was here earlier. Then when I got back, the cat was here. I figured I'd see what she was looking at. The sun was shining. It sparkled."

"Did you see the person who was here?" Tommy started downward, toward the knife.

"No, Dallas chased him. Or her."

"Dallas?"

"Dallas Prinze. He was with me when we saw the person."

The forensic guy paused. "You know Dallas Prinze?"

"Yeah. We were in a boat and coming to the lighthouse, and we saw somebody. Dallas is up there, somewhere." I waved at the cliffside above me.

"I'm sure we'll find him." Tommy prowled around the area where the knife was, pulling something from his toolbelt. A camera, I decided. He paused a few feet away from the knife, took pictures, then to my surprise, he took pictures of me where I sat on my rock, watching.

"Hey, what's that for?" I demanded.

"I wanted to make notes about your route from the knife to where you are. We may need to eliminate your footprints or handprints."

"Handprints?" I checked my hands, which were not exactly clean. "I didn't put the knife there. Why would I do that? It's my knife. Why would I incriminate myself?"

"Ma'am, I've met all kinds of people. You might be surprised."

"I suppose I would be although I've met all kinds of people, too. I'm a baker, and you should meet a couple of the bridezillas I've worked with."

He grinned. "I can imagine." He continued his prowl, snapping pictures.

"I suppose I can go back now," I said. "Now that you're here."

He reached for his buckle. "You can use my rope."

I waved a hand and scrambled to my feet. "I got this." I climbed upward, his sputtering protests behind me. I ignored him and picked a path to the top, angling toward the steps where I spied Detective Usher standing.

He watched me with obvious disapproval when I dragged myself onto the last rock. I jumped toward the step, slipping under the bannister to face Usher.

"I told you to wait," he commented.

"You did, and I didn't." I pushed past him to stand next to the porch. "Where's Dallas? Is he okay? He took off running after the person who put the knife there."

"You saw somebody put the knife in that spot?" Usher looked at Tommy, who was still taking pictures.

"Well, no, but the knife wasn't there earlier and now it is, and we saw somebody. Obviously, somebody put the knife there."

"There's no obvious about it." He took my arm in a none-too-gentle grip. "Let's talk, shall we?"

I considered struggling but decided that might be resisting the police. I grabbed my bag then let him lead me to the Jolt. It was now past nine o'clock, and daylight was fast vanishing. The motion light came on outside the bakery when we approached. "We should look for Dallas," I said. "What if something happened to him?"

"I have officers canvasing the whole area. We'll find him." Usher went to the bakery door and tried it. "Do you have a key?"

I dug into my purse and found the new set of keys and the spare set to give to the students. "We recently got the locks changed," I explained, letting him inside. "I plan to stay here to meet the students when they come on duty tonight. Normally we hide a set of keys outside, but I think maybe I need to meet them from now on."

"That won't be necessary. Show me your knife drawer again, please."

"Why won't it be necessary?" I led the way to the left side of the kitchen and the knife drawer.

"We think we know who vandalized your shop. I don't think they'll be back."

"Seriously? You know already who killed Mrs.—" I drew a blank on her name.

"Dronning. We don't think the two are related." He opened the knife drawer and examined the interior.

I wondered about fingerprints, then I remembered the forensic minions who had processed the place hours earlier. That made me realize what a long day it had been, and I yawned. "What are you looking for?"

"Where were you earlier tonight?" He closed the drawer and removed the small memo pad from his jeans pocket.

"I was across the lake, at the new restaurant. Dallas' restaurant." I watched him write something in the small book. "Why? Am I a suspect?"

"How long were you with Mr. Prinze?" Usher regarded me with that calm, inscrutable look I was coming to know well.

"He came to a meeting I had here at the shop. Then he and I drove to his restaurant. He volunteered to let me use the bakery there for work I'm doing." I considered launching into more details but decided the detective didn't need to know about the intricacies of cake preparation.

"That was generous of him." Usher watched me, apparently expecting a reaction.

"Yes, it was."

"As I said earlier, he's a special friend, isn't he?"

I leaned against the counter, stifling another yawn. "It's the cake for his restaurant I'm working on. I suppose he has a vested interest in making sure I have what I need for it."

"Hmm." Usher didn't seem impressed by my logic. His gaze went past me to the door.

Dallas came in, followed by two young police officers in khaki pants and dark shirts. Dallas limped toward me. "I lost him, Tug," he said with a grimace. "I almost caught up to him at the park, but a boat was there, and he took off."

"I'm glad you're okay." I glanced at Usher and was surprised to see his eyes on the officers, not Dallas.

A message passed between the different police officers, then Usher said, "Thanks for the help, Mr. Prinze. We'll need to get a statement from you about what you saw, then you'll be free to go."

"Are you sure? Tug, do you need any help? I don't like leaving you here alone if somebody is prowling around." Dallas met me at the counter and regarded me with a worried look. "Maybe I'll wait until the students arrive."

Before I could answer, Usher said, "That's okay, sir. We'll be here for an hour or more. We'll make sure Miss Gallant is safe."

"It's okay," I said hastily, cutting off any argument from Dallas. "You've done more than enough, what with letting me use the restaurant and all."

"Are you sure?"

"One of my men will go back with you in the boat," Usher said. "Just to make sure you get back safely." He smiled so briefly I wasn't sure I even saw it. "We wouldn't want our local celebrity to have any problems."

Dallas stiffened next to me. I put a hand on his arm and gently steered him toward the door. "I'll come to the restaurant tomorrow and put on that last coat of buttercream for your cake. I'll get volunteers, too, to help with the cupcakes. What time do you want them there?"

My diversion worked. He walked with me to stand on the small portico outside the bakery. "Two o'clock would be good. Do you have a special recipe you want me to use?"

I put my arm through his and pulled him toward the steps and the dock. "I'll send it with the students. We'll do a cream cheese frosting."

"Rats. I wanted to discover your secret buttercream recipe."

I gave his arm a shake. "No such luck." I spied Shrimp and King Queen at the steps. "Your other escort awaits you. Maybe you should adopt them."

"Not until I get my house built. I'm staying at a rental now. I don't like leaving you alone."

"I'm not alone, silly. Don't worry about it. The police said they know who did the break-in. They must be close to wrapping it up."

He stopped, dragging me to a halt with him. "So soon?"

I couldn't decipher his expression. He seemed confused or maybe worried. "That's what Detective Usher said."

"Good." We got to the steps, and he paused at the top, the two cats prancing ahead of him downward. "I'll see you in the morning." He went down a step then turned to me. "Good night."

It seemed like the most natural thing in the world to lean forward and give him a quick kiss. "Drive carefully." I stepped back, and the police officer passed me, following Dallas. The two cats bounded out of the rocks and dashed after them.

I watched the men get in the boat and cast off. The two cats sat on the dock, the last of the sun making them into silhouettes. Dallas waved. I waved in return then went to the Jolt and Detective Usher.

True to his word, the police stayed until my fitness alarm went off, followed by Daria, Doug, and Pete arriving. The officers stayed outside, clambering around on the rocks with high-powered lights. Several also walked the path to the park, their flashlights like giant fireflies that they swung to and fro.

I stowed the new set of keys in a different location, between the Jolt and the shed on a small hook that normally held a flashlight, which I transferred to the shed. I showed the keys to the students, then we discussed the night's baking. As I was leaving, I asked, "I need a couple of volunteers to work tomorrow afternoon at the Prinze restaurant. Do you know anybody who might be available?"

Three hands shot up.

I laughed. "You guys can't do it. You'll work a shift tonight, then you have class tomorrow and a shift tomorrow night."

"Wrong-o," Pete said with a grin. "We're on summer break. I'm only taking one class, and it meets on Mondays."

"Same for me," Daria said. "My class was on Tuesday."

"This is our chance to work in a high-end restaurant. That's worth lost sleep," Doug added.

I gave in. Who was I to argue with youthful optimism? I gave them the address and details about where to park, and they promised to be at the restaurant at two the next afternoon. I left them to their nightly work, assured that tonight, at least, we'd have a normal work schedule.

Usher and his minions had folded up their equipment and left. I staggered back to the lighthouse and into bed for a few hours of sleep.

Thursday dawned hot and humid. I worked on the cakes for Saturday, bringing the layers and frosting to room temperature and prepping the cake boards. Once I finished that, I worked on doing the frosting and decorations for the shop. After that the Saturday cakes were ready for leveling and a crumb coat. I was pushing it, but I would be busy that afternoon at Dallas' restaurant, and I needed to get it done.

I made sure I had enough flowers and seashell ornaments for the cakes, then I decided to take a break and go for my swim. I went through the shop, waving to Shelly, who worked the Thursday/Friday/Saturday morning shifts. As I walked along the path, I tried to see what the police searched for the night before, but everything appeared normal. Bees buzzed, flowers bloomed, and the air was thick with the aroma of lakeshore and grass.

I had a leisurely swim, going to and from the swim platform with alternating strokes, flipping onto my back for the final leg. I stared up at the sky, my mind as abuzz as the flowers above me.

What was happening with Dallas Prinze? He kissed me twice, which was two times more than I had ever expected to be kissed. Granted, they were friendly, buddy-kind of kisses, but still—what was that about? Add that to the break-in and the old lady's death, and I felt like I'd been dumped out of a boat and was topsy-turvy in the waves.

I paddled about for a few minutes, then I came to shore. Regardless of how upside-down my world was, I had a cake to deliver, two cakes to prepare, and Dallas' cake to design. A full day of work awaited me. I wrapped a towel around me, sarong-style, dragged on my Crocs, and headed back for the lighthouse.

I was deep in thought and nearly walked straight past Lily. She stood in the shade of the lighthouse, near the dock steps. I stopped when I saw her staring at the spot where her grandmother died. I was going to express my condolences, but she scowled at the dock as if it were chiding her about something. Then she saw me, and a smooth façade slid into place, a crisp business persona replacing the chastised girl.

Any sympathy I had for her dried up immediately. I checked my fitness tracker. "You're early," I said. "By about an hour."

"You said you'd be awake and available. We can do our business, then I'll be out of your way for the day." She acted as though standing at the murder scene of a relative was the most natural thing in the world. "I'm sure you're busy." Her gaze swept my disheveled form up and down, then she straightened her shoulders. Her pale blue linen shirt hung in a straight line from her breasts to her crisp navy capris. Even her navy sandals and her flippin' toe polish—dark blue with little white stars painted in the middle of her big toes—matched her ensemble.

I was acutely aware of my tangled hair, scuffed and battered red Crocs, and the cheap-o beach towel that clung damply to my equally cheap-o swimsuit. "Sure," I growled. "Come in." I stomped past her to the Jolt.

"Aren't you going in through the store?" she asked, wheeling to follow me.

"I don't want to scare the customers." I didn't look to see if she was behind me. I went in through the kitchen. The students were gone for the day, hopefully to go home and get some sleep before showing up at Dallas' restaurant for an afternoon of cupcake making.

"This is a nice little operation," Lily said as we walked through the space. "Small but adequate for your business." She paused by the dry good locker. "That's a unique way to secure your flour and yeast."

I stopped by our jerry-rigged system. The lock was jammed by whoever broke in, and Pete broke it off in order to get into the cabinet. I ordered a new door, but it hadn't arrived yet. Until it did, we used a metal pole duct-taped against the front to keep the doors closed and plastic sheeting on the whole thing to ensure moisture didn't get in.

"We had a break-in. Some asshole messed with my inventory."

"Oh, yes. Dallas mentioned that someone smeared butter everywhere and emptied milk in your fridge. That must have been messy."

"That's an understatement." I led the way to the back staircase, waving to Jamie who was at the front of the Jolt. He shot me a startled look when he saw Lily, then I gestured her ahead of me. "I'll talk to you later," I called.

"You can count on it," he replied.

I followed Lily up the stairs, going ahead of her at the top to open the door to the catwalk. "That's convenient," she said. "It gives you a nice in and out of the lighthouse."

"It was here for the keeper, and we decided it was useful." I opened the door leading into my kitchen. "Have a seat on the couch. If you don't mind, I'd like to change before we talk."

"This won't take long." Lily meandered through the kitchen, ending up near the cooler where today's wedding cake sat, awaiting delivery. She leaned over to stare at it. "Isn't that charming?"

Her nearness to the cake made me nervous. I bustled to the counter and set out my cake box and assembly tools. "I'll be delivering that to the reception hall in a couple of hours. I hope you don't mind if I work on getting it prepped."

As I expected, this diverted her attention to watching me set up the delivery case. "I always wondered how bakers did that," she said when I opened the heavy cardboard box, unfolding it until it was flat on the countertop.

"It's easier to load it this way." I always put a cheap rubber jar opener on the bottom to provide a non-slip surface. I glued it in place with a squiggle of white school glue. "I line the sides with special foam to keep the cake cool, especially when it's hot and humid, like it is today." I busied myself with cutting foam sheets to size. "I don't mean to rush you, but I do have a lot to get done today. Would you mind summarizing the contract? Or maybe you can leave it with me, and I'll review it." *Hint, hint.*

Lily pulled a folded piece of paper from her stylish navy tote bag. "Dallas insisted on having a minimal set of criteria for your services." She set the paper on the counter, her voice lingering on the word *services*.

"I'm sure I'll be able to live up to his standards." A little voice chanted in my head, *this is a good deal, don't get mad. She's just a flunky. This is a good deal.*

"I suppose Dallas made this restaurant, here in the middle of nowhere, sound like his idea of returning to his roots."

I barely heard her while I skimmed through the wording on the contract. "I don't understand. He's paying full market price for my cakes and cupcakes. Normally a restaurant wants a discounted price so they can make a profit."

"It's because of you, of course."

Her icy, sneering tone was like a chain, jerking my head up. "What?"

Her gaze was on the window and the lake in the distance. "He's in over his head. We should never have taken on this restaurant. High end dining isn't doing well in big cities. Why did he think it would do well here? And now that we're here, he's doing what he always does. He finds a local woman and tries to seduce her."

Oh, damn. This was it. This was Lily's Big Moment. How to handle this? I put a hand on my damp swimsuited chest. "Me? He hasn't done anything like that."

"Oh, please. I've seen how he is with you. It's the same thing that's happened time and time again. He finds someone, then he comes back to me." Lily shook her head, her artfully tousled hair swaying with the motion. "I know how it is. It's easy to believe him. I've followed him for most of my life. We're soulmates, Dallas and me. He needs me, but he needs validation from other women, too."

There were so many things wrong with that statement I wasn't sure where to start. I began with the obvious. "Why do you stay with him?" I crossed my arms, trying to protect myself from the bitterness that seemed to flow out of her.

"I love him. I've always loved him. I feel like he gives me a purpose. I mean, working for him, helping him with his career and his life—it's what I live for. It's a part of who I am." Her gaze was fixed somewhere beyond me, and I know she was seeing a bright and shining future for her and Dallas. "You know how it is between lovers. Everything is shared."

"Lovers?" I cut foam for the sides of the box, using that to avoid looking at her. The worshipful look in her sea-green eyes was both sad and frightening. If Dallas was to be believed, this was just delusion on her part.

Then a niggly little voice said, *but what if she's telling the truth? What if Dallas lied?* Why would I think that? I had no reason to not trust him. Why did I trust her and not him?

Because she's a woman, I answered myself. Because women are often used like this and discarded. Because it's easy to believe.

"I suppose he said it was over. Said it happened briefly. That's what he told the other ones. But think about it. Why would someone hire an ex-lover to work for him? Wouldn't that be too awkward? Of course, I understand how to work with him, and it's easy for him." She fiddled with a bit of foam I set aside, flexing it and bending it with her long, elegant fingers, the nails painted the same blue as her toes. "Sirena handles the busy work and I handle the finances—and Dallas."

"Busy work?"

"You know—permits and blueprints and those kinds of things."

"What do you do then?" I hurried on when I saw her eyes narrow. "I mean, don't you need to handle those kinds of things?"

"I usually work with the local businesses to make sure we fit into the community." Lily pressed the foam piece into the counter, seemingly intent on squishing it flat. "You certainly have made a life for yourself here. Dallas is impressed with you. He talked about how you've built your business. You cater to gays, you donate food for the homeless, and you run a support group for overweight women. What are you—a saint?" Lily's voice was faintly derisive.

"I'm a decent human being," I snapped. "I was marginalized when I was fat, and I was almost homeless, twice. I haven't forgotten what it feels like."

"I had no idea," she said dismissively. "Well, it doesn't matter. You'll be like the other ones. He'll get the restaurant going, he'll have a brief little fling, then we'll leave." She tapped the paper I had dropped to the counter. "This is his way of assuring that he'll have your affections while we're here."

My vague feeling of sisterhood with her vanished. No one bought my affections, and if that's what she and

Dallas assumed they were doing, they had another thing coming. "I'll discuss it with him. I want to make sure he understands the true cost of what I'll be providing."

Her cool, composed demeanor cracked, just slightly. I saw it in how she clutched the foam piece, clamped in her fist. "That might not be wise. It might be awkward."

I squirted more glue onto the sides of the box and fit the foam boards onto it. "I've survived many an awkward moment in my life. I'm sure I'll survive that one." I met her gaze squarely. "I'll be at the restaurant this afternoon. He and I can discuss it then."

"Oh. Well, yes. I'm sure you can discuss it. I hope you're not offended," she said with obvious insincerity.

"Offended? Not at all." I knelt to pull out several heavy platters I kept for this purpose. I set them on the foam pieces to weight them down. "I want to make sure everyone understands the terms of the contract." I put the glue and foam knife in the drawer. "Thank you for hand delivering it. I'll review it and discuss it with him this afternoon."

"What time will you be there? Perhaps I can attend, too. We can discuss any changes that are needed."

"Around two or so. I need to work on the cake for your party tomorrow." I went around the counter and put the contract on my cluttered coffee table. "If you don't mind, I have to get to work now. I appreciate you coming so early. It's certainly freed up time in my morning." I waited expectantly for her at the end of the counter.

She joined me, setting her bag on the coffee table to root in it, extracting a magazine, a large bulging wallet, and several other items, tossing them on my already littered coffee table. "I haven't gotten around to changing my calendar from my Franklin to my phone," she said softly, finally finding one of those pricy customizable leather planners with multiple tabs and color-coded sections. It was small and decorated with flowers on the outside and fat with papers stuffed into it and colored sticky notes stuck at random spots. She opened it and flipped through several pages. "I doubt if I can be there at two. I'm sure you and Dallas can come to an agreement about what's needed."

"I'm surprised you don't have everything online," I said while she flipped and searched.

"This is more than a datebook." She closed the book and clasped it to her chest. "This is my life."

"I'm sure it is." I smiled as falsely as she did, waiting patiently while she reloaded her tote. I escorted her to the stairs leading to the shop. "You can exit this way," I explained. "It's more convenient for visitors than going through the Jolt." For a minute, she looked like she'd protest, but instead she slung her bag on her shoulder and went down the steps. I followed, stopping at the bottom. "Thanks for coming. I know how busy you must be."

"Like I said, Sirena handles the busywork. I mostly handle the money and Dallas and his whims." She regarded me with wide, innocent eyes.

"I meant with your grandmother's death." I couldn't resist a slight chiding tone when I said it. "You're probably occupied with settling her estate. Your work with Dallas would need to take a backseat to that, I'm sure."

She yanked open the door. "Of course."

I glimpsed the busy store behind her, then she was gone, the door slamming behind her. "Good riddance to bad rubbish," I said to her back before going upstairs.

So Dallas was trying to buy my affection? That was bullshit, obviously. But why else would he give me such generous terms in a contract? I re-read the contract, signed by him with a messy-looking signature that would do a doctor proud. Why would he insist on those kinds of terms?

I hashed it out in my head while I showered, changed clothes, and finished prepping the delivery. I boxed up the cake just as Mike Beach, my driver, came upstairs. I never drove my own cakes. Instead, I hired Mike, who was a retired semi-truck driver and instructor of Long-Haul Truck Driving at Spirit Lake Technical College.

"Ready to go?" he asked. "That's a small one."

I suppose to someone his size the two-tiered cake with the flowers flowing around it was small. Mike reminded me of Dwayne Johnson except Mike was fifteen years older than The Rock and he still had a sparse sprinkling of gray hair on his round head.

He lifted the two-tiered cake and headed for the catwalk doorway, a procedure we had used dozens of times before. I followed behind with the sheet cake for the guests and a bag with the cake stand and assorted decorating tools dangling on my arm. I'd learned, the hard way, that it paid to be prepared for any disaster, big or small, on wedding day.

We made our way through the Jolt kitchen to the small minivan that Mike kept garaged for me at his home and used only for cake deliveries. He placed the plastic box on the special padded non-slip surface in the rear, and I got in the back to keep an eye on things while he drove.

"I heard about the break-in," he mentioned, steering along the drive toward the main road in town. "Some folks in town are mighty pissed off about our cakes."

Our cakes. "I guess they'll have to learn to live with it."

He drove for a few minutes then said, "I got flak at school about it."

"What?"

"Yeah. A couple of the guys there gave me some crap about delivering cakes for queers." He met my outraged gaze in the rearview mirror. "Their phrasing."

"What did you say?"

"I told them it didn't hurt anybody to deliver a few cakes. And it's not like gay people are the only ones you bake for. Besides, they're people like everybody else. What's the problem with making a cake or two?" He blew out a moist noise. "Assholes. I told 'em that if they tried anything, I'd make sure they lost their license."

"Tried anything? What do you mean?"

"They were blowing smoke." His gaze flickered right to left, and now that I noticed it, he appeared far more cautious than usual.

"Is someone going to do something to stop us?" Oh my God. That's all I needed was a crazed idiot ramming my delivery truck.

Mike met my panicked gaze in the rearview mirror. "No worries. We got friends. They're keeping an eye on our route. Nobody's messing with our cakes."

I wish I believed him.

Chapter Ten

I aged ten years on that drive to the reception hall on the other side of town, despite Mike's repeated assurances that everything was okay.

"I told a couple of guys at the school about being harassed, and they said they'd handle it," Mike said, moving the cake from the van through the back door of the hall. "Ain't nobody messing with our deliveries, today, tomorrow, or whenever."

"But that's—you shouldn't have to—how can I—" I was so discombobulated I didn't even know where to start. "That's not fair," I finally said.

He walked in with the cake and spied the setup, already decorated with the bridal colors. "Ain't a problem. We got it handled." He set the cake box on the table and stepped back. "Do your magic now, Tug. I'll get the sheet cake."

I didn't know what to say. Instead, I threw my arms around what I could of him and hugged tightly. "Thank you."

"Folks deserve a happy wedding day," he said. "No matter who they are."

I released him, wiping at my tears. He was right, damn it. I sucked in a deep breath and went to work. Mike stood off to the side, watching and offering occasional comments. 'A bit more to the right' or 'that one's too tall. Maybe use the shorter one.'

Twenty minutes later I stepped back from the cake then walked around it, surveying it from each side. The bride at the top gazed downward for her groom, who peeked up at her through the sugar paste foliage. A bluebird was perched on the bride's shoulder and other birds—orioles, finches, and cardinals—were nestled among the flowers, watching everything. I even added a loon, sitting in a tiny 'pool' of blue at the bottom of the first tier. The main colors were an exact match for the tablecloth and the napkins on the guest tables.

"Oh, is that my cake?" The bride, a short plump girl in a frothy white gown, swooped into the room, followed by a bevy of young women in pastel dresses. There was oohing and aahing and profuse thanks, then Mike and I swept up my tools and went back to the van. "A successful morning," I said, leaning back with a sigh.

"Don't you worry about a thing," he said, driving with considerably more enthusiasm than he did earlier. "I got Saturday's deliveries covered, too. My guys made sure those assholes knew they don't mess with our business, but they'll keep an eye on things just in case."

"What did I do to deserve such friends?" I touched his hand. "Thank you."

"You and Jamie are a breath of fresh air in this town. Glad to help." He flipped on the radio, tuned to his favorite Sixties channel, and we both hummed along to the Beatles.

Mike dropped me at the lighthouse, promising to be there bright and early on Saturday for our two deliveries. I went inside, successfully bypassing Jamie, who I knew wanted to gossip. I went to the kitchen and worked on the Saturday cakes, getting the first buttercream layer done and the cakes put into the fridge. By then it was after one-thirty and past time to drive to Dallas' place. I stuffed the contract in my purse, bundled together the ingredients I needed for the frosting, and headed out.

As I drove, I considered the wording of the contract lying on the seat next to me. Did Dallas think I couldn't compete and that's why he gave me special terms? Why didn't he treat me like a regular vendor? I remembered Brooke's comment about how Dallas came here to help his hometown. Was this part of his attempt to appear to be shopping locally? Was this a token gesture of his to make it look like he was including local business in his venture?

The more I considered it, the more insulting it seemed. My frustration ratcheted up a notch when I left Denmark and drove along the strait connecting the town with the ritzier neighborhood comprising the Upper Lake. Porsches and Mercedes joined me on the road, sleek sharks surrounding my poor little minnow of a Ford. Chic, trendy shops lined the road, catering to tourists and the wealthy who lived on the Rich Side of the lake.

You're So Vain came on my iPod, plugged into the stereo system, and I grinned. What an appropriate song for this place and time and for my frame of mind. Traffic was beep and creep along this stretch of road as BMWs and big Cadillacs angled for their share of pavement. I think, too, most people drove through this narrow stretch only to be seen in their fancy cars because it seemed like every other traffic light somebody slowed to wave to somebody else or pause for a quick chat and a 'say hi to Stuart for me, Ciao!'

The SUV in front of me was an enormous dark gray Mercedes SUV driven by a blonde wearing a baseball cap. It was impossible to see her face because what the cap didn't hide, her oversized sunglasses did. I swear, she must have known everyone in town because whenever a car approached, she slowed and languidly waved her tanned left arm at the passerby. The heavy traffic seemed to flummox her because she drove with little fits and starts that had me tapping my brakes to avoid sullying her pricy bumper.

One such stop nearly toppled my tub of frosting and tools off the seat and onto my less-than-pristine floor. I cursed her loudly and the driver of the car next to me shot me a startled look. I didn't care. I just wanted to get out of this stupid affluent-thick neighborhood. The snobbery was giving me a headache, but I was hemmed in by construction surrounding us. I let my car inch ahead while I played what I'd say to Dallas in my head.

What if—just what if—he was making a play for me? It was ludicrous to consider it, of course. Yes, I was modestly attractive, but, well, look at me. No sense of style, second-hand furniture, haircut by Cheap Clips, and fine wine by the box. He lived here, amongst the Richers, sipping six-dollar coffee and sampling brioche and biscotti while driving their high-priced gas guzzlers through town.

As though sensing my increasing frustration, Blondie Trophy Wife in front of me sped up, moving at a reasonable rate of speed. I glimpsed construction barrels on my right. There were no workers in sight but, apparently, they were widening this—

"You bitch!" I slammed on my brakes when Blondie suddenly skidded to the left, the rear of her SUV blocking the lane and making me spin my steering wheel to the right. I aimed for the space between two construction barrels, my car clipping one on my right. I jounced and skittered across uneven pavement, winding up in a side street that was torn up for repaving.

"You stupid ugly bitch," I snarled while I navigated potholes and dips, aiming for a church parking lot on my left. I held my breath when I approached the lip of the lot, praying my car would survive the climb. Something scraped and whined on the car's underbelly when I drove up, up, and finally, with a small crash, landed in the lot.

I rested my head on the wheel then twisted in the seat to check the road. I didn't see the Mercedes at first, then I glimpsed it driving ahead, merrily leading a string of cars down the road. "You idiot!" I yelled, even though I knew she was too far away to hear.

I sucked in a deep breath, debating whether to check for damage or proceed on the hope of none. I saw the nearby church and decided to depend on the power of prayer. I whispered a few entreaties and drove to the exit on the opposite side, leading to a paved street. My car appeared none the worse for wear, although I heard a rattling noise that hadn't been there before.

I didn't see an obvious way to get back to the street I'd unceremoniously departed. This was lake country, and roads tended to twist around natural obstructions like streams, bays, and inlets. I knew if I didn't get guidance, I would end up far from my destination. I rooted around in my purse and found my phone.

A minute or two later I was staring at a map on the screen. If I was lucky, I'd get back to the main road within a few turns. I drove, phone on the seat next to me. Then I got to the "Road Closed" sign and realized it wouldn't be that easy. Construction Season was in full swing, and I was in the middle of it.

Twenty minutes later I finally got back on the main road and became embedded in the crawling traffic. Another ten minutes, and I pulled into the parking lot at Dallas' restaurant. Several cars were there today as well as cars in the lower lot, near the delivery door. I hurried inside, a half-hour late.

Dallas was near the ovens in the middle of the room, a white apron covering his chest and legs. Today he wore jeans and a dark blue T-shirt and navy sneakers. When he saw me, he waved an arm toward the students, who were in the bakery section, all wearing identical aprons with the Prinze logo. "We started on the cupcakes," he said. "The yellow ones are in the oven and the guys are whipping up the frosting now."

Daria looked up from a mixing bowl. "I hope you don't mind," she said with a glowing smile. "We know how busy you've been."

Pete straightened, holding a two-dozen muffin tin. "Isn't this a great kitchen? Our class needs to do a field trip here. The other kids would love to see a joint like this."

I dropped my bags on the center prep counter. "Not every culinary establishment is like this one," I said, struggling to keep the anger out of my voice. "It's better not to get anybody's hopes up." Dallas was bent over the oven. "What recipe did you use?"

"The guys said this is your usual yellow one. We didn't do the chocolate ones. They said you have a special cocoa you use for that." He straightened, frowning. "Something wrong?"

I ran a hand through my hair. "I'm hot and tired and pissed off at the world. Better not to talk to me." *Because if you do, I'll bite your head off.*

"Sorry. I was hoping this might cheer you up."

He was so deflated that I almost forgave him the contract. Then I remembered Lily and the bravado I heard in her voice when she talked about Dallas and his other women. "Yeah, well, it's been a bad day." I busied myself with arranging my tools on the prep table, pausing to bask in the air-conditioning that kept the kitchen cool even with the ovens going full blast.

"Sorry to hear that." Dallas went to the bakery section, joining the students, but he had a puzzled frown.

"What's it like to be in a movie?" Daria asked him.

"It's like any job. You show up and somebody tells you what to do."

"How many did you do?"

I glanced over my shoulder. They were working, filling cupcake tins, piping frosting, or pulling pans from the oven. As long as they kept working, I didn't care what they talked about.

"A dozen or so." Dallas peered into a mixing bowl. "Too thick?" he asked Doug.

"Drizzle test. Lift the spoon. If it flows, it's too thin. If it clings, it's too thick. It's someplace in between. What was Brad Pitt like? You worked with him, didn't you?"

Dallas lifted the spoon. The white frosting trickled downward. It looked just right. "Yeah, I worked with him. He's funny. One time…"

I tuned out the voices and focused on the buttercream icing I was creating. I wanted a special flavor for the party, and I wasn't sure what I needed. Something with an undertone of sweetness. Like Dallas. I watched him laugh and joke with my staff. He was a nice guy. Yeah, he was handsome, but the main thing was that he was a good guy.

Unless he was an asshole, a little voice in my head said. Was Lily telling the truth? He was amazingly handsome. It was easy to imagine that he cheated on her. Who wouldn't want to have a fling with one of Hollywood's most eligible bachelors?

I shook the idea aside. I needed to focus on this damn cake. It was critical that I get it perfect if I wanted to impress the Richers who'd be attending the party. I didn't have time to design an elaborate sculptural cake. Maybe I needed a different flavor for the Hollywood frosting than the one for the lake frosting. Yeah, that might work.

The lake frosting should be refreshing, I decided, adding a half-cup of the special vanilla powder I kept on hand mixed with the finely milled powdered sugar and the organic butter that I always used in my buttercream. I tasted it. Not quite right. I added a dash of cream and more vanilla powder then a drop of citrus to the mixture. I stirred it and tasted. Perfect.

I set that bowl aside and took up the rest of the frosting in the other bowl. Hollywood. What would that taste like? Artificial, I decided. Not *too* artificial, or people would choke. But they needed to taste the difference between one cake and the other. I went into the pantry and checked the bottles there. As I expected, it was well stocked and well organized. Whoever set this up knew what they were doing.

I spied the large bottle of vanilla extract. I'm sure the *pâtissier* would quibble with me, but most commercial vanilla was at least 35% alcohol and tasted that way. It would do perfectly for the artificial flavor. Most Americans wouldn't notice it until they tried a slice of the cake with my special buttercream made with powdered vanilla, not an extract.

I went back to the kitchen and removed the sheet cake and tiers for Friday's cake. I set up my cake boards then went to work on applying the first layer of artificial buttercream to the layers. As I worked, I listened to Dallas and the students. He didn't sound like Mr. Big Shot, but his stories about working in Hollywood were certainly impressive, as were some of the names he dropped. Well, none of that mattered. He and I would have a business relationship and nothing else. I was a professional, and that's how I demanded to be treated. I washed my tools and focused on the sheet cake with its coating of real buttercream.

They wrapped up the cupcakes a bit sooner than I wrapped up the second layer of buttercream. "Thanks, guys," I said after they washed up their equipment and joined me at the prep counter. "I couldn't have done it without you. Now go home and rest so you can work tonight."

Daria peeled off her apron, but Dallas shook his head. "Nope, you keep the aprons as a souvenir. Any time you want to come and putter around in my kitchen, give me a call." He winked at me. "I won't take you away from Tug, though."

Doug smiled knowingly. "No worries, man. She's got first priority."

The others added their agreements and headed for the door. "I'll see you tonight," I called. "Don't forget the new keys."

They waved acknowledgement and left. "That's a good crew," Dallas said, leaning on the counter next to me to watch me smooth on the icing.

"I'm lucky to have them. I can't pay them what they're worth, but they're getting college credit from working with me. I suppose it evens out." I eyed the cake in front of me, smoothing one of the edges. "You can probably pay them far more than I can."

"Are you afraid I might poach them?" He reached for the buttercream bowl, but I shifted it away from his reach.

"Of course I am. After all, you're the rich guy come back to town, opening a fancy restaurant with high-end fixtures." I gestured around the kitchen with my offset spatula. "Look at this place. I've never seen a kitchen like this in a small restaurant."

"I like to do things right." He edged closer to me, and I resisted the urge to avoid him, instead focusing on the cake. "I want this to be a place I enjoy coming to."

I finished the coating. Dallas put his hand on mine and took the spatula from me. "Don't rush away." He leaned closer, setting the spatula on the counter.

I stepped back, torn between wanting to push him away and worry for the cakes making me hesitate. "What are you doing?"

"I'm trying to kiss you." His eyes were fixed on mine, and I felt like a fish on the hook, with nowhere to run.

"I won't betray Lily." I took another step back and went to the sink.

"Betray Lily? What?"

"You know what I mean. She told me. You and she are, you know, together."

"Is that what she said?"

I spoke above the running water. "It's obvious, isn't it? You two have been together for all these years."

"Is that what she told you?"

"Sirena told me, and Lily told me. They both said you and Lily had been together for—"

"Sirena. She's been leading Lily around for years."

"I don't know what's going on." I wiped my hands on a towel, as much to still their trembling as to dry them. "I know you're accustomed to, well, to having women be attracted to you, but we need our relationship to be business." I couldn't decipher his reaction. Anger, confusion, and maybe—sadness. I stumbled on to fill the awkward silence. "Lily told me that you and she have been together for years."

"Lily lied," he said quietly. "I told you that she and I were not in a relationship anymore. Is there a reason you believe her and not me?"

"It's just—" I jammed the towel into my back pocket to dangle on my butt. "Dallas, why are you doing this?"

"Doing what?"

"This restaurant. Trying to kiss me. All of it."

"I wanted to come home. That's why I opened the restaurant. And I think you're attractive, and I hoped you were attracted to me. Obviously, I was wrong."

"But don't you see? It makes sense that you and Lily would be together." I don't know why I was defending myself, but I was. Then I saw what I was doing, and that pissed me off. "For heaven's sake, I'm not the kind of woman you'd want to be with."

"Is that what Lily said?" He shook his head sadly. "Do you have such a low opinion of me? What have I done to make you think that? You assume that because I'm handsome I can only be attracted to someone like you perceive me to be—tall, slender, good-looking, and rich. You assume I'm shallow and I can't see someone except in those terms."

I wanted to protest, then I stopped. He was right. If he'd been anyone but Dallas Prinze, I would have— What? Flirted with him? Taken his teasing seriously? Maybe.

"You're so preoccupied with protecting yourself that you don't even see it when people want to be close to you. I know you were stereotyped when you were overweight. But you're not that person anymore. Quit acting like it. Quit putting up barriers and assuming people perceive you in a certain way." He began walking away. "Just close the door when you're done. I'll come back later and lock up."

"Dallas—" An apology died on my lips. I considered going after him and throwing the contract in his face, then I decided that he might not even see why I saw it as an insult. Maybe it was a ploy on his part to get me to fall into bed with him.

Good heavens. I leaned against the prep counter. I had honestly never considered Dallas in Those Terms. He was always just a nice guy, Mr. Hollywood, a shining star beyond my reach.

But was he in reach? I used the towel from my back pocket to dab my sweaty face. Who was I kidding? This was Lily's imagination combined with a fit of nostalgia on Dallas' part. I sucked in a long, steadying breath. I had work to do. I would prove to everyone that I was a professional and could handle the work. Forget the romantic bullshit and focus on the job at hand.

Steadied by that rationale, I put the cake layers into the cooler to chill. I had the glimmer of an idea of making a small replica of the restaurant, which would sit at the far end of my sheet cake lake. I sketched ideas on the back of the contract but it wasn't exactly what I wanted. I decided to put that aside for the moment and focus on assembling the two-tier cake. I pulled my dowels and cake boards from my bag and got ready to work.

"Lily said she discussed the contract with you today."

I whirled. Sirena stood in the serving area entryway. She wore a tailored and chic pantsuit, a far cry from the wrinkled, poorly fitting suit from the other day. "I didn't hear you come in."

"I just got back from meeting with the city council. I had a presentation to make." She crossed the room to stand across from me at the prep counter. "What are you doing?"

"Setting up part of the cake for tomorrow. If you don't mind, I need to concentrate. It's hard to do that when people are talking." I removed the three layers for the bottom tier from the cooler. I placed one on the cake board then put on an even layer of frosting, stacking the others on top with more frosting to "glue" them together.

I gently pressed the cake board for the top tier into the frosting then removed it, using that as my guideline for inserting the first dowel into the bottom tier. I marked the dowel, removed it, then cut the five other plastic dowels to the same size. I inserted them quickly then put a layer of frosting on the top and put on the cake board for the top tier.

I repeated the process for the smaller three layers comprising the top tier, using three dowels. I covered the entire finished cake with a thin layer of frosting that would serve as my base coat. Tomorrow afternoon I'd do the true decorating, once the cake was chilled. I stepped back to evaluate my work and saw Sirena watching me.

I don't know why, but her gaze unnerved me as nothing this day had done. It reminded me of the time I was swimming and a water snake caught me by surprise. It watched me with the same cold evaluation I saw in Sirena's eyes. "I didn't know it was such an elaborate process," she said, nodding to the cake.

"It's like architecture. There's a lot that goes on under the surface."

"Like people." Her eyes took on a distant look then she shook her head. "You know Lily is under a great deal of stress. That contract she crafted might not be the best reflection of her work."

"I beg your pardon?" I paused, a dollop of the artificial buttercream poised above the cake. "I assumed the contract was Dallas' idea."

"Oh, he gave her guidance, but the actual wording is Lily's, I'm sure. She handles financial matters for him. I didn't get a chance to review it." Her pink lips, artfully lipsticked, thinned and added to my memory of that lake snake.

"It did have unusual terms in it." I focused my attention to the cake, smoothing the icing.

"I'm sure that was Lily." Sirena tilted her head right, then left. "What color will it be?"

"This part is pale gray. The sheet cake will be blue."

She wrinkled her nose. "Gray? That's not an attractive color for a cake."

I forced myself not to hit her. "It will be covered with sugar flowers and other decorations. You won't even notice it." I took the cake back to the cooler and considered getting the sheet cake to work on it. But I didn't feel like experimenting with Sirena standing there. Instead, I studied my earlier drawing on the back of the contract.

"How is the investigation going? I'm sure you're getting tired of having the police underfoot."

"Underfoot? They're not bothering me at all. I think they're ready to wrap it up. At least, that's what it seemed like to me the last time I talked to the detective." I glanced at her and saw Sirena frowning, her eyebrows drawn together in a straight line like a gash across her forehead. "I'm sure that will be a comfort to Lily. I'm sure she'd like to know who did that to her grandmother."

"Yes, I'm sure it will be." Her expression changed to something resembling sympathy.

"Are you about done, Tug?"

Dallas stood in the doorway, silhouetted against the sun. "Sure. Let me put my tools away."

"Thanks. I have some things to do tonight." He moved out of sight.

Sirena watched me for a second then she said, "You shouldn't blame Dallas for the things that Lily does. He's not responsible."

"She works for him." I kept my head down, scrubbing my spatulas and cake lifters with single-minded intensity.

"But she doesn't pay much attention to what he wants." Sirena walked to the service exit, pausing there. "I hope your cake comes out the way you want." There was a wistful tone in her voice. She stared at the outside door, where Dallas had stood.

"It usually turns out the way I plan it."

"Lucky you." Her lips curved briefly, then she left.

Now what the hell did that mean? I didn't bother to try to decipher her enigmatic words. I finished quickly, tucking my tools away into the bakery cabinet and the buttercream into the fridge. I left the restaurant, closing the door behind me. I paused at the office door and knocked. "Dallas? I'm leaving."

He was standing at a file cabinet, his back to me. "Thanks. I'll lock up."

I hesitated, but he didn't turn. I closed the door and drove away, my head spinning. Believe him? Believe Lily? Believe Sirena? Or don't believe any of them? My life was getting way too complicated, I decided.

I stopped by my usual auto shop on the way home, and the guys put my Ford on the lift. "No serious damage," the technician said after an examination. "A few scrapes and a dent or two but nothing to worry about."

That was a relief. I drove home, bone tired and facing a night of cake decorating. I wanted to flop on my couch and put my feet up, but instead I set to work on one of Saturday's cake after dialing up the correct playlist.

I deliberately concentrated on the music and the cake, using that to push other concerns from my brain. I smoothed on the final layer of buttercream, then I crafted several undersea creatures to decorate it along with flowers and wisps of sea foam that I was particularly proud of. The highlight of the cake would be the glorious mermaid who would sit at the top, poised to slide down to the bottom tier. She'd go on tomorrow, after I delivered it.

I put everything in the cooler to chill then took a break to eat leftover casserole before tackling the second cake. This playlist was far more romantic, and I found myself sliding into a sort of wistful melancholy while I worked on the decorations. By the time I finished, it was dark outside, I had a headache, and I was happy to shut off my iPod and sink on the couch with a bourbon.

I swung my feet up on the coffee table, dislodging the newspaper and other effluvia. That's when I saw the fat flowered planner, lurking under a magazine that wasn't mine. Damn. Lily left her crap here. I nudged the magazine with my foot, and the planner, balanced precariously, dropped to the floor, scattering sticky notes and pages everywhere.

I considered letting it lie there until morning, but I knew it would annoy me even more then. I knelt down, scooping up wayward paper and trying to arrange it in a semblance of order before stuffing it back in the book. As I did, I glimpsed Dallas' name in Lily's big, looping handwriting.

His glossy black hair was so beautiful in the starlight. I loved the way his body was with mine. He's made me feel things I never knew it was possible to feel. It should be illegal for a man to be so sexy and loving. I'm so happy we're together. He makes my life complete.

"Damn it. I don't need to read about her love life." I dropped the papers on the table, but once again they scattered and a photograph slipped out. It was Dallas, tall, dark, handsome—and naked. He was talking to someone behind him. I don't think he knew someone was taking his picture. His long dark hair was mussed, and a towel was draped on his broad, tanned shoulders.

I was going to jam the photo back into the book, but a little demon made me set it on the coffee table. I opened the planner to put more papers in when I saw Sirena's name on a page in Lily's handwriting, underlined heavily. A list of initials and numbers were on the page, some crossed out and others underlined. *Vegas* was there with more initials and what might have been casino names—*Mirage, Stardust,* and the like.

I stuffed it into the planner and dropped the fat little book on the coffee table. I scooped up the picture of Dallas and went upstairs, where I kicked off my shoes. I set the picture on my dresser, dropped onto the bed, and fell asleep for four hours of tossing and turning.

I managed to stumble through my morning routine like a robot, working on autopilot. I went for a swim, praying that would shock my dazed brain into something that resembled consciousness. I had three cakes to finish today, two for Saturday and the one for Dallas' dinner party. I had to be in top form for that.

I paddled to the swim platform then flipped onto my back to drift, staring at the cloudless sky. The drone of a boat in the distance was the only disturbance. Well, that and my brain. The words from Lily's diary kept playing in my head. I imagined a romantic scene with Dallas, his long sleek hair damp and—

Wait a minute. I tipped over and treaded water. Dallas had silver hair. He'd been gray or silver for almost a decade. And that picture—he had long dark hair in that picture, swept back from his forehead. He wore his silver hair now parted on the side.

Was that an old picture? An old memory? I began to swim to shore when I realized the sound of the boat was much closer. Too close.

I bobbed in the wake, twisting to see the prow of a runabout, aiming for me.

Chapter Eleven

I didn't see who was driving, which meant they might not see me, either. I discarded any idea of waving to get their attention and dove as deep as I could, heading for the swim platform.

The runabout cut through the water above me, so close I swore a propeller blade swooshed against my back. I pushed through the lake, churned with bubbles from the boat, praying I was going in the right direction. It took several strokes before I saw the anchor line for the platform, snaking downward. I swam a few more strokes and came up under the heavy-duty plastic rectangle, gasping for breath in the small air pocket formed where the braces held the decking above the waves.

I heard the boat puttering on the lake side of the platform, going back and forth. Then the engine kicked in hard, and it apparently sped away, throwing up enough of a wake that I was swamped. I ducked again and kicked cautiously.

I rose to the surface and hazarded a quick look. A family was entering the park, two kids and parents running for the beach. That must have been what caused the driver of the boat to turn around. It was now heading into the lake, looping around the point. I caught a glimpse of the registration number painted on the bow then it was gone, the spray from the water hiding the boat and its occupant. I silently repeated the registration number while I paddled to shore where I sank to the beach and wrote it in the sand.

Did somebody just try to kill me? I collapsed on my towel, shivering. I was wearing a red-and-yellow striped swimsuit, bright enough to be spotted by any attentive person piloting a boat. Plus I was near the bright yellow swim platform which had several buoys bobbing nearby, indicating swimmers might be near.

I tugged the beach towel around me. What the hell was happening? I managed to pick up my phone and take a picture of the numbers in the sand, then I staggered to my feet. Maybe I was being paranoid, but I would damn well call the police.

An hour later, Detective Usher was in my kitchen, sipping a cup of coffee. "We'll run the registration for the boat," he said, jotting the numbers from my phone sitting next to him on the counter. "But I don't think it's the same person who vandalized your lighthouse. We have him in custody."

"What?" I peered at the detective around the cake I was decorating. I hated combining business with business, but I had too much to do and too little time. I tucked a flower into place. "You mean you know who messed with the bakery and poisoned the cats?" I had a brief spasm of guilt when I said that. I hadn't checked on Shrimp and King Queen lately. I made a mental note to do that before I left for the restaurant.

"No, we know the person who shot at your lighthouse. The same person took a swing at a couple of mailboxes with a baseball bat." Usher watched me above the rim of his mug, and I was surprised at the look of mischievous humor in his usually deadpan eyes.

"Did someone see the jerk doing it?"

"No, one of the mailboxes he took a swing at is anchored in the ground on a concrete post. The driver of his car didn't stop, and the guy swinging the bat broke his arm. And his bat. They called for help, and the patrol officer who came put two and two together." Usher tried, and failed, to look regretful. "These two good old boys have written letters to the editor about the filthy gays in town, and folks in their neighborhood said they've heard nasty talk at the parties these guys have."

I added a flower, dabbing buttercream in place to anchor it. "Did they confess?"

"Oh, yeah. They seemed proud of the fact they tried to hurt every business that had a gay client. The flower shop, you, the caterer. They made a big mistake going after the pastor though."

"Why do you say that?"

Usher smiled. "He's the one with the mailbox anchored in concrete."

I grinned. "Score one for the Christians."

"Indeed." Usher set his mug on the counter. "We're close to figuring this out, and I don't want you to worry. We expect to make an arrest as soon as we've verified our evidence."

"All of this—you mean the poor lady who died as well as my shop?" I stepped away from the cake lest I mar it by a sudden action. "That was fast. I mean, don't these kinds of things take weeks to solve?"

"We've had help from the state, and we gathered evidence that helped us narrow the field of suspects." He regarded the three-tier cake. "Is it supposed to look a bit off-center?"

"Yep. The grooms insisted on it. They said their whole relationship has been a bit off-center, so why shouldn't their cake reflect that?" I rounded the counter to view it from Usher's angle. The two marzipan grooms appeared to be chasing each other uphill on the cake, two small dogs following behind them. "Yep. That's what I was looking for."

"You're very talented." The detective went to the steps, and I followed. "It takes imagination to design cakes like that."

"I enjoy doing it. I'm lucky to have a job I love in a town I love." I walked with him to the shop. As soon as Shelly saw me, she gestured me closer. "Thanks for coming again. I appreciate the help you've given me."

"That's part of my job." He examined the cupcakes in the display case. "I may need to take dessert home. I've been away a few times lately."

"Whatever you want," I assured him. "It's on the house."

"Nope. I'll pay like anybody else. But thanks for offering." He studied the cupcakes, and I went to Shelly, who leaned on the counter.

"There's a guy outside," she said. "He said he had a custom order for you. I told him we didn't order anything from The Crabby Cove but he insisted he had a delivery. He's around back, near the Jolt."

"Now what?" I sighed. "Take care of the detective, would you? I'll go see what the Crabby Cove wants with me."

I went to the porch and out the side door near the steps. I walked around the base of the lighthouse toward the Jolt and stopped when I saw an older man, stooped and white-haired. He was nudging a replica of the lighthouse in place, positioning it under the overhang between the Jolt and the lighthouse. A flat-bed cart was behind him and had probably been used to transport the heavy-duty miniature of my home. The old man's look was quintessential Lake Guy with chapped skin, rough hands, faded jeans and shirt, and battered sneakers.

"Excuse me," I said. "I didn't order that." The small lighthouse was about as tall as me and perfectly proportioned, about three feet in diameter at the bottom and narrowing to the top, which was a small cupola with balcony. It was the spitting image of my lighthouse except where mine had windows, this one had small doorways on the first and second floors.

"It's not a bad job if I do say so." The old man leaned back and examined the small structure then shifted it a bit to the left, facing more east than west. "If you put up a screen near it in the wintertime, it'll be protected from the snow."

"But I didn't order it." I regarded the marvelous little replica.

"Yeah, well, a fella came in and said he wanted a rush job done and asked if I could do it." The man regarded me with sharp, bright blue eyes. "Just a regular looking guy, you know, wearing cutoffs, sneakers, and a T-shirt. Told me what he wanted, and I said sure, I can do that. Everybody knows Tug's lighthouse. Then he asked if I could do it in a day or two, and he said he'd pay what it took. That's when I knew who he was."

Dallas. It had to be him. "Because of the money?"

"Nah. Because everybody knows I don't put one person ahead of another on my schedule. That means he must not be from here." The man leaned back, hands jammed in his jeans pocket while he rocked back and forth on his heels.

"And yet—" I pointed at the lighthouse. "Here it is."

"Well, he said it was for Tug, to help her out, so yeah, I did it. I heard somebody tried to poison your cats. Assholes." The old man grinned. "Besides, I like seeing you put those uppity Richers in their place. That guy, he said you might be having your cakes and things at his restaurant. And he asked about a few things I got at the Cove. Said he might need some at that place he's setting up."

"He said he wanted to use local food." I peeked into the miniature lighthouse. "This is clever. I hope the cats can figure it out." The doorways were covered by heavy white plastic flaps which swayed when I touched them.

"Once it gets cold or wet, they'll figure it out. Yeah, he said he wanted to wait a bit before he got to setting up his place. Said he wanted to get the food going first. I told him he was on the right track if he was using your cupcakes. They're the best in the county."

"Thank you. I'm glad you like them."

"Is this where you want it? He said to put it between the lighthouse and the coffee shop where it'll be out of the wind."

"Sure, this is fine." I tapped the top of the small cat house. It had an open cupola where the searchlight should be with a balcony like mine around it. The cupola and balcony combined was large enough for a cat to sit on and enjoy the view. "Thank you. I sort of inherited the cats, and I wasn't sure what I'd do with them in the wintertime."

"It's good of you to take care of them." The old man began to trundle his cart around the lighthouse, heading for the parking lot behind the Jolt. "Most folks, they see a discarded animal, they don't do squat. You got a good heart to be taking care of them. Well, speak of the devil." He paused to look back at the mini lighthouse.

The cats were approaching it warily, moving away from the shade near the Jolt's entrance to examine this intrusion on their territory. Shrimp appeared more eager to investigate, circling around the structure and even poking at the lower door with his head. When it swung back at him, he leapt in the air.

"Yeah, it may take getting used to," the old man said, continuing his amble to a minivan parked in the lot. "Put food in there, and they'll figure it out. Don't leave food out overnight, though, or you'll draw the coons."

"Damn. You're right. I've fed the cats in the shed, but I'd better feed them someplace else."

"The cats will get the hang of your schedule. Set food out every day at the same time, and they'll show up." We got to his vehicle, a black van with The Crabby Cove logo—a merry-looking crab holding a hammer in one claw and a saw in the other—painted in bright colors on the side. "I didn't mind helping Roy Prinze's kid. Roy was a good businessman back in the day. He treated his people right. Better than old King Malone did, that's for sure." Mr. Crabby Cove pulled a ramp from the back of the van.

"I never had much to do with them," I said. "My family wasn't in that kind of tax bracket."

The old man snorted disdainfully. "King of the lake, that's how Malone acted, like he owned the world and everybody else was his employee." Mr. Cove pushed the cart up the ramp with a couple of shoves, following it to secure it in the back with a rope strung through sturdy loops at the side. "Malone was a mean one, that's for sure. I guess it's no wonder his wife ran off like she did. I heard tell his girl might sell the dress shop in town."

"I didn't know they settled the will. Her grandmother only died a couple of days ago, out there on the dock." I gestured to the lighthouse.

"That must have been a shocker for you." He jumped down and slammed the doors shut. "Adella was a tough old broad. The way she browbeat that girl…" He shook his head. "Nowadays somebody would call Child Services. Back then, folks said she was being strict. I suppose Adella was worried the girl would end up like her mother."

"I was pretty young. I didn't hear about it. I heard that Lily and her grandmother were close."

Mr. Crabby swung up into his cab. "They might have been close, but there was no love lost between 'em, that's for damn sure. Adella didn't approve of her granddaughter setting up a house with a guy she wasn't married to. Of course, that kind of stuff happens anymore, but it sure stuck in Adella's craw."

I began to point out that only Lily believed that they were 'setting up a house', but he waved a hand airily. "After meeting the guy today, I'm pretty sure the girl is lying through her teeth. He didn't seem like the kind of man who would put up with a conniving little witch like her." My shock must have shown on my face because he added, "She's been short-changing people hired to work at that restaurant she's managing. I told him today he'd better get himself a different manager or his help is gonna quit before it even opens." Mr. Crabby nodded wisely. "He didn't seem too surprised to hear it. I guess he's smarter than folks are giving him credit for. Maybe he feels sorry for her and that's why he's putting up with it. But I'll lay you odds she won't be sticking around. Denmark doesn't seem like a big enough pond for a big fish like her."

"They'll both go back to Hollywood, don't you think?"

"Nope. He bought a house off of Storybook Cove. He's staying put."

I looked at the lake, shading my eyes with my hand. "He'll be there?" I pointed across Priest's Bay. Who knew? Maybe Marty, my clerk, got the gossip right.

"Yeah, pretty much so. He said he bought a house that needs fixing up. He'll be hiring local folks to help him get it in shape." Mr. Cove started the van. "You need any other little projects around here, you keep me in mind. I got all kinds of odd and ends that might look nice in that lighthouse of yours." He winked and backed up.

I went back to the replica, my mind in turmoil. Dallas was staying in town and Lily was leaving? Sure, he mentioned it, but I didn't believe him. But why didn't I? I watched Shrimp examine the mini lighthouse, sniffing around it cautiously. He reminded me of myself, standing back to view things from a distance until I was sure it was safe.

Was Dallas right? I'd lost so much weight, but was I still thinking like a Fat Girl? Was I counting on rejection? I pushed open the lower plastic door, and Shrimp went inside, King Queen watching from a few feet away with a look of such suspicion I chuckled. She stalked forward cautiously, going to the door where her companion vanished. When he came back out, she immediately pushed past him, wedging herself through the small opening while he went above to explore the upper floor.

I left them to it and went back upstairs to work. Two hours later I was done with the Saturday cakes. I boxed them and put them in the cooler, then went up to my bedroom to inspect clothing for tonight's event.

Despite what Lily said, I was determined to put in an appearance at the party to touch base with the movers and shakers. I had two "dressy" outfits, one for spring/summer, one for fall/winter. I found the spring/summer one, still in its dry-cleaning bag, and the matching green sandals in my closet. I tossed my party duds and my baking tools in my car and was off.

I rehearsed what I would say to Dallas when I saw him, but as soon as I visualized his face, I also visualized his naked body as seen in the photo still sitting on my dresser. Damn. The photo. The stupid planner. It was still sitting on the coffee table. Oh, well. If Lily hadn't bitched about it by now, it wasn't that important.

But the picture gave me the exact idea of what I wanted for the cake. I'd been agonizing about it for the last few days, unsure how I would portray what I wanted to portray—Dallas and his feelings about his Hollywood life. The picture was perfect, and I knew what to do to make it come together.

I walked through each step in my head while I drove to the restaurant, which today was far busier than the previous days. The kitchen was awash in personnel getting ready for tonight's party. The rich aroma of roasting meat was in the air, and the *chef de cuisine*, a portly gentleman with bright red cheeks matching his bright red hair, stood off to one side, watching his sous-chef, an impressive woman with curly black hair and a no-nonsense manner, handle the actual operation of the kitchen.

I introduced myself to both. "Yes, it's good to have you here for the evening," the chef de cuisine said with a mischievous twinkle in his pale blue eyes. "Your cakes have excited curiosity. We cannot wait to see what you craft for our special night."

No pressure, I thought. I made my way through the various stations which tonight were manned by their respective *chef de parties*, a fancy word for people who managed roasting, fish, grilling, and sauces. A very big kitchen might have as many as eleven chefs who handled these specialties. I counted four here with the same number of *chefs de commis,* the junior staff who worked with the *chef de parties.*

I went to the pastry station and set my tools on the counter. A small box sat there with a card attached. I opened the card. *I'm sorry if I offended you. Dallas.* I lifted the box lid and found a fitness band in two parts. On the buckle side of the band pink tugboats chugged on a sea blue background, puffs of heart-shaped pale gold smoke coming out of their smokestacks. On the adjustment side was a lighthouse, pale blue with gold trim, like mine.

I unclasped my current band and quickly slid the new one in place. I raised my arm, admiring the tugboats while they merrily made their way to the lighthouse.

"I know a guy who does stuff like that. I asked him if he'd design it for me." Dallas stood near the cooling rack, watching me. His pale blue dress shirt was rolled up at the sleeves, exposing his tanned forearms. The navy pants he wore matched his navy Crocs, typical chef-wear. "I have to say something, Tug. I was thinking about this the other night, when I listened to the ladies talk at your support group. Your world view is that you're fat. That affects everything you do. It's always there."

No one appeared to be paying attention to us. We were in a relatively private spot in the kitchen, away from the usual flow of traffic. I scooted over farther away from the main aisle, and Dallas followed me into the small bakery area. "That's because it's important in today's society," I said. "People are judged because—"

"No, that's not what I mean." He bit his lip as he considered his words. "A person's world view defines what they will and won't see. If a person is poor and has always been poor, they're trained from birth not to see certain opportunities. They simply don't exist in that world view. Do you see what I mean?"

I'd studied sociology, and I understood the concept. "Children who are raised with abuse view that as normal. They have no other standards of judgement."

"Something like that, yeah. In your world view, a man like me can't be attracted to a woman like you."

He stood in front of me, his eyes intent on my face. "I'm asking you to expand your view to include someone like me. If you can, we might have fun."

He was right. For the first time I allowed my mind to acknowledge what my heart already knew. It was irrelevant about his appearance. Yes, he was amazingly handsome. But that didn't matter. Dallas Prinze was one of the best human beings I'd ever met. "Okay," I said, stepping closer. "I'm willing to try."

His eyes widened. "Really?"

I put my arms around his neck. "Thank you. For the cat lighthouse, for the fitness band, and for believing in me." I stood on my tiptoes and brushed a kiss across his lips.

He embraced me, our bodies tight against each other. "I didn't offend you?" His eyes, so dark and expressive, examined my face anxiously.

"No. You surprised me. I didn't know how to react."

"Do you know now?" He lowered his head.

"Yes. But now I have a cake to prepare. You'll have to wait to see my reaction." I gently disentangled myself from his arms. "I'd love to have help with the cake, though."

"Does this mean I'll learn the secret of your buttercream?"

I laughed. "There are only four ingredients, silly. It shouldn't be that hard to figure out." I went to the bakery cooler and retrieved the tiered cake and the sheet cake to bring them to room temperature. "I can't believe the lighthouse you had made. It's perfect."

Dallas went to a nearby sink and washed his hands then pulled on a clean white chef's coat from the stack of coats hanging on the wall near the ovens. "They needed a house, and it seemed like a nice way to manage it. Two floors. Two cats." He came back to me and whispered, "I'm not sure what the upper floor looks like in your lighthouse, but I assume there's somewhere to sleep up there."

"If you play your cards right, you might even see it."

He grinned. "Hot damn. I can't wait."

"Well, you have to. We have a cake to get ready." I checked my tools, mentally creating the embellishments for the Dallas cake. "I need white chocolate, a piping bag and number nine, ten, and eleven tips. I also want marzipan and food dyes." The tiers began taking shape in my mind. "We'll need a couple of knives for carving and—" I considered a new element to add to the cake. "And I'll need a couple of jumbo piping tips, too." I shooed him away. "Get going. You're my *chef de commis de pâtissier* today."

"Yes, ma'am." He gave me a mock salute and spun away, heading for the pantry.

I got the tub of buttercream I stored the night before, dipping in a spoon to taste test it. After everything that happened this week, I wasn't taking any chances on a malicious asshole ruining my Big Dessert. But both tubs—artificial and Tug's—were fine. I set them nearer the ovens which were going full blast so they'd come up to temperature faster.

I dug my phone out of my purse and did a fast search for the iconic Hollywood sign. I breathed a sigh of relief. No special font, no special curlicues or colors. Easy to do. Dallas came back with the ingredients I requested, and I put him to work on making the cupcakes we'd give to the diners tonight. I concentrated on coloring the buttercream to the shades I wanted.

We worked in companionable silence for a time. He finally put his cupcakes in the oven. "You know, your friend at the dress shop was right, in a way. I did come back here to be a big fish in a small pond, but it's because I want to be a part of a community. I can't do that in a big city. But here, I can make a difference. My money and my influence can maybe help someone or help the community. That's why I came back. I want to be a part of something. And maybe be a part of your life, too."

I stirred the white chocolate, which I'd microwaved. It wasn't quite melted and I put it back for another few seconds. "It's been a long time since I had anyone in my life. I'm not sure where you'll fit."

His dark eyes took on a mischievous look. "Fit?"

"Oh, please. You know what I mean." I took the bowl of frosting and poured it into the piping bag. "You always were a teaser."

"And you were always Tug On Task." He watched me pipe the letters for the Hollywood sign on parchment paper. "What are you doing?"

"You'll see. But you won't see it until it's ready. I want it to be a surprise. For now, you can spread another layer of buttercream on each cake. Blue on the sheet cake and pale gray on the tiered."

"Aye, aye, Captain." He bent to the task, humming. I recognized the tune. *Ooh La La* by the Faces.

"I heard you bought a house on Storybook Cove."

"Yeah. I'm going to remodel it." He laughed softly. "Some night I'll blink at you across the bay. Maybe we can work out a code."

"Lighthouses used to have a signal code. We can bring it back in style." I finished piping the letters and put the "sign" into the freezer compartment. I worked on the model of my lighthouse next, coloring part of the marzipan pale blue and part gold. I created the lighthouse by wrapping the food paste around an oversized piping tip then put it in the fridge to chill.

By then the cupcakes were out of the oven and ready to frost. I had Dallas do that while I worked on my Dallas figure for the sheet cake. "Four ingredients? You're sure you don't have a secret ingredient?" Dallas asked while he piped on the buttercream.

"Nope, it's the usual. Vanilla, powdered sugar, butter, and cream." I kept my back to him, hiding the little marzipan man I was crafting. "You know, it's odd. I keep thinking four questions about Lily's grandmother, like four ingredients in a mystery."

"What?"

"Why was she at the dock? How long was she there? Where did she come from? And who would want to kill her?" I turned back to the marzipan body I was shaping, getting the basic form done—torso and legs of a man on a beach, a towel around his mid-section. The Hollywood sign was behind him while he waded into the water, toward the lighthouse.

"I'm sure the police have theories."

"Oh, I know they do. From what the detective told me today, they're close to closing the case."

"Today? Why were you talking to him today?"

I hid the little marzipan Dallas under a napkin. "When I was swimming, a boat almost ran me over. I reported it to Detective Usher."

"What?" Dallas stared at me, his face ashen. "Somebody tried to run you down?"

"Yep. Out at the public beach." He seemed shook up and I added, "I wasn't hurt at all. I dove deep enough. I got the registration number and gave it to Detective Usher."

"I need to—" He set down the piping bag. "I have to do something. I'll be back." He brushed by me.

I watched him stride through the kitchen, heading for the outside door. What the hell got into him? I hurried after him, catching up just as the *chef de cuisine* handed him a clipboard. "Dallas, is everything okay? What's going on?" I watched him sign his name and hand the clipboard back to the chef. I glimpsed what he wrote and snatched it from the chef. "Wait a minute. Is this your signature?"

The chef and Dallas both stared at me like I was insane. "Yeah, it is. Why?"

I examined the sharp, angular signature, the two Ls like a little goalpost. "That's not the same as the contract."

"What contract?"

"The one Lily gave me. The one you signed."

"I never signed a contract. I told her to draft one for me to review."

I thrust the clipboard back at the chef and ran back through the kitchen to my purse. I rejoined Dallas, following him from the kitchen to his office. I handed him the contract, folded and creased. "You signed this one."

He skimmed it. "I would never offer terms like this. I expect a thirty-percent discount. We always have a thirty-seventy split with any outside vendors. I never pay full retail."

"Twenty," I countered. "Twenty-eighty negotiable after a month."

"Lily." He dropped the contract on his desk. "Last night I told her I was done. I was selling the restaurants. I wouldn't need her to work for me anymore. I contacted Sirena and told her the same thing. She said she wasn't surprised. She heard about the problems, too."

"About the workers?"

"Yeah. I knew Lily was having problems with the staff. I didn't want to interfere, but—" He tapped the contract. "This is bullshit. If she's pulling crap like this with our other vendors, then we'll be in real trouble. I don't understand why she's doing it."

"What did she do when you said you didn't need her anymore?"

"She told me—" Dallas looked past me. I turned.

Lily smiled brightly at me. She wore a beautiful yellow sundress that laced up the front with spaghetti straps and a flowing, chiffon-like skirt. "Our guests will be arriving in few hours. How's our cake coming along?"

Chapter Twelve

"What do you want, Lily?"

Dallas' voice was so cold I shivered. I expected Lily to react but she didn't. "Want? I want to make sure everything is perfect for tonight, of course." She came into the office, the door closing behind her.

"What is this?" Dallas snatched up the contract and held it up.

"Let me see." She joined him at the desk, her body pressed against his. Dallas shifted away from her, his face as still as marble. "Oh, that's the rough draft of the contract for Tug." She gazed innocently at me. "Did you sign it?"

"No, I didn't. I wanted to discuss it with Dallas." I wasn't sure how to interpret her coy, innocent act. Did she believe I didn't know what she did?

"This is an insult." Dallas crumpled the contract and tossed it toward the wastebasket. "I asked you to give Tug favored vendor status. We would try her desserts at the restaurant on a limited basis, to give the public a chance to appreciate them and build anticipation for them. We'd go to a regular status after a month."

"That's what the contract outlined." Lily sounded genuinely confused. "Why is that an insult?"

"I told you to offer Tug the standard commission. Why did you lower it?"

"You said she was to have favored status." Lily's faint smirk told me her opinion of that idea. "I assumed that's what you meant. I can draft another contract. That's easy to do."

"So you can forge my signature on that one, too? Like you've done for most of our vendors?" Dallas came around the desk to stand with me. "Tug, perhaps you should leave. Lily and I need to have a serious discussion. I know you have a lot to do for tonight."

He didn't leave me any option. "I'll get the cake ready," I said, wheeling to leave the room. I stopped, though, when a notion popped into my head. "Lily, you mentioned the milk spilled in my refrigerator at the kitchen."

She frowned. "I don't remember that."

"You did. When you gave me the contract. How did you know what happened?"

"Dallas told me."

He shook his head. "I didn't know about that. Tug said it was vandalized. She never told me the details."

"How did you know about it, Lily?" I demanded.

"Sirena must have mentioned it." Lily walked to the desk, picking up a piece of paper and making a show of examining it. "It's not important, is it?"

Dallas put a restraining hand on my arm. "I need to talk to Lily. Go back to your work. Don't worry about this."

I hesitated.

"I know you don't like to let other people handle your mess but this is my mess, Tug. You got caught up in it. Let me deal with it."

He was right. I headed for the door.

"I didn't mean any harm, Tug," Lily called after me.

I paused at the door to look back. Dallas had frustration, anger, and pity mingled on his expressive face. Lily appeared bemused, as though this was only a minor problem and would be resolved soon.

I knew how this would appear to any outsider and how Dallas had gotten stuck in this trap. A woman like Lily was always given a free pass for any errors she made while a man like Dallas would always be held responsible for errors, real or imagined. It was discrimination as subtle as that levied against those who were gay, overweight, elderly—anyone who was stereotyped by society.

I came back and stooped to snatch the contract from the floor near the wastebasket. "I'd better hold on to this in case you need legal proof about the forged signatures." I saw his relief in the way Dallas' tense shoulders relaxed. "Let me know if I can do anything to help."

"Stay out of this." Lily's voice was low and bitter. I held her gaze for a moment, my skin crawling when I saw the hatred in her blue eyes. "It doesn't concern you."

"It concerns me a great deal. Especially if you're the one who's been causing me headaches lately." Her eyes widened, and I saw that my wild accusation had hit home.

"I'll handle this, Tug." Dallas made a little shooing motion. "Go get my cake ready."

"Aye, aye, Captain." I gave him a mock salute and left, pulling the door closed behind me. I stopped outside, sucking in a deep, steadying breath. The tension in that room had morphed onto me, and I forced myself to relax, to let go of the anger. It was Dallas' fight.

The loading dock was quiet, all the action going on in the kitchen. The sun was still high on the horizon, the long fingers of light leading to the dock. Four boats were tied up there, two runabouts and two fishing boats with outboard motors. I studied them, my earlier suspicions starting to solidify. I stopped when I saw the dark gray Mercedes SUV parked off to the side.

"That bitch." The damn car was a dead ringer for the one that caused my unplanned exit from the road the previous day.

I strode through the doors and into the kitchen. I needed to talk to Detective Usher. This was no longer only Dallas' fight. If Lily was targeting me, then he needed to know. I reached the bakery area and saw the half-finished cupcakes. The *chef de cuisine* walked past, eyeing my work. Damn. I needed to finish tonight's business first and police business second. Lily wasn't going anywhere.

I picked up the piping bag and quickly finished the cupcakes, getting them boxed and in the cooler for the night's party. I kept one eye on the doors while I worked, expecting to see Dallas any minute. But an hour ticked by, and he didn't reappear.

It was three o'clock by then, and I had a cake to assemble. I applied the final buttercream coat to the sheet cake then added white 'waves', swirling the buttercream so it appeared frothy. I carved a 'hill' on the tiered cake, adding several faux trees made of fondant and brown buttercream to resemble earth. Next, I applied my Hollywood sign, consulting the pictures I called up on my phone to make sure I got the right placement. I created a 'road' of piped dark gray frosting along the tiers, then I put the cake in the cooler. I would add the white lane markers later.

"Very clever," the *chef de cuisine* commented. He and the *sous-chef* had abandoned any pretense of disinterest and were nearby, watching me. "I wondered why the tiers were in such a drab color." He raised an expressive eyebrow. "It appears you do not have a high opinion of Hollywood glamour."

"I'm not sure it has any glamour," the *sous-chef* said in a low voice. "I've worked there. It's not a pleasant place."

I straightened from my marzipan Dallas. "I'm glad to hear you say that."

She eyed my Dallas, complete with swim trunks and towel on his shoulder, his gray hair and goatee leaving no doubt who he was. "It's an excellent place for those with no soul."

"It's not that bad, is it?" the *chef de cuisine* chided.

She shrugged eloquently and gently touched the small Dallas figure. "Ask those who leave. They'll tell you."

The two went off to inspect the prime rib, and I breathed a sigh of relief. The tricky part of the cake was coming up. I created a space for my Dallas figure's feet but didn't place him yet. I'd do that upstairs, once the cake was in place. I put the sheet cake into the cooler and sat on a stool, trying to ease my sore back muscles. I took a drink of water then checked my fitness tracker. Four o'clock, on the dot.

I approached the *sous-chef,* and she commandeered two of the staff to help me lift the cakes onto a cart then into the elevator for transport upstairs. I rode with the cakes while the staff raced up the steps to meet me above.

This was the first time I'd been in the actual restaurant. The elevator brought me to a small auxiliary kitchen, with warming lights for food from the kitchen. The two kitchen helpers wheeled the cakes through the area quickly, getting the precious cargo away from the heat as fast as possible. We came through double doors and into the main dining room, an expanse of windows overlooking the lake.

A bar was opposite, on my right, with staff already setting up for the upcoming party. Sirena was there, supervising the placement of placemats and glassware. She was gussied up for the evening in a flowing dress that disguised her bulky figure. It was various tones of golds and greens, which went well with her overly red hair, coiffed today into a springy, artfully tousled mass.

As soon as I came into view, she made a beeline for me, moving cautiously on her green high heels. "The cake needs to be assembled immediately, over there." She gestured to the long table near the windows already set with a pale gold tablecloth, plates, and silverware.

"I'm getting ready to finish it now." I held up my bag of goodies.

"Finish it? Good heavens, what do you need to do?" She consulted a bejeweled watch on her wrist. "The guests will be arriving in less than an hour. We asked several of the more prominent investors to come early for a private tour."

"No one mentioned that to me," I snapped, my good mood evaporating. "I was told four o'clock."

"And it's after four now. Get busy and get it done." She gestured to the young men with me. "You—set it in place."

"Be careful as you go," I cautioned. "There's carpet and tile mixed here and the cart might get snagged."

"Not to worry," one of them assured me. "We'll take it slow." He winked broadly and began gently inching the cart forward.

"We need to—" The bartender called her name and Sirena hurried away.

"Good riddance," the server muttered.

"Is she a problem?" I followed beside the cart, keeping an eye on the floor in front of it while the two guys trundled it around the perimeter of the room.

"She acts like she owns the place. Everybody knows the only reason she has a job is because the boss feels sorry for her and Blondie."

"Blondie?" I caught a glimpse of Sirena, who appeared to be instructing the bar staff on how to rearrange the food on the bar top. They were obviously none too happy with her ideas.

"The other one. All she does is process paperwork. From what I heard, it's a miracle we have food tonight and chefs to cook it. The Tyrannical Twosome have pissed off almost everybody below decks."

"I suppose they're worried about making sure things go smoothly tonight."

"Yeah, right. They don't give a shit about this restaurant. If I didn't know better, I'd say they're setting it up for failure." The server gently lifted the cart above the lip of the carpet/tile intersection, coming to a rest next to the windows. I held my breath when the two young men hoisted the tiered cake then the sheet cake into place.

"Can we watch?" one of them asked as I removed my accoutrements for placement.

"Sure. It's only a matter of assembling now." I positioned my Dallas into the holes I'd carved at the shoreline of the sheet cake lake before smoothing the icing around him to make it look like the waves were lapping up his bare legs. Then I positioned the lighthouse at the far end of the sheet cake, the beam from its beacon shining on him.

I quickly piped white driving lanes onto the tiered cake then positioned it behind the sheet cake. The first thing people would see was Dallas, poised to enter the water with the Hollywood sign looming behind him, above the lake.

I touched up the buttercream coating with dabs from the piping bags I brought with me, piping greenery and flowers here and there, as well as small rocks for the beach. At four-thirty I stepped back. "It's ready."

"We'll bring up the cupcakes," the helper promised. "Are you attending the party?"

"Damn. I forgot." I dug in the pocket of my chef's coat and found a bunch of business cards, setting them near the plates. "There. Yeah, I'm going to dinner but I'm not sure where to change. Is there a ladies' room around somewhere?" I touched my frosting-spattered clothing and remembered, belatedly, that I didn't bring any makeup with me except the meager touchup collection in my purse.

"You can use the staff lounge. It's downstairs. Come on."

I followed them down the service stairs and back into the kitchen. "Staff lounge is that way," the helper said, pointing toward the exit doors. "On the left, when you come in."

"Thanks." I ducked into the pastry bay and dropped off my tools then got my purse and went outside to my car. I paused by the office and knocked. No answer. Where was Dallas? I didn't have time to worry about that. I took my outfit and went back into the kitchen, going into the staff area. It was a large square space with lockers lining the walls. Straight ahead was a spacious restroom where I washed my face, did what I could for makeup from the purse supply, and changed clothes.

My outfit was a simple shimmery sleeveless top in pale greens and blues. The palazzo pants were navy, and a lace over-blouse was decorated with green mermaids and blue mermen. Matching sandals gave me about an inch or two of height and were comfortable to boot. I finger-combed my hair, surveyed myself in the mirror, and decided I was passable.

I tossed my baking clothes in a handy spare garbage bag, threw it into my car, then I hurried through the kitchen to the service stairs. I wanted to get upstairs and make sure nobody sabotaged my cakes. I slipped into the dining room, which was starting to fill with people, most of them holding drinks and taking appetizers from the waiters who ambled about. I hurried around the perimeter to the cakes where several people were grouped, commenting on the pyramid of cupcakes in their boxes and the central cake.

Everything was as I left it except for the addition of the cupcakes, stacked neatly with my logo prominently displayed. I evaluated the cake from different angles, moving around the gawkers, and decided it was good. Relieved that all was well, I looked around the room—

And saw Dallas and Lily talking to a group of people, drinks in their hands and looking so carefree I did a doubletake to make sure I was seeing correctly. Dallas wore a dark suit that fit him to a T, and Lily was in a slinky mist-green dress that clung to every curve, a wispy shawl draped across her chest. I felt like a senior citizen next to her finery and the outfits on a few of the people drifting around the room.

I got a glass of a wine-type drink from a server and made a beeline for the bar where appetizers were displayed on trays. What the hell was going on? Dallas had acted like Lily was about to be canned and here they were, chatting and talking with guests. I gobbled a dab of cheese on crackers followed by a champagne gulp.

I meandered around the room, listening in on conversations and nodding occasionally when someone acknowledged me. The clientele appeared to be Upper Crust Richers. They had that bored, restless look that I associated with the wealthy. Granted, I had little interaction with them, but I saw them occasionally at various town functions, and this crowd seemed like the usual assortment of Up and Comers.

"Hey, I wondered where you were."

Dallas was heading toward me, cutting through a crowd of Richers like a boat moving through surf. Lily was behind him, attempting to catch up. Someone delayed her and she stopped, her gaze on Dallas even as she spoke with the guest.

I headed toward the end of the bar to swoop up another glass of wine. "I delivered the cake as required. I just wanted to drop in and check the party before I leave." I nabbed an enormous olive stuffed with mushrooms and popped it in my mouth.

"You're staying for dinner, aren't you?" Dallas kept his back to most of the company, giving us a little pocket of privacy.

"Oh, I don't need to. I think I've seen enough." I gulped wine and reached for another canape.

Dallas slid the plate out of my reach. "What's wrong? I thought—you said we—is something wrong?" His warm brown eyes searched my face.

I avoided him, my gaze bouncing around the crowd. Lily watched us while she spoke with a guest, her eyes narrowed in suspicion. "I see you and Lily have come to an understanding."

Dallas frowned. "What do you mean?"

I slugged back my wine. "You and she seemed pretty cozy there."

He began to smile, a slow, curving of his lips. "You're jealous."

"Oh, bullshit." I finished the glass of wine. "It's just that you said she was fired and then I saw you and her chatting it up with your big-shot friends."

"She is fired. And tonight's her last night. I told her if she helps me pull off this dinner, she gets a good-bye bonus. It's in her best interest to make sure this party is a success." He watched me take another glass from a nearby waiter. "You're jealous," he repeated.

"I am not." I sipped the wine. "I'm confused. You and she were so chummy."

"Chummy?" He stepped closer to me. I tried to step back, but the bar was behind me, preventing me from moving. "You think we're chummy?"

"Well, yes. You were standing close to her and—"

Dallas took the wine glass from my hand and set it behind me on the bar. "As close as this?" He angled nearer. The warmth from his body and a faint whiff of a spicy, musky aroma reached me.

"I suppose." I wiggled back but he only came closer, and I had nowhere to go.

"That wasn't chummy." He put his hands on either side of me, leaning on the bar. "This is chummy." His arms were pinning me in place where they gently squeezed my arms. Dallas lowered his head to stare into my eyes.

"Stop it," I whispered. "People are watching us."

"Let them."

"But—" A nearby society matron gaped at us, a piece of shrimp dangling from her fingers, poised near her lips. "People will say that's why my cake is here," I whispered desperately.

"Damn." Dallas leaned back, still close but not touching me anymore. "You're right." He seemed bereft and so chagrined that I knew instantly that he had never even considered that. It was another one of Lily's lies.

That's what made me say, "And you know what? I don't care what they think." I put my hands on his lapels, pulling him to me. "I don't give a damn." I stretched up and kissed him.

"I knew you were priceless," he whispered when I finally released him.

"Oh, I have a price." I hooked a finger in his belt and gave it a shake. "But I think you can afford it."

He threw his head back and laughed, one of those big guffaws of his that always made me grin. It reminded me of sleepless nights at school when we were in the kitchen, struggling to finish the latest assignment. Dallas was the one who kept us going with his laughter, his teasing, and his infectious good spirits.

"Come on," he said. "We're getting ready to eat. I want you next to me."

"Are you sure? Aren't we assigned a seat?" I scanned the tables in the middle of the room, their silver and crystal glassware glittering.

"Nope. You're with me." He grabbed my hand and pulled me to the head table nearest the cake. "I like my cake, by the way."

"Wait until you taste it." I brushed past a woman who appeared outraged that I, a total stranger, was being kidnapped by the host. I relished the moment with heartfelt glee.

"Is that the special effect you promised?" He pulled out a chair for me.

"Dallas, I wanted to have Mrs. Maris sit next to you." Lily appeared at Dallas' side, moving between us. I stepped back or else bump into her.

"I'd like Tug to sit here." Dallas gestured to the other guests who were approaching the table. "She can tell us what it's like to bake such a marvelous cake." He turned to me. "You don't mind, do you?"

Lily's expression was frozen, eyes wide with surprise.

"I don't mind at all," I said, sliding into the chair. "I may bore people with the details."

Waiters began to bustle around, setting salad plates at each place setting. I slipped into my chair, nodding a greeting to the silver-haired gentleman on my left. Dallas sat on my right and Lily sat across from us at the eight-person table.

Dallas kicked off the conversation with a memory from our days at culinary school, and I chimed in, describing the cake-making process and debunking the foolishness of those baking competition shows.

We were finishing up our prime rib main course when the conversation took an odd direction. "Our daughter has decided to take up martial arts," the man sitting next to Lily declared. He appeared to be in his late thirties with a thick head of dark hair and a tan that he would come to regret in future years when his skin got leathery. "I don't understand why a teenaged girl would be interested in fighting."

"So unladylike. That is odd." Lily had a sly look. "Perhaps she's being influenced by her peers. Who knows what kind of pressure is being brought to bear on children nowadays with the changes our society is experiencing?"

The man next to me nodded. "In my day, girls dated boys, and there was none of this gender nonsense that's going on now."

"Perhaps it's always been happening, but now we're becoming aware of it," I pointed out.

"I doubt that." He sipped his wine, setting down the glass with a little too much emphasis. "I'm sure if I'd been around someone who was unsure of their sex, I'd know it."

"I'm not sure I'd know," I said. "After all, bigoted attitudes were supported by law. If I'd be arrested for being gay, for example, I'd hide it."

"But now the law lets anyone flaunt it." Lily dabbed her lips with her linen napkin. "Maybe it's not about identity. Maybe it's payback."

Dallas started to speak, but I beat him to it. "Can you blame anybody if it was? I certainly wouldn't. Many roles are being redefined in today's world, and I'm sure it's confusing for everyone involved. I know when I was growing up, women often didn't have a self-identity. Their identity was tied to their roles in life—wife, mother, daughter, confidante."

"Those are important roles," Lily said with a chilly condescension. "Very fulfilling roles."

"I'm sure they are," I said. "But often women are asked to undertake those roles before they have an opportunity to decide what they truly want to do in life. They're expected to pick up a role without having a chance to explore options."

"That's their choice, though," Dallas said. "They don't have to do those things."

"I don't know if a man would understand." I put my hand on his wrist, forestalling his protest. "I mean that literally. Unless you're raised as a female, you might not be aware of the pressure put on us to be a certain kind of person. My father, for example, always assumed I'd marry, settle down, and have a family. I wasn't taught anything about careers or how to pursue my own interests."

I saw a dawning realization begin in Dallas' brown eyes. "People are molded by their families," he said. "Their world view."

"That's not such a bad thing," Lily said. Her voice sounded faintly shrill, with an edge to it. "Don't you think it's good to be part of a team, part of a couple?" She was sitting straighter in her chair, her spine rigid. I recognized that posture. I'd seen it before in women when we were getting close to an uncomfortable truth.

"If that's my choice, then yes, it is," I said. "But what if it's been decided, a long time ago, that I should be a certain kind of person? What if I never even considered another kind of life because of what was told to me while I was growing up?"

"That doesn't matter," she stated. "Sometimes people are meant to be together."

Dallas leaned back, his eyes wide and his body stock still. He finally understood the extent of her fantasy.

For some reason, I remembered Coral and how she filled in the background first on her coloring app. *It makes it easier to see what's hidden,* she told me once. *If you see the background, you see how the other parts fit together.* Lily's background made it easy to see what was hidden. An abusive father, a pathological need to be paired with a man.

I squeezed Dallas' wrist, struggling to find a way to get off this explosive topic. "I disagree," I said, keeping my voice calm and mild. "People need to be given choices that make sense for them. This gets back to why I support those people who are marginalized, like the obese and transsexuals and gay people. They've been categorized by people who think they know the answer about what it takes to be normal. We need to learn to accept people as they are and work to help them become the best person they can be." I forced myself to smile. "But that's enough of such weighty talk for now. Let's have cake, shall we?" I pushed back from the table. "Dallas, you need to cut the first slice."

"I've heard that you've designed cakes for gay people," the matronly lady said with a disdainful look at my cake.

"Yes, I have that honor." I wanted to stand, but Dallas put his hand on mine where it rested on the table.

"Tug is an equal opportunity baker," he said in a quiet voice.

The people around us quieted, maybe hearing the suppressed anger that I heard. Lily laughed unconvincingly. "She does have the reputation for having the best bakery on the lake." She lifted her glass in a mock toast.

"I have to admit, I do cater to gay people," I said. "And to white people, black people, fat people, thin people, rich—" I paused. "Okay, not rich people. I've even been known to not charge for a cake if someone can barter with me. How do you think my lighthouse was painted?"

"Oh, the lighthouse," she said with a dismissive smile. "Such an unusual place for a business."

"We have standards at the Club," the man with the matron said. "We feel more comfortable around people who are similar to us."

I raised an eyebrow. Dallas' hand pressed hard on mine, and the words *Like misogynists and racists* died on my lips. He shoved his chair back and stood. "That reminds me. I wanted to reveal my mural. Why don't I do that now, then we can enjoy Tug's beautiful cake."

He strode to the windows behind the cake and, for the first time, I noticed the brown paper taped on the three or four feet of wall above the windows. "I have to admit that I was naïve. I assumed that if someone wanted a cake," and he nodded at me, "or a meal or a home or a job that it didn't matter if they were black or white or gay or transsexual. I assumed that if a person did the work or paid the bill then they would be accommodated. I knew, of course, that there's inequality in the world, but I never knew how deeply ingrained it is until Tug and some ladies I met revealed to me how widespread it can be and what its effects are."

He reached up and grasped an edge of the brown paper. "Tug opened my eyes to a world I didn't know exist. I want to let everyone know where I stand on this issue so there will be no doubts as to who is welcome in this restaurant." Dallas pulled on the paper, and it peeled away, revealing a ten-foot-long mural painted above the window. My lighthouse was at one end and the restaurant was at the other end. In between were boats and fishermen and swimmers. On closer examination, a few of the couples on the beach may have been same sex, several ladies were plump, and a few of the swimmers and fishermen were black or maybe Hispanic.

And above it all was a long, bright rainbow, connecting the restaurant to my lighthouse.

I jumped to my feet and began to applaud. Several other people scattered around the room did the same. Slowly—reluctantly—everyone else stood and rendered tepid applause. I didn't care how hard they clapped. I added enough noise for those white assholes.

Dallas raised his arms in acknowledgement. "Let's have cake!" he shouted. "I think it's time to celebrate!" He gestured to me. "Come on, Tug."

I edged my way around the disdainful Richers and joined him at the cake table. "Make sure everybody gets a small slice of each," I said when Dallas lifted the knife. "It's important to compare the flavors."

He grinned at me then made a cut into the top tier, deftly moving the Hollywood sign to one side. "I'm saving that for something special," he said in a low voice, for my ears only. "I have another dessert in mind where that will come into play."

My arms and other parts of me broke out in goose bumps at the sensuous look in his eyes. "I can't wait to see what you have planned."

Dallas cut a small slice of cake from the tier then one from the sheet cake below it, leveraging both pieces onto a plate. He handed the knife to the waitress who was nearby then he sampled the cake, starting with the Hollywood one.

He frowned at me. "This isn't your usual cake."

I wiggled my eyebrows. "That's Hollywood for you."

He took a bite of the lake cake and grinned. "Yep. That's yours."

"That's the difference between real and artificial." I glanced at the people milling about the room, many of them shooting us dirty looks. "Do you think they'll notice?'

"Screw them. If they don't have the good sense to recognize quality when they taste it, they deserve whatever they get." Dallas looped his arm around my shoulder, setting down the plate and moving us away from the people lining up for their turn.

"Make sure they get a bit of each cake," I instructed the waitress. "They need to taste the difference."

"Will do," she said.

"I want to go to my new house after the party," Dallas said, smiling and nodding at people while they came and went. "Want to come over?"

My phone, tucked into a pants pocket, thumped me. I pulled it out, praying I didn't have a new crisis to deal with at the store. But it was from Detective Usher, a short text message.

Boat registered to Prinze restaurant. On my way.

"What's that?" Dallas saw the phone.

I tried to stuff the phone back in my pocket, but he caught a glimpse of the message. "It's nothing. Only an update from the police."

"The boat." His arm tightened around me. "Is that the one that ran you down this morning?" Dallas released me to look around the room. "I'll be back."

"What is it? What's wrong?"

"Lily was gone this morning." His gaze swept the crowd, searching.

"She said she can't drive a boat, though."

"Wait here." Dallas cut through the crowd with single-minded intent. He headed for Lily, who stood near the door leading to the staff staircase and elevator.

She saw him coming and pivoted gracefully to avoid an elderly man. I followed Dallas, who was delayed by several guests. Lily must have seen me because she paused and shot me a look of such pure malevolence that I hesitated. Then she was gone.

Chapter Thirteen

I beat Dallas to the dining room entry, blocking his access to the staff stairs. "What are you doing?" I demanded. "Why are you chasing after Lily?"

Before he answered, Sirena bustled to us, pushing through the crowd. "The police are here and are demanding to speak with Mr. Prinze. I asked them to wait for you outside. We don't want our guests seeing them." Several diners were watching us with avid curiosity. A couple were in danger of dislocating their necks from leaning forward to eavesdrop.

Dallas hesitated, looking to his right where Lily had vanished. I knew what he was thinking. Go after Lily or handle this public relations mess?

Common sense won out. "I'll talk to them," he said. "Sirena, can you find Lily? I need to talk to her, too. I think she went to the kitchen."

Sirena hesitated. "If she's not here, I should stay with the guests. Someone needs to make sure things are running smoothly."

"If things aren't running smoothly, it's a fault in planning," he snapped. "Find Lily and tell her I need to talk to her." He brushed by Sirena, and she overbalanced. I steadied her to keep her from stumbling.

"I've never seen him upset like that," she said. "What's happening?"

"Just find Lily." I started to follow Dallas then paused. "I forgot to mention it to her. Tell Lily I have her planner-calendar thing."

"What?" Sirena was so stunned I was afraid she might have a swooning fit.

"Her calendar manager. She left it at my house."

"That's impossible," she croaked. "Lily never lets it out of her sight."

"Well, she must be blind then because it's sitting on my coffee table. I forgot to bring it over. Tell her I'll drop it off tomorrow." I hurried after Dallas.

"Your cake is marvelous," a stately looking gentleman said as I passed him. "Are you available for family events? Our daughter is engaged, and she and her fiancée are coming home for a visit. We'd love to have a cake at the dinner to welcome her."

I hesitated. "Her? Your daughter?"

"No, her fiancée. Sheila." The old man lifted his chin defiantly, as though daring me to comment on his daughter's choice of life companion.

I had a sudden epiphany, one of those brief moments of clarity that flash through a person's brain. How many dreams did parents have for their children that were dashed when a child came out as gay or transsexual? What secret desires did parents have for the future for their progeny—and for themselves— that were washed away or set askew? Imagine the strength it took to accept such a future and embrace it.

"I'd love to do a cake. I think it's marvelous that you're having a dinner." I fumbled in my back pocket and found a crumpled business card. "Please give me a call, and we'll work together to design something special for the occasion." I held out the card and squeezed his hand when he reached for it. "Please. Call."

He examined the card. "Our town needed someone like you," he said gruffly. "Thank you."

I watched him rejoin an older woman with beautifully coiffed silver hair. He said something and she smiled at me, deep dimples at the side of her perfectly outlined lips. *Thank you,* she mouthed.

I nodded in return and pushed through the heavy front entryway, barreling ahead. I ran into Detective Usher where he stood with his back to the door, confronting Dallas. "What's going on?" I demanded. "Whose boat is it?"

"Just wait there, please." Usher was all business in his black jeans, gray shirt, and dark gray sport coat. He was like a storm cloud above the lake on this otherwise beautiful summer day with the sun setting behind us and the picture-perfect waves.

"I will not," I said, crossing my arms. "If you're talking about the boat that almost hit me, then I want to know who it was."

"It's okay, Tug," Dallas said. "Just wait for me and—"

"Quit pulling the macho man bullshit on me. I want to know what's going on. I was the one who was shot at. I was the one whose bakery was trashed. I was the one with a dead body on her dock." I glared at both men. "I think I need to be included in any discussions about the crap that's been happening to me."

Usher regarded me with his impenetrable gaze then he said, "I understand your feelings. If Mr. Prinze doesn't mind, then I don't."

"Doesn't mind what? What's going on?"

"Can you answer my question, Mr. Prinze?" Usher said. "Where were you on Wednesday morning?"

"I was with Tug. I went to the beach to swim."

"When did you arrive?" Usher asked.

"I'm not sure. Maybe six o'clock."

"That's early for a swim."

"I always swim that early," I interrupted, anxious to break the tension between the two men. "If I do it first thing in the morning it gets done. Otherwise, I never seem to get around to exercising."

Usher nodded, but I know it was an automatic reaction. He wasn't listening to anything I was saying. His attention was totally on Dallas. "Did you drive by the dock at the lighthouse on your way to the park?"

"The dock? My dock?" I visualized the boat route in my mind and knew what Dallas would say before he said it.

"Somewhat. I mean, I was in the channel and I did drive by it. But not near it."

"What did you see?" Usher had his little notepad open and jotted something in it.

Dallas' checks flushed dark red above the trimmed edge of his goatee. "I wasn't sure."

"You did see something?" Usher insisted.

"I saw two people on the dock. I couldn't tell who it was from a distance."

Usher focused on his notepad, jotting something. "Why did you call in an anonymous tip about a fight in progress? We traced the call to your cell phone."

"A tip? What?" I turned to Dallas. "You called the police that morning? But I called them and—" Then I remembered. Usher arrived at the shop so quickly. I assumed it was because he lived nearby, but— "Why didn't you tell me?"

"He didn't say anything because he hoped he was protecting you." Usher's cool, calming voice cut through the fog in my brain.

The words didn't make sense at first. Then I saw the desperate look in Dallas' brown eyes. "You thought I killed her? Why would I do that?"

"I wasn't sure." Dallas sounded desperate. "But it was your dock, and you argued with her." His hands clenched at his sides, opening and closing reflexively. "I didn't know what to think."

Usher jotted in his notepad, eyebrows drawn together. "You said you saw something when you boated past."

"Yes."

"Did anyone see you?"

Dallas and I both faced the detective, equally surprised. "Why does that matter?" I asked.

"An alibi is always useful," Dallas said softly.

Usher met my gaze. "You have an air-tight alibi. The students in your kitchen vouch for you, the emergency veterinarian, the grocery store clerk in the Twin Cities—all corroborate your story." He tapped his notepad. "But we don't have anything for Mr. Prinze."

My poor brain was reeling, processing everything he said. They checked up on me. They talked to those people. Good heavens, did Usher think I might have killed that old woman because of a discussion about religion?

I was avoiding an even deeper fact, one I hated to articulate.

Did Dallas think I would murder that old woman?

I shoved that to one side for the moment. "Why would Dallas want to kill her?"

"Lily Monroe inherited a substantial estate. Mr. Prinze and Miss Monroe are partners. Perhaps he was hoping for a share of her inheritance. Can you tell us, Mr. Prinze—would an infusion of cash be useful?" Usher waited for an answer with that unrelenting patience, like a fisherman angling a hook slowly through the water.

I remembered Lily's voice. *He's in over his head.* It was when she came to the lighthouse to talk about the contract. There was something else she mentioned, a comment—

"Cash is always useful when starting a new business venture," Dallas said. "I plan to sell my other restaurants and focus on this one. Until I close those sales, I'll need to cut back on expenses." He spoke with confidence as though managing multi-million-dollar deals was a simple matter of time.

"You offered to sell those restaurants to Miss Monroe and Miss Winchell. Do you have a backup plan if that sale doesn't go through?"

For the first time, I saw a hint of doubt in the way Dallas' shoulders tightened, straining the fabric of his expensive tailored suit. "I'm sure I'll be able to find a buyer."

"I did a bit of research. Your restaurant in Las Vegas isn't performing as well as your other one in California. And the one in Kansas City is not doing well, is it?"

"No, it isn't." Dallas' voice was level, but I was sure I heard an undercurrent of uncertainty.

"Do you have any idea why?"

"If I did, I'd fix the problem."

"So instead you're selling the restaurant to Miss Monroe?"

"I was giving Lily and Sirena the right of first refusal."

"Because they're friends of yours."

"Because it only seemed fair. They worked with me to get those restaurants successful. It seemed polite that I offer them an opportunity to buy into what they worked so hard on."

"I see." Usher checked his notes again. "You didn't answer my question. Did anyone see you on Wednesday morning?"

"I saw a couple of fishermen and waved to them, but we didn't talk. No one at the motel saw me leave. The boat is docked at the restaurant, and it was early. Nobody was there. I didn't speak to anyone until I saw Tug."

Usher jotted something. "With a substantial inheritance, Miss Monroe will have no trouble obtaining the financing she needs to buy the restaurant in question. Perhaps I can chat with her. Is she inside?"

"I think so," I said. "The last I saw of her, she was downstairs. Maybe checking with the sommelier about the wine."

"Thank you." Usher went to the door.

"Am I free to go?" Dallas asked. "I mean—do you want me to come to the station or something?"

"No, that won't be necessary. I spoke with Davey Drake. He runs a fishing service, and he said he saw you that morning a little before six o'clock. I guess you have an alibi after all." Usher went into the restaurant, followed by another person who I assumed was a police officer.

"Well, shit. Why did he make me go through that?" Dallas clenched his fists.

"To see if you were telling the truth or not, I suppose. You didn't think I killed that old lady, did you?" I wasn't sure whether to be appalled or surprised. I settled for mildly angry.

"Of course not. But I was afraid it would look bad for you. I ran from the park to your place to make sure I got there before the police did." Dallas paced in front of the door, his head lowered. "I don't know about Lily, though."

"What about Lily?"

"I know she knows how to handle a boat. Lily used to drive for us when we went waterskiing, back when we were in school. I saw her in one of our runabouts the other night."

"The other night? You mean—"

"Yeah. It was late, maybe nine or ten o'clock."

I breathed a sigh of relief. "The old woman was killed after that, I think. You said she was cold to the touch."

"I don't think that means anything. I remember reading someplace that it only takes ten or fifteen minutes for the skin to feel cold after death. I think. Maybe I read it wrong." He grimaced. "That detective made it sound like she was killed early in the morning, but I'll bet she was there all night. I didn't see blood underneath her. The rain might have washed it away."

"But where did she come from? Why was she there?"

"I don't know. I guess the police will figure it out." Dallas gave an impatient shrug. "I have to go back inside and play host. Will you promise me you won't leave until I can go with you? It doesn't feel safe to have you at the lighthouse alone."

A fast *no, that's okay* died on my lips. He was right. Even if the police had caught the vandals, I still had a murder on my doorstep. "Sure," I said. "I'll come in and wait for you."

"Good. I was afraid I'd have to convince you."

"Not where my safety is concerned." I walked with him to the door where he paused.

"I'm sorry about this, Tug."

"About what?"

"If Lily—if she tried to hurt you, it's because of me."

I shook my head. "If she tried to hurt me, it's because of a warped idea she has about you. That's not your fault unless you lied to me and you and she are in a relationship."

He put his hands on my upper arms to pin me in place, staring into my eyes. "Absolutely not. I wouldn't lie about that."

I examined his face and saw only honesty and openness. "Good. I don't want any lies to come between us."

Dallas pulled me closer. "Honey, I don't want anything between us."

I nestled into his embrace. "I like the way you think." Our lips met in a long, lingering kiss, then I reluctantly stepped back with a sigh. "Time for you to go talk to your guests."

"I'd rather stay here with you." He leaned toward me again.

"Go." I gave him a little shove. "You need to schmooze. We'll have time later on tonight for shenanigans."

"Shenanigans?" He grinned. "Oh, I can't wait to see what that entails."

We went into the restaurant and were immediately swept into the swirl of socializing. Dallas was pulled away by various groups, the center of attention. I spoke to several people then faded into the background. I was happy to do so. I had too much to think about, and I needed time to process it all. I let everything bounce around in my brain without trying to even make sense of it all.

Would Lily try to hurt me? Was her fantasy so real to her that she needed to get me out of the way? Perhaps the bigger question hadn't even been considered—was she capable of murder? The victim was her grandmother. Why would Lily want to hurt the old woman? If she was capable of murder, then she was surely capable of attempting to injure me or…

I hesitated to put it into words, but it kept coming back. Lily tried to injure me and maybe kill me. That boat coming toward me was no accident. She had to see me there in the water. A collision would have injured me enough that I would have drowned.

Lily knew how to manage a boat. She was, at least theoretically, capable of running me over. She'd inherit an estate from her grandmother. Dallas needed money. His restaurant in Vegas was struggling.

Vegas. I saw something about Vegas recently. Where did I see that? It was written somewhere. It came past me quickly, a note or—

The memory escaped me. Did it matter? Something nagged at me, saying it was important, but I wasn't sure why.

I wandered around the venue, pausing now and then to chat. An hour or two later most people had left or were on the way out. "I'm going to the kitchen," I said to Dallas, who stood near the door to chat with people while they left.

"I'll be there in a minute. I want to thank the staff."

What a nice gesture. I squeezed his arm in acknowledgement and went down the back stairs. The kitchen staff were bustling about, closing it up for the night. It was a familiar routine, and I savored it for a brief moment—the dishwashing station going full blast, the manual washing being done at the oversized sinks, chefs putting away equipment, and surfaces all being scrubbed.

"Make certain items are returned to their correct locations," the sous-chef barked, striding around the room. "All knives, pans, pots must be accounted for. Return goods to their proper storage areas. We will not start our tomorrow with a messy kitchen."

I went to the bakery station, prepared to clean up my mess, but it sparkled as though it had never been touched.

"We decided you had enough to do," the *chef de cuisine* said, approaching me from the center prep station. "We decided to tidy up for you."

I doubted that he did any tidying, but I thanked him anyway. I was relieved. I'd planned on at least a half-hour of serious scrubbing. I could relax, at least a little bit. Then I spied Sirena near the exit door, walking toward me, and my hopes for relaxation vanished.

"I'm worried about Lily," she said without preamble, inserting herself between me and the *chef de cuisine*.

"Thank you again," I said to the chef. I turned to Sirena. "Did Lily leave? Did Detective Usher see her?"

"I think so. She left a while ago. It's been busy." Sirena touched her hair nervously, patting it into place. "I lost track of time."

Dallas entered the kitchen, greeting the *chef de cuisine* then moving to the *sous-chef* and the other *chefs de partie,* following the kitchen hierarchy that was as rigid as the rules set by Debrett's Peerage for the aristocracy in England.

"I'd better find Lily," Sirena said. "I hope she doesn't blame—you know she's still upset about her grandmother."

I didn't care about Lily, but a response seemed expected. "I hope she'll be okay. I'm sure that plus her career problems are causing her stress, but I'm sure she'll find a good job."

"Job?"

"Dallas mentioned that tonight was her last night working for him." I belatedly remembered that it was Sirena's last night, too. "I mean, I'm sure you'll both find other clients. Restaurant management is such a huge task. Most people want to focus on the creative side of it, not the business side."

I don't think she heard me. Her eyes had taken on a glazed look. "Yes, I'm sure. I'd better find her. We need to start making plans." She strode away from me, cutting through the staff gathering around Dallas like a fiend of hell was chasing her.

I wondered if Lily had even shared the news that their firm was fired. Oh, well. Not my problem. I watched Sirena leave then joined Dallas as he shook hands, thanking people for their hard work. Chefs, servers, dishwashers—everyone was greeted and their efforts acknowledged, thanking them for their contribution to the success of the evening.

It was after ten o'clock before we shook free. "Do you want to come to my place for a drink?" I asked, stopping at my car.

"I was hoping you'd ask." Dallas put a hand on my open door. "Why don't I drive us in the boat?"

"Or I can drive, and you can follow me."

"Hmm. Maybe you can give me a ride." He leaned closer. "And then you can drive me home tomorrow."

I hesitated.

He winked at me. "Tomorrow is only an hour or two away, you know." He kissed the tip of my nose and leaned back.

I saw the dare in his dark eyes. "Well, when you put it that way—hop in." I laughed at his surprised look.

"I didn't think it would be that easy," he admitted, hurrying around the car to the passenger side.

"Are you calling me easy?" I drove onto the mostly empty roads.

"Not at all. Just…unpredictable."

We were silent for a few minutes then I said, "You know, I've been thinking about our contract. Instead of charging a flat percentage maybe we can barter for my desserts."

"What?"

"I do it all the time with people." Actually, I'd only done it once or twice but I'd been thinking about it. If he was short on cash, maybe this would give him an out. "I could have an employee dinner at your restaurant two or three times a year. You treat me and my staff, and I give you a discount on my bakery goods."

"How many staff?"

It was pitch dark and hard to see his expression, but he sounded intrigued, not offended. "I figured seven staff plus me and Jamie and his wife, so ten total. A fifty-dollar dinner for each is five hundred dollars. Do that two or three times a year, and it adds up."

He was quiet for a long moment. "What kind of discount?"

"Oh, I don't know. Maybe we split it fifty-fifty instead of thirty-seventy, at least for a year or two until we see how things shake out." It wasn't enough to make up for my costs, but I'd absorb the loss. "I want a display of cupcakes near the checkout. People can buy something to go." The more I considered it, the more appealing it was. Many restaurants had desserts near the front so people coming in anticipated what was available, and people leaving took home something to enjoy.

"Let me think about it. I like the idea."

"It might benefit both of us. I can advertise that my cakes and pies are being served at your restaurant, and you can advertise that you're featuring my desserts on your menu and in any other advertising you do."

"Mutual benefit." His hand caressed mine where it rested on the gear knob. "I like it."

I shivered with anticipation. "Good. Like I said. I do it with other folks."

"Maybe you can do the baking for the restaurant at my kitchen. That way it won't intrude on your bakery for your store."

"I was worried about that," I admitted. "We don't have much capacity."

"We can decide on an arrangement where you can use the space at a certain time of the day or days of the week. If we're serving your bread and dessert, I shouldn't need that space as much as I normally would if we were handling it."

"Good. Thanks." We drove in silence for a few minutes then I said, "It went well tonight."

"Everybody pitched in and helped," he replied. "This group feels like a team, more than any of my other restaurants."

"Who hired the staff here?" I asked.

"I did. Why?"

"Who did the hiring at the other ones?"

He was quiet for so long I wasn't sure he heard me. Finally he said, "Sirena and Lily."

"I heard some of the staff complain about them." I drove onto the road to the lighthouse.

"Yeah. I guess it's a good thing they won't be working with me anymore."

He sounded glum, but I guess I didn't blame him. He and Lily had been together for a long time. It must feel odd to be in his situation.

"I should be relieved," he said. "Instead I feel sorry for her."

"They'll be fine. I'm sure Lily can find another job if she wants one." I pulled into the parking lot next to the two student cars already there. "I'm going to check on the bakery."

I led the way to the Jolt and then past it, to peek around the corner. I gestured Dallas nearer. "There's your lighthouse."

"Mine? Wow. That's cool." He approached the two cats, heads poking from the model to see who was intruding on their space.

I ducked into the bakery and verified that everything was going well. When I came out, Dallas wasn't at the lighthouse model. I rounded the side of the real lighthouse and found him standing at the top of the steps, hands in his pockets while he stared at the lake. He turned when he heard me approach. His necktie was undone and hung around his neck, the collar of his shirt open. The moonlight seemed to catch in the silver of his hair and his goatee, making his high cheekbones stand out in sharp relief. He really was one of the handsomest men I'd ever seen in my life.

"I love the lake at night," he said, holding out his arm.

It seemed the most natural thing in the world to go to him and let him pull me against his side. "I like it in the wintertime. I like seeing the ice form and break up. The waves are different in the winter."

"It's more elemental then. I know what you mean."

We stood in comfortable silence for a time. "Do you want to come in for a drink?" I asked, slipping from his embrace and unlocking the porch. He followed me inside. "Is bourbon okay?" I was nervous, not sure how to act. It was years since I'd had any sort of romantic entanglement. What should I do?

"Bourbon is fine. It's good to be here, Tug. I always feel relaxed around you. It's low key and easy."

My anxiety dissipated. This was Dallas. I didn't have to act. I just had to be me. I went into the lighthouse, hurrying upstairs to my kitchen. I splashed bourbon into two glasses and put them and a small bowl of chips on a tray. When I took our little feast downstairs, I found him on the deck overlooking the lake. He was at the farthest edge, at the point where the deck jutted above the rocks forming the base of the lighthouse. His suit coat was draped over a chair, and his sleeves were rolled up. He appeared to be at home after a hard day at the office.

It felt like the lake surrounded us and we were suspended above. I settled into a chair next to him, my legs stretched next to his. The lake lapped against the rocks below us, a dark presence barely seen through the Plexiglass panels on the railing. We sipped our drinks for a time, then Dallas said, "You said it went well tonight, but I was busy and wasn't sure. Are there things I need to improve?"

"In the kitchen? Sure, there's always room for improvement."

"Tell me. I value your opinion about that kind of thing. You have a great setup here, and it runs so smoothly. I want to pick your brain to find out your secret."

I shook my head. "No secret, only common sense." I took a sip of bourbon then said, "I noticed one server was paying too much attention to the men and not enough to the women. It was noticeable."

"Really?"

"You're a man. You wouldn't notice it. There're other things, too."

"Like what?"

I launched into a recitation of the small things I saw that might help things run better. It didn't take long but when I was done, he said, "See—I knew you'd have ideas. Maybe I need to hire you as my restaurant manager."

"No way," I said firmly. "I'm happy where I am, but thanks anyway." We lapsed into a companionable silence, punctuated by the waves lapping against the rocks below us.

"I always had kind of a crush on you, Tug."

I tilted my head to regard him. "Why didn't you act on it?" I knew the answer, but I wanted to hear him say it.

"It wouldn't have been cool," he admitted. "When I was a kid, I cared about that kind of shit."

"Yeah." Even after all these years, his honesty stung. "You couldn't be seen with the fat girl. People would have made fun of you."

He dug into his pants pocket and pulled out his keyring. "I kept it."

I took the proffered keys. "What is—" Then I saw the worn braided bracelet dangling from the key clip. My friendship bracelet. The one he tore off my wrist when I saved him from drowning, long ago.

"I knew it was you," he said. "I've always kept it. It's my good luck charm. If it wasn't for you, I wouldn't be sitting here."

I ran the bracelet through my fingers. "Why didn't you say anything?"

"You didn't say anything. I wasn't sure if you wanted anyone to know." He took the keyring from me when I held it out. "I wish I had the confidence then to do what I wanted to do. I feel like I'm finally doing that for the first time in a long time. I don't want to stay in Hollywood." He sipped his bourbon. "I'm glad I found you again. Maybe this time I can act on what I want to do instead of worrying about what other people think."

"What if I was still overweight?" I asked. "Would you care about that?"

"Nope," he said immediately. "It doesn't matter if you're thin or fat or anywhere in between. What matters is who you are, not what you look like." He leaned closer. "Do you think I'll get a tour of the lighthouse tonight?"

"If you play your cards right."

He examined my face, his dark eyes shadowed by the night. "I feel like this is right. A missing piece of my life has been found. It's not just you but it's this place. I'm finally home."

"That's how I've always felt," a shrill voice said behind us.

I twisted in my chair. Lily stood in the shadows in the porch, near the entryway. She wore the same stylish green gown she wore at the party, with stiletto heels and a filmy shawl.

"Where did you go to?" Dallas asked, glancing back at her. "The party was a real success, and you had a large part of making that happen."

"Her cake is what made it a success." Lily took a step forward, her body tense and rigid, hands held at her sides. Something about her posture made me uneasy, but I couldn't put my finger on it.

254

"I'm sure my cake was an interesting part of the evening." I faced the lake again, unwilling to be a party to any unhappy scenes. Why did she have to spoil my night?

"I always loved you, Dallas. From the time we were young, I loved you. My grandmother told me that you and I were meant to be together. She said that I must have done something to drive you away from me. What did I do? How can I fix it? Is it because of her? She's different than the other ones, isn't she?"

I shifted uncomfortably in my chair. The honest confusion in her voice was pitiable.

"I told you, Lily. There hasn't been anything between us for years. I hired you to work for me, that's all. You need to let go of that fantasy and get on with your life. You need to find someone who can love you the way you want." Dallas put his hand on mine on my chair. "Leave us alone, Lily."

"You're the missing part of my life, Dallas. Grandmother told me that when I found the right man, I'd feel whole. That's how you make me feel."

Dallas looked at me and shook his head. "I don't know what to do," he said softly.

"Lily, you can't rely on another person to make you happy." I twisted in my seat to watch her reaction.

"I was happy with Dallas." Lily came into the light cast by the security lamp at the top of the stairs, a few feet from the veranda. "I was happy until he met you again."

"I'm sure you were, but life changes."

"Yes, it does." She came on the deck, and that's when I saw the butcher knife in her right hand.

Chapter Fourteen

Dallas was farther away from her because he was on my left. When he saw the knife, he pushed back his chair, jumping to his feet. "What are you doing, Lily?" His voice was soothing and calm, and I thanked God for it. I was feeling anything but calm.

"I wanted to make sure things went back to the way they were." She stood about five or six yards from us, her body as stiff as a statue except for the knife, which she held near her breasts, the blade pointing downward. "But that won't be possible. It won't be possible because of her."

I stood, unsure if my presence might cause more harm than good. What should I say? *Life goes on even if your heart is broken? Don't worry, you'll find someone else to love?* Obviously, she never did. She was fixated on Dallas, and she wouldn't consider anyone else. I struggled to think of something to say that wouldn't make her even more upset than she already was.

Dallas was cautious, taking small incremental steps to approach her. "Lily, you know I care about you. It's only that—" He glanced at me beseechingly.

"It wouldn't be right," I said, standing with my back to the lake. "Dallas wants to stay here, but you're meant for the big city."

Lily ignored me, instead focusing on Dallas. Except she wasn't focused. She had a vague, distracted look. "I was afraid this would happen. She's different than the other ones."

"There weren't any other ones," Dallas snapped. "It was in your mind."

I shook my head. *Don't argue with her,* I mentally implored. *Don't upset her any more than she already is.*

Lily took a long step forward, and I leaned back from the implied threat. The guard rail was at my back, pressing against my butt. "Of course there were others. That's why you never came back to me."

"Listen to what you're saying." Dallas inched forward. "It's been years since we were together, Lily. Tug had nothing to do with that. We split up because of us, not because of her."

Lily listened, nodding mechanically. I wondered if she was drugged or high. She seemed absent, other-worldly. "None of that matters. I'm meant to be wherever you are. Sirena and I talked about it. You're nothing without me. She knows it. Why don't you?"

I suddenly saw how I had stereotyped Lily and thus disregarded the intensity of her fantasy. I'd dismissed her as a hanger-on, a woman without any ambition, a woman who was nothing without a man. But here she was, acting on her dreams, taking command. My preconceptions had been based on her appearance—the pretty blonde, the sexy assistant, the airhead. Why didn't I look beneath the surface?

She tied her life to another person's dreams, and now those dreams were dissolving and she had nothing left. I'd been lucky. My obesity had precluded any meaningful relationship, and I was forced into making my own dreams, forced into being alone during my growing-up years. If I'd been young and beautiful at that time, I might have done what my parents wanted me to do. I would have married someone and let his ambitions set my path.

"I'm sorry, Lily," I blurted. "I didn't know how hard this was for you."

"Hard?" She took a step forward. "You have no idea."

"No, I don't."

That seemed to make her pause because she frowned, her perfect eyebrows drawn together. "I don't want the damn restaurants, Dallas. I went into this business because of you. If it hadn't been for you, I'd still be a dancer, I'd be a singer."

Dallas drew breath to speak but I beat him to it. "I'm sure you would have been a success, too," I said. "I'm sorry you felt you couldn't continue your career."

"Of course I couldn't. Dallas needed me to manage his business."

"You and Sirena," Dallas said softly.

"Sirena?" Lily croaked a bitter little laugh, and her gaze fixed on him. Something flickered in her eyes, an intensity that made my skin crawl. "She's been more of a liability than a help. I've managed her mistakes for years. I'm getting tired of it. She's the one who's pushing me. I told her I was done with it, though."

"That's not what she told me," I said, anxious to divert Lily's attention. "It sounded to me that she spent most of her time reviewing contracts and working on details."

"She lied." Lily came forward. "Sirena has done nothing except hold me back. She's kept me from what I wanted to do. But she won't hold me back anymore."

Dallas inched forward again, and I took advantage of Lily's distraction to peek past her. The entry to the porch was on her right, the door closed. On her left was the guard rail, and next to it was the stairs. She blocked the only exit.

The only human exit.

Behind her, King Queen oozed through the narrow gap between the veranda and the stairs, where the guard rail began. The workers left about a six-inch opening in order to secure the rail to the deck material. I always wondered how the cats managed to find a way onto the veranda when the entry door was closed. I now had my answer.

King Queen poked through the opening, squirming to get her chubby hindquarters in. I swore I heard a faint POP when she finally got all the way through. The portly cat prowled forward, intent on these humans who were here at night in what had once been his—her—secret domain. Then I saw why the fat cat appeared so smug and self-satisfied. A mouse dangled from her mouth. The feline headed for Lily, who was the nearest available human who might appreciate the ability of the huntress.

Not to be outdone, Shrimp pranced into view, lithely jumping up on the rail and walking with nonchalant ease behind Lily, balancing on the narrow beam. I longed to snatch the small cat lest he plummet over the side, but I didn't dare. Shrimp strolled along, his gaze intent on Lily and King Queen, who paced behind Lily.

"Tug would never understand," Lily said, the knife inching up and down in front of her breasts in slow, hypnotic movements. She walked toward us, her stiletto heels clicking on the faux wood flooring, echoing hollowly. "Tug never loved anyone the way I loved you. She never gave up everything for the man she loved."

"No, I didn't. I never had that experience." I pressed against the guard rail, hearing the lake behind me where it pulsed against the rocks, a hissing, insistent sound. "I never loved anyone like that."

"And you never will." She took another step closer. "You never will."

"Don't hurt Tug." Dallas was a dark shadow ahead of me, a large, solid bulk. I saw the flex of the muscles in his forearms when he shifted position, and I knew he was tensing to jump for her.

"She won't hurt me," I said, praying my confidence would convince her. "Lily knows that I'm not any kind of competition for her."

Lily's attention snapped to me, and Dallas used the distraction to inch forward again. "She's right," Lily said softly.

Her eyes were wide, empty of emotion. She appeared blind, as though she stared at a distant future only she saw. Lily raised the knife and positioned the long edge of blade at her throat. The tip pointed downward, toward her heart. Then her hand shifted, and the tip of the blade touched the top of her breasts, somewhat exposed in the thin gown she wore.

I saw it then. I saw her plan. Lily would kill herself, and Dallas would have the guilt of her death on his conscience. He would blame himself and castigate himself that he hadn't done something to stop her. Her death would kill any chance he and I had at happiness.

If she couldn't have happiness with him, she'd make sure no one would.

The realization sped through my mind in the time it took to blink.

Lily met my horrified gaze. "I won't hurt Tug," she whispered.

King Queen chose that moment to drop her mouse at the feet of the nearest human, which meant it landed on Lily's stilettos. The mouse gave a startled squeal when it escaped, scrambling to flee from the human feet around him and the feline predators chasing him.

Shrimp sprang off the rail, jumping in front of Lily to attempt to capture the escaping mouse. King Queen, not to be outdone, dove on top of the smaller cat, and the two erupted into a hissing match. The mouse scurried about, trying to avoid being rolled on by the cats or stepped on by the human.

Lily whirled, but one of her high heels snagged on a crack in the wooden flooring. Her body twisted, hitting hard into the Plexiglass surround. Dallas put his arms around me and turned, shielding me from an attack. I saw Lily out of the corner of my eye, her arm upraised. I don't think she recognized that Dallas was vulnerable. Her attention was solely on me.

Lily's arm began to come down. I twisted in Dallas' arms and kicked out, hoping to startle Lily. She tried to get away from me, but her foot was still trapped by the flooring. Her leg twisted and she cried out, releasing the knife. Shrimp, who had broken free of King Queen, pranced toward it, alert to the possibility of a new diversion.

I desperately twisted again, bumping into the small cat. He yelped and bounced away, his body hitting against Lily's legs. Still pinned, she tried to shake him free and only succeeded in contorting her body. With a strangled shout, she tore her foot loose of the shoe, teetering on one foot that still held a three-inch heeled shoe. Lily fell back. The guard rail wasn't tall enough to keep her upright.

She dropped over it into the night.

The two cats, startled by the clumsy nearby humans, raced away. The mouse took advantage of the moment to squeeze through a crack and vanish.

Dallas and I reached the rail at the same time and leaned over.

Lily lay on the rocks below us, water washing onto her body.

****

It took hours for the police to be done with us. Dallas and I gave our statements multiple times to multiple people, I suppose to check if we were lying. I had called Jamie, and he came and handled the bakery, promising to sell the goods in the Jolt because the police closed the lighthouse for the day.

It was seven a.m. before Dallas and I had a chance to talk privately. "You look beat," he said, enfolding me in his arms.

I leaned into his embrace. "I am. But I have two cakes to deliver and a shop to manage."

He brushed a kiss against my lips. "And I have a restaurant to manage. I'm lucky we're not opening officially until next week. Let's try to get together later today, okay?"

I sighed. "Give me a call tonight. I hope to be caught up on everything by five."

"Good. I want a tour of your lighthouse." He grinned at me then walked away, meeting the police officer who would drive him back to his car, still at the restaurant.

I forced myself into my usual routine, thankful that it was Saturday. That meant I only had to wrap up this week's cake and had nothing big to decorate for the immediate future. I boxed up the two cakes that were due, then Mike Beach and I successfully delivered them. Even though I was cross-eyed with exhaustion I managed to finish the decorations at each venue. The cakes were well received. I guess I didn't screw up.

It was afternoon before I got back to the lighthouse. Detective Usher was still there. "We'll be wrapping up soon," he said. "You can go inside."

"Thanks. I need a nap." I yawned, my jaws expanding so wide I heard a pop.

"You can open the shop tomorrow." He hesitated. "I'm sorry this happened. It's not your fault, you know."

"I know, but I still feel responsible, at least somewhat."

He frowned then said, "You'll hear anyway. I don't think it matters if I tell you. Lily had a psychiatric history. When she was younger, she was treated for a dependent personality disorder. She struggled with it all her life. We found several kinds of medication, and apparently she had a doctor in California who was treating her."

Dependent personality disorder. That made sense. Her fixation on Dallas was not only because of love but also because of illness. "I remember when we were in school, a teacher told me she had anger issues. I wonder if that had anything to do with it."

"That's sort of the flip side of a dependent disorder. A person with that kind of disorder has a difficult time managing emotions and is reliant on another person, a stronger personality, for direction. When the ill person feels the stronger personality has let her down, they have trouble adjusting. Lily's illness caused her to assign Mr. Prinze a dominant role in her life, so much so that she may have had no sense of a future when he finally convinced her that he had no interest in being with her."

"I'm sure he had no idea about the depth of her illness. Or that she was even ill at all. Lily hid it from him very well."

"You saw it, though," Usher commented.

"I didn't realize the extent of it. I just assumed Lily was longing for a relationship that ended long ago."

"Our medical people told me that her disorder may have made it difficult for her to accept that as her reality."

"But what about—" I hesitated. "I can understand why Lily would try to get back at me. She saw me as a threat. But her grandmother?" I remembered my four questions: why there, how long, where from, and who.

"Our theory is that she killed her grandmother in a fit of rage. From what some of the locals tell me, they had a troubled relationship while Lily was growing up. Her grandmother made no secret of the fact she felt that Lily had ruined her life by staying with Mr. Prinze. Mrs. Dronning made disparaging remarks about Lily and her inability to have what her grandmother considered a normal relationship. Apparently, they argued several times since Lily came back here. Sirena Winchell mentioned it and told us how distraught Miss Monroe was about it."

"She was also set to inherit money, you said."

"Yes, a large sum. That kind of money might have given her a sense of independence. I don't know if that was her motivation, though. I don't know if we'll ever know for sure. I was unable to talk to her at the restaurant yesterday evening. She was already gone when I tried to find her."

"But Sirena said—" I struggled to remember but the memory vanished. "But how did they get to the dock? Why my dock?"

"I can answer that for sure. Mrs. Dronning had a small boat. She grew up around watercraft, and she was an accomplished boater. She followed Lily to your lighthouse and confronted her on the dock. Lily had taken one of the boats from the restaurant and came here to vandalize your bakery."

"I thought she had," I said. "I was going to tell you my suspicions earlier, but I got sidetracked. Was it her on the rocks? With the knife?"

He hesitated, and I had the sense he was debating what to say. "Her fingerprints were on the handle. Mr. Prinze suspected that she was upset about you, but I don't believe he knew the extent of her anger."

I remembered Dallas running after the person that night. "Did he see her?" My stomach did a sick flip-flop.

"I don't think he did. If he had, he would have told us. I think he might have wondered about it, but—" Usher hesitated, frowning, again searching for the right words. "I think Mr. Prinze honestly has no idea how a person could act the way Lily Malone did. He seems to be one of those people who always believes the best of someone."

Poor Dallas. Good heavens, what he'd gone through—worried for my safety and worried that Lily might be the cause of my injuries, yet unable to believe that she might be capable of it. Such a shocking revelation must have made him realize how little he truly understood her. I remembered how he acted at the dinner the night before, when we talked about gender roles. His world was upside-down and inside-out.

"The men we arrested earlier had an alibi for the time when your bakery was vandalized. Therefore, we knew it was someone else. She seemed like a logical suspect, especially because she was upset about you and Mr. Prinze."

"I assumed it was the same person as the one who shot at my lighthouse. What happened to the boat?"

"We found it drifting. Miss Monroe must have set it loose."

I nodded tiredly. My head was stuffed full of bits of information, rattling around like confetti. It was connected but was in pieces.

I think Usher saw my exhaustion. "I'm sorry you and Mr. Prinze got caught up in her problems. It caused difficulties that had nothing to do with you."

Difficulties? That was an understatement. I thanked him and went into the empty shop. I dragged myself up the stairs, paused at my kitchen to peer groggily around, then went up the final flight and dropped onto the bed, so tired I felt it in every bone.

As soon as I closed my eyes, an image of Lily's face appeared on my mental view screen, so desperate and lost. I'd never had such a dependence on another human being. I doubted if I ever would. Dallas and I were independent people, each of us with a life shaped long before we got together. We'd forge a different kind of relationship. I hoped.

I fell into a restful doze, thankfully not punctuated by any bad dreams. When I woke, it was hazy outside, with a dense fog pressing against the windows. My bedside clock said it was six-thirty, but it felt much darker than that. I stumbled around, disoriented, but after showering most of the cobwebs were pushed away. I pulled on my bathrobe and went on the balcony, the lake a sound, not a sight, below me. In the distance I saw a faint light go on and off in a regular cadence. My phone, charging next to my bed, rang and I went inside to get it.

"Did you see my signal?" Dallas asked. "I waited until I saw your lights come on. I wanted to make sure you got to sleep."

"Is that you?" I asked, going back to the balcony.

"Yep. See. On. Off. On. Off. Those little bugs with the lighted butts got nothing on me."

I laughed. "Where are you?"

"At my new house. Are you ready to receive visitors?"

I spied my discarded towel and clothing in my messy bedroom. "Sure. I'll tidy the place up a bit."

"Don't do it on my account. I'm standing on the porch of a rundown old house that hasn't been updated since Elvis was alive. I won't be judgmental."

"Then come over," I said. "I'll make sandwiches."

"How about leftover prime rib and potatoes?"

"I like the way you think."

"On my way."

I went up to the cupola and flipped on the high-intensity light. Then I dressed in linen capris and a sleeveless top covered by a gauzy linen blouse that matched my pants. I slipped my feet into a pair of flipflops and raced down the steps. I was as light as air. The vandalism was done with, the death of the old woman was solved, and Dallas and I had a possible future together. Life was good again. True, Lily's death would hang over us for a time, but I knew that we'd get through it together.

I paused in the shop to savor the silence. This was the time of the week that I called "Tug Time". Last week's cakes were delivered, the night crew wouldn't arrive for several hours, Jamie was gone. Tomorrow I'd set up next week's cake schedules and start the whole process again. But for these few precious hours I had no tasks, and I was alone.

Except for Dallas.

I came through the patio door to the porch, flipping on the lights there then to the veranda to flip on the dock lights. It was too foggy to see anything across the lake, but I trusted that he would find me. The lighthouse beacon alone was probably enough. I leaned on the newel post at the top of the steps, staring into the mist.

I had no idea how the Sexiest Man in America not only found me but also found me sexy. He was right about so many things. I prided myself on being inclusive and open-minded, but I had categorized him and Lily, assigning them to a 'type' who I assumed would act in a certain way.

Both of them shattered my assumptions. Now she was dead, and I was minutes away from a potential future with a man I respected and liked. Would it lead to love? I had no idea, but I was certainly willing to step on that path and see where it would go.

I was deep in my musings and didn't hear Sirena until she was a few yards away from me, coming around the Jolt from the parking lot. She was dressed in dark slacks and a dark knit top, her pale face appearing disembodied in the foggy air.

I hurried to meet her. "I'm sorry about Lily," I said when I reached her.

"It's a tragedy, isn't it? She was such a tortured soul." Sirena walked to the stairs and the veranda. "I did what I could to help her, but I wasn't able to reach her. She was fixated on Dallas."

"I know. There was nothing anyone could do."

"I was wondering…I saw the police here earlier and I didn't want to bother you. Do you still have Lily's planner?"

I stared at her blankly. "Her what?"

"Her planner. You know, her calendar planner."

Vegas. The word sprang into my mind. I saw something in Lily's planner about Vegas. A note or something about Sirena and Vegas. "Oh. That. Yes, I do. Why?"

"Lily kept details about our contractual details in that planner. She kept many handwritten notes that I need to check about our restaurants."

"But you're not working for Dallas anymore," I said. "Maybe I can give it to him. The information might be useful for him."

"No, no, that wouldn't be good at all. I'll go through it and put together a summary for him. Do you have it here? I'll take it if you have it." She smiled but it was forced. Or maybe it was the yellow lighting from the security lamp at the top of the steps.

"Yes, it's upstairs. But I think I need to check with Detective Usher before I hand it over." I wasn't sure why I said that, but it seemed right. "After all, it isn't my property. It belongs to a woman who died, and it's part of her estate."

"I'd rather not have the police pawing through my personal business." Serena sounded truly pissed off. It was hard to see her face because she kept moving in and out of shadow.

My mobile phone, tucked in my side pocket, thumped. "Excuse me." I saw Detective Usher's name on the screen. "I need to take this call." I didn't give Sirena a chance to object. I put the phone to my ear and descended one step, trying to get privacy. "This is Tug."

"Miss Gallant, we've discovered new evidence I think you should know about."

I sensed movement on my left. Sirena was poised at the top of the steps. I went down again, and as I did, I heard a faint put-put of a motor on the lake. "Thanks for calling me," I said.

"Sirena Winchell is in deep financial trouble. We always do a financial check on everyone involved in an investigation. That's how we discovered Mr. Prinze's problems. That led us to Miss Winchell, who was in charge of the financial arrangements for his restaurants. It appears she owes a substantial amount of money to rather unsavory people. We also found probable illegal transfers of money from the restaurant accounts she controls."

"If you would please give me the planner," Sirena said from the top of the stairs.

"Excuse me, I'm busy. This is an important call. It's from one of my bridal customers." I went down another step. "The Vegas restaurant?" I whispered into my phone.

"Yes, that one and the one here in town. She had clients other than—"

"I'm rather busy," Sirena said, coming to a step to stand above me. "If you don't mind, I'll take that planner. I'll give it to the—" She paused, staring at the lake. The sound of a motor was louder now.

"—but those owners retained a tighter control on their finances than he did," Usher said.

"I'm talking with—" I smelled perfume, wafting to me on the still air. Sirena was on the step immediately above me.

"—some of the medication Lily Monroe had in her possession—"

"I told you this was a private call. Wait a minute, Sirena." I went to the interim landing midway to the dock.

"—apparently changed the medication. It's an initial analysis, but Miss Monroe wasn't taking the anti-anxiety—"

"Where is the planner? Is your shop unlocked? I'll just run in and get it." Sirena was poised just inches from me, her gaze going from the dock to me to the lighthouse. "Is it unlocked?"

"Who's with you?" Detective Usher demanded. "Are you okay?"

"I don't know," I said in desperation. "I have Lily's calendar planner in my shop and Sirena wants it."

"I'm on my way," Usher said. "Don't let her have it. Take care."

I lowered the phone. Sirena whirled to go up the stairs. My flipflops tangled with a rough edge of wood and made me almost pitch face down. I abandoned the shoes and scrambled after her. "Sirena, wait! The police are coming. Don't try to—"

She stopped. I ran into her, luckily ricocheting away onto firm ground at the top of the stairs, the path at my back.

"Lily was a stupid, malignant little bitch," she hissed. "I couldn't buy him out without Lily's help, and she couldn't get the money from the old lady."

"Her grandmother?" I inched backward, the cold earth under my bare feet.

"That old bitch told Lily to get away from me. She told Lily that she'd go to the police if Lily didn't quit working for me."

My beleaguered brain spun crazily. "How did she know about your mismanagement?"

Sirena flinched, glancing to her right at the lake where we both heard the motor. "Lily kept records, and she told the old bitch. Lily knew that if Prinze sold the restaurants to us, she'd never see him again. I was counting on her to get the money for me from the old woman. After that, I didn't give a shit what Lily did." Sirena's face, highlighted by the light from the porch and the top of the stairs, was twisted into a mask of hate and anger.

"What did you do?" I backed up another step, peeking past her to the Jolt, praying I'd see a police car pulling into the front drive. It was dark, though, like the darkness behind me where the path wound along the top of the bluff to the park. "You're in debt, aren't you?"

Sirena's entire body seemed to sag, like a balloon deflating. Her shoulders hunched and, for an instant she was pitiable, a woman defeated and worn down by the world. But then she straightened, her body taking on substance like a snake rising to strike. I cringed back, not sure whether to dash down the steps or leap for the nearby rocks to avoid the blow I sensed was coming. "Debt? That doesn't begin to describe it. Lily kept track of it. I had no idea she knew but she did, that stupid bimbo."

"If she found out about your embezzlement, she wasn't stupid, was she?" I don't know why I was defending Lily but I felt compelled to. Lily—trapped by her illness and her love for Dallas, manipulated by her grandmother and Sirena, unable to break free. "She knew, didn't she? That's why you changed her medication. You wanted her to attack me. You wanted things to continue the way they'd gone at the other restaurants." I leaned toward her, anger giving me courage. "You knew Dallas cared about me. You knew he would—"

Sirena slapped me so hard I reeled. I choked when all breath left me and, for one blinding moment, I saw stars.

"You're as stupid as she was. He doesn't care about you."

The sound of the boat drowned out her voice. The fog amplified the motor noise. That always happened on the lake. I knew Dallas was still several yards away, but it sounded like he was at the dock, shrouded in the mist below us.

Sirena glared at the lake, then she looked at the door leading to the porch and from there to the lighthouse. Where did she think she would go? The police were on their way, Dallas was nearby, and I was a witness to what she said.

A witness. Sirena seemed to realize it at the same moment I did. She headed toward me, and I tried to dodge, but the flowers lining the path stopped me. I couldn't get by her. I ran, loping along the path and ignoring the pain of pebbles on my bare feet. As soon as I left the circle of light from the stairs, I made my way through the shrubs at the top of the bluff and crouched, praying she hadn't followed me.

My prayers were not answered. Sirena walked above me, her phone raised with the light shining on the path. I huddled a few feet away, curled into a compact ball. The bluff here was more of a slope, and I might be able to get to the water's edge without injury. I reached out to test the ground behind me, and my fitness band lit, showing me the time.

And showing Sirena where I was.

She lunged at me and hooked her hand on my collar. "You're not ruining my life," she grated, dragging me upright. "There's no proof of anything but that stupid planner.

"What are you doing?" I asked desperately. "This is crazy. The police will know it was you. I told them you were here."

"They can't prove anything." She tried to drag me toward the lighthouse, but I dug my feet into the damp earth and pulled back.

Sirena overbalanced and pitched forward, catapulting past me down the slope.

A police siren warred with the sound of the boat coming to the dock. I didn't wait to see what happened to Sirena. I whirled and raced toward the stairs, almost falling when I tangled with my abandoned flipflops. I reached the end of the dock as Dallas was pulling in, leaning in to tie his bow line. I jumped into the small cabin cruiser and straight into his arms. We collapsed on the deck when the boat pushed away from the dock, the line dangling in the water.

"Wow. That's quite a welcome," he said, his arms around me where I sprawled on his chest.

His face was already precious to me after so little time. I kissed him, my passion mingling with fear, pity, remorse—a thousand emotions seemed to coalesce into one simple fact: I was in love with the Sexiest Man in the World, and I think he loved me.

When we finally separated, I heard voices shouting from the steps above us. Dallas caressed my back where I lay on him. "Why do I get the feeling my tour of your lighthouse is going to be delayed again?"

"Not for long. I promise." I reluctantly rolled off him and sat up.

"Good. I'm determined to get the secret of your buttercream frosting." Dallas scrambled to his feet then helped me up. Reaching behind the captain's seat, he lifted a small cooler. "I brought the Hollywood sign. I have plans for this."

I looked up into his laughing, mischievous eyes. "There's more where that came from."

"I like the way you think."

I looped my arm through his and we watched Detective Usher come on the dock, waving to us. "We may have to postpone for a bit, though."

"I can wait. I'm not letting you slip through my arms this time."

I squeezed his arm against me. "I guess it's your turn to rescue me."

Four Months Later

I set out the computer tablets on the table and took one last look around the shop. Halloween decorations gave the place a festive feeling, from the black-and-orange streamers on the countertops to the witch and Frankenstein cookies in the display case.

The resident felines, napping in their baskets in the corner, added to the atmosphere. Queen Fisher and Mr. Shrimp each had a hollowed out 'pumpkin' sleeping cozy made by Mr. Crabby Cove. The cats entered their private abode via the pumpkin mouth, a large O that gave it the look of startled surprise.

After speaking with the inspectors at the Health Department, I discovered that having the cats in the store was acceptable. They were not allowed in the bakery or in my upstairs kitchen, so Dallas helped design a clever system where the cats could enter my bedroom and the light at the top of the lighthouse via an external tunnel, a true catwalk. The cats loved it, I was assured that no mice were taking up residence anywhere on the premises, and the shop patrons adored them.

Voices drifted to me from outside. The Wednesday Night Gabby Girls were approaching. I heard Dallas' deeper voice among them. The first time he joined us as himself, I was amazed when the girls simply welcomed him to their midst. No one appeared intimidated or shy

277

around him. "He's your boyfriend," Coral explained when I asked her later about it. "So he must be a regular guy."

They entered the shop, bringing with them a burst of cold air. "I can't believe you didn't prosecute," Coral said as she shed her jacket. "That woman embezzled money from you."

Dallas met my gaze over Coral's head while he gathered the coats from the Girls. "I figured she had enough problems with all the money she owed." He stowed the coats on hooks near the door and added his own to the mix.

"She deserved more than a broken leg," Pearl declared, taking the Android tablet and heading for the table. "I hear a lot of gossip at the library, you know, and she shortchanged a few people who had a vested interest in your restaurant."

"I took care of that." Dallas joined me at the table, sitting next to me and setting his own tablet on the table. He and I spent Monday, Wednesday and Friday evenings at the lighthouse, and Tuesday, Thursday, and Saturday at his home, a.k.a. the Work In Progress or WIP. Sunday night was for relaxing wherever we ended up.

"How was your day today, honey?" he asked, putting his arm on the back of my chair. His brown turtleneck sweater made his gray hair and goatee stand out in sharp relief and highlighted his dark brown eyes.

I felt his warmth through the arm near me, and I leaned closer to him. "Busy. I'm glad we can use your restaurant for our baking. Business is booming."

"Well, I still say she deserves more than a bit of jail time," Brooke griped.

"As you well know, we don't always get what we deserve." I said it mildly, but I privately agreed with her. Both Dallas and I suspected that Sirena had a hand in Lily's obsessions and maybe had more than a hand in Mrs. Dronning's death. But there was no proof and, in the end, we kept our suspicions to ourselves and let the police handle Sirena. Her financial mismanagement cost Dallas, but friends of his from Hollywood stepped in and helped. The sales of his other restaurants were finally complete, and he was free to focus on Spirit Lake completely.

"I saw the restaurant got a writeup in the Star Tribune," Fleur said. "It was a nice article."

"Four stars," Coral said. "The critic loved that potato side dish." She nodded at me with a knowing look.

"Tug's Taters. Who knew such a pretty guy could cook?" Brooke grinned at Dallas. "I'm particularly proud of that name."

Dallas laughed. "I knew you ladies would be able to help me find the right name."

"Almost as good as the Prinze Pastry," Coral said, not to be outdone. "I've heard the restaurant sells out every night."

"We do," Dallas said. "I've seen her make it, and I still don't know how she does it."

"It's just a lot of layering and folding." I was proud of my buttery pastry, an old recipe I discovered that I tweaked to use my special vanilla flavoring. "It is time-consuming, but worth it. And it's fun to cut out different shapes depending on what our theme for the day is."

"People call ahead of time and reserve their desserts," Dallas said.

"Who knew that recipe would be so well loved?" The ladies exchanged a look. "What?" I demanded.

Dallas cleared his throat. "I, uh, I picked out the picture for tonight's coloring exercise." He glanced at the Girls, who nodded emphatically, as though encouraging him. Brooke even made a little shooing motion, urging him on.

The tablets were on the table, none of them on. "I loaded a mandala for tonight, but if you have one you'd like to use…"

He removed his arm from around me and fumbled with his tablet, turning slightly so I didn't see what was on the screen. I shot a suspicious look at Brooke, who merely smiled innocently.

"I thought that maybe—" He tapped nervously at the tablet in between wary peeks at me. "You know, we've known each other for a long time, I mean in school and this past summer we spent time—"

"What is it?" I asked.

"I hoped maybe…" Dallas looked around the table, at the floor, at the cats who were sound asleep—anywhere but at me. "I mean, you and I know each other, and I wanted—"

"Just show her already, you big wuss," Fleur said, slapping him on the arm. "She won't bite. She's Tug."

He blew out a long sigh then thrust his tablet into hands. "There."

I examined the screen. It was a simple picture, a tugboat docked at a lighthouse with a big heart on the side of the boat. "Go ahead. Color some of it," Brooke urged.

I tapped the red color circle at the bottom of the screen, and the heart as well as smoke shaped lettering coming out of the smokestack was highlighted.

I love you.

Will you marry me?

I tapped the highlighted parts, not sure I was seeing right. "What? How did—"

"I know a guy who did it for me." Dallas' dark eyes were fixed on mine, beseeching. "I wasn't sure how to ask you. I was afraid—I didn't know—I wasn't sure—"

The letters and the heart on the screen were now bright red. I dropped the tablet and threw my arms around him, almost knocking over the table, the chairs, and both of us. "You idiot," I said. "Of course I will."

His eyes were so intent on mine I felt like I was being pulled into his soul. "I love you, Tug."

"You're just marrying me for my buttercream," I whispered.

"Oh, no. I already know the secret of your buttercream." He put his lips against my ear. "You make everything with love. That's your secret."

I touched his face. "Yep. You figured it out." I pulled him to me and resolved to never let go.

A word about the author...

J L Wilson writes mysteries with a touch of romance—and romance with a touch of gray. She has a few dozen books out there to keep you entertained. Check http://bit.ly/JWilsonBooks to see all her books—or check her website (jayellwilson.com) to find out more about her doings.

Thank you for purchasing
this publication of The Wild Rose Press, Inc.

For questions or more information
contact us at
info@thewildrosepress.com.

The Wild Rose Press, Inc.
www.thewildrosepress.com